All the Light There Was

Books by Nancy Kricorian

Zabelle

Dreams of Bread and Fire

All the Light There Was

All the Light There Was

A NOVEL

Nancy Kricorian

SHE WRITES PRESS

C-6

Published 2014
Printed in the United States of America
ISBN: 978-1-63152-905-4
Library of Congress Control Number: 2014935239

All the Light There Was was originally published in hardcover by Houghton Mifflin Harcourt in 2013.

For information, address:
She Writes Press
1563 Solano Ave #546
Berkeley, CA 94707

For Nona and Djuna

All the Light There Was

I

BY THE TIME MY brother and I arrived at Donabedian's Market, our mother was waiting on the sidewalk outside the shop, having commandeered the grocer's wooden handcart, which was loaded with gunnysacks of bulgur, net bags of onions, liter tins of olive oil, along with miscellaneous brown-paper parcels tied with red string.

From behind the plate-glass window, Baron Donabedian waved to us as he and his assistant were busily ringing up sales. Half the neighborhood's housewives had joined the effort to empty his shelves.

"Missak," my mother said, "you and your sister take this cart home. I have more errands to run. Maral, help your brother carry everything up the stairs."

My brother asked, "What's all this?"

My mother said, "Food."

"Right," he answered. "Are we starting a restaurant?"

"Don't be smart." She tugged at the sacks on the bottom,

checking that the pyramid of goods was securely settled on the cart.

"How did you pay?" I asked.

She shrugged. "The money in the cracker tin."

My brother and I exchanged glances.

For as long as I could remember, at the end of each week my mother had climbed the step stool in our tiny kitchen to put coins and small bills into the gold and red cracker tin on the top shelf of the cupboard. She was saving to buy an electric sewing machine that would replace the ancient and venerable Singer pedal machine she used to do piecework as a vest maker. She had a newspaper advertisement showing the different electric models, one mounted on extravagant marble, one with an elegant sewing table, and the one she had set her heart on, which was a simple black model on wood that came in a leather-covered carrying case. She coveted the small electric light affixed to the body of the machine.

My mother said briskly, "After you take everything upstairs, Missak, you return the cart to Donabedian as soon as possible. Maral, put the spices in the jars, and the sugar on the top shelf. The rest goes wherever you and Auntie Shakeh find space."

That was how our war began. It didn't start with blaring newspaper headlines announcing a pending invasion, nor was it signaled by the drone of warplanes overhead. Our war commenced that afternoon when my mother stockpiled groceries so that, no matter what this new war might bring, her family would have something to eat.

• • •

As the trickle of people fleeing Paris turned into a torrent, my father decided we would remain in our apartment in Belleville, an eastern district that at the time still retained some of its character as an outlying village. Schools across the city were closed, and at the order of the authorities, children were being bused out of town to safety. Many stores were shuttered, and their owners loaded cars and streamed toward the peripheral exits. My father wagered, however, that remaining where we had a roof over our heads and where he could keep an eye on his cobbler's shop was safer than wandering across the countryside to God knows where. As he said, "We're staying put. The last exodus we saw led straight to hell."

That afternoon Missak and I pushed the handcart up the hill on the sidewalk past our neighbors—the French from the Auvergne and other rural provinces, along with Armenians, Greeks, and Eastern European Jews who had flocked to France for its promised liberties, and all of them looking for employment in Belleville's factories, shoemaking ateliers, and tailoring workshops. We wended our way through half a dozen languages as street vendors and their customers engaged in commerce at the end of the workday. As the war moved ever closer, most of the residents of Belleville chose not to join the mass flight from the city.

My brother and I made a number of trips up the five flights to our apartment, where we deposited the provisions at Auntie Shakeh's feet. She stood in our front hall wringing her hands. While Missak went to return the hand truck, I climbed on the stool to put the sugar on the top shelf, as my mother had instructed. Next my aunt and I dragged the sacks of bulgur from the front hall to the bedroom that we shared. With much effort, we wedged two of them under my bed and the other two under hers.

"That's a lot of bulgur." My aunt wiped perspiration from her face with a hankie.

"Enough to last until we won't be able to stand the sight of it on our plates," I said.

"Don't talk like that, Maral. We will be grateful for every bite." My aunt's tone was uncharacteristically severe.

Missak stumbled back in, panting under the weight of more packages, having made his final trip up the stairs with my mother at his heels. My father arrived just behind her.

"Do you feel better now?" my father asked my mother.

She nodded. "I found some more rice, and I bought machine needles, hand needles, and three dozen spools of thread. But I know there's something I've forgotten."

"The animals," my brother said.

"What animals?" my mother asked.

"You know, the pairs of animals two by two," Missak answered.

My mother dismissed him with a toss of her hand. "Talk to me in two months, Mr. Wise Guy."

That night my mattress, which usually dipped in the middle, hit up against the hard bulk under my bed. I turned from side to side, trying to find a position that felt less as though I were lying on top of a boulder. I slept fitfully, waking a number of times in the night worrying about the sacks of bulgur that seemed in the dark as sinister as carcasses. Some time toward morning I dreamed that I was standing over a cooking pot someone had left on the stove in the kitchen. I watched a bubbling lamb and tomato stew that rose and rose until, to my horror, it overflowed the pot and like scalding lava spread over the kitchen floor.

Ten days later, when the Germans marched down the rue de Belleville, Missak and I watched through the slats of the closed blinds of the Kacherians' apartment, on the third floor of a building two blocks from ours. Missak; his best friend, Zaven; Zaven's brother, Barkev; and I were crowded around one window, while Mr. and Mrs. Kacherian with ten-year-old Virginie between them were at the other.

As the first tank rolled down the hill, none of us breathed. The tanks were followed by armored trucks, and behind the trucks came tall German soldiers in black uniforms, their boot heels hammering the cobblestones in cadence. When Zaven leaned toward the window for a better view, his shoulder pressed against mine. I had never been so near to him before. I glanced at him sideways, so close that I could see the beads of perspiration on his temple. I stayed perfectly still, prolonging the contact between us and wondering if he felt what I did. When I noticed that his older brother, Barkev, was staring at me, I was ashamed. I quickly turned to peer through the slats at the columns of troops.

Suddenly Virginie exclaimed, "How handsome they are!"

Her father, who never raised a hand to his children, unthinkingly slapped her face. "Handsome? They are the Angels of Death."

. . .

At dinner that evening, my mother said, "You have no consideration for anyone else. How do you think we felt when we realized you were gone?"

My brother said, "We only went two blocks, to the Kacherians'."

"Only two blocks? You could go two steps at a time like this and have disaster fall on you," my mother said. "I know you think you are a grown man because you have a few wisps to shave, but let me remind you that you are sixteen years old, and your sister is even younger."

My brother rolled his eyes.

"And it's done?" Auntie Shakeh asked.

"Not a shot fired," my father answered. "Paris is an open city. I couldn't see the Germans from the shop, but I heard the boots. That's a sound you will never forget."

And the sound of those boots reverberated in my head for months and then for years, and sometimes even still. This is the story of how we lived the war, and how I found my husband.

2

WHEN WE RETURNED TO school that autumn, there were portraits of Maréchal Pétain hanging in all the classrooms. He was promoted as a French war hero, but you could sense the strings of the German puppet masters behind his uniformed shoulders. There was a new uneasiness circulating in the halls and classrooms. But our teachers, their eyes ringed with sadness, strove for normalcy. We girls soon settled into the routine of our studies.

In early November, as my brother and I paused on the landing outside our apartment, he thrust a slip of paper into my hand. It said *The Boches will not honor the 11th of November; meet at 6 p.m. at the Arc de Triomphe.*

"Are you going?" I asked.

"Zaven too," he whispered.

"Then Jacqueline and I will go," I whispered back. "Will you say anything?"

"Are you crazy? And not a word from you either."

I tucked the paper into a notebook inside my school satchel.

"I know how you like to tell your mother everything," he added in a low voice. "But you're not six years old anymore."

As our father's heavy tread started on the stairs below, my brother opened the door to the apartment.

"We're here," Missak called, switching from French to Armenian.

We dropped our school bags, hung our coats on wooden pegs by the front door, and changed our shoes for slippers.

Our mother swept past wearing an apron and carrying a towel-wrapped pot. "Your father should be here any minute now."

My father arrived and announced, "To the table. I could cleave a spit-roasted lamb and eat the whole thing myself."

Missak said, "I could eat a lamb, a pig, a small cow, and wash it down with a liter of milk . . ."

"Azniv, this boy isn't getting enough food," my father said.

"No one is. That poor Jewish baby across the way is this thin." My aunt held up her pinkie finger in demonstration.

We sat down to supper in the cramped front room that served as dining room, parlor, and workroom, as well as Missak's bedroom. Around the wooden table, which had leaves that folded down so it took up less space between meals, were arranged three straight-backed chairs and two stools. Covering the uneven floorboards was an Oriental carpet that had once been claret-colored. The two windows that looked out over the street were dressed with heavy blackout curtains.

My mother spooned food onto the plates. "All I have left

are bulgur, a liter of oil, and the spices. Thank God for the Nazarians' onions . . ."

Our dinner conversations now revolved around food: how hard it was to get it, the long lines at the shops, the often-empty shelves, and schemes of how to find more and different things to eat. Missak had used his slingshot in the Buttes Chaumont to bring down a few ducks, but with the arrival of cold weather, the game birds had disappeared. Our father sometimes bartered his services for food, but not often enough to make much of an improvement in the daily ration. Earlier in the season, I had bicycled to Alfortville a few times to see the Nazarians, my mother's cousins, who grew vegetables in their backyard. Before I headed home, I loaded the bicycle's basket with shoes that needed repair, and I attached to the back fender a box filled with tomatoes, peppers, onions, and fresh mint. But we ate mostly what we could purchase with our ration cards: tasteless items such as rutabagas that were customarily fed to barnyard animals, ersatz coffee made from chicory, and a sticky mess concocted from wine-press grapes that was optimistically called jam.

In addition to long conversations about food or its lack, dinner featured my father's nightly diatribe against the *maréchal*, whom he referred to as "that lying goat."

"It isn't enough that the Germans are stealing our wine and chocolate—people can live without wine and chocolate, but now"—here he slammed his hand on the table—"that lying goat is letting them make off with our wheat and potatoes."

My mother pleaded, "Be careful, you're going to knock over the glasses. And not so loud."

"You don't think the Lipskis agree with me?" he shouted.

After the dishes were done, I sat at the table with my books in a stack beside me. Across the table, Missak scratched on his sketchpad with a pencil. In another corner of the room, my mother worked the foot pedal of the sewing machine, and its arm stuttered up and down, thrusting the needle in and out of the fabric. Auntie Shakeh's metal knitting needles ticked against each other as a sweater grew from a fat, round ball of wool. The volume on my father's radio was turned so low that he had to lean forward in his armchair to catch the words that were an indistinguishable murmur a few feet away.

I pulled out the slip of paper Missak had passed to me.

Missak slid another scrap across the table to me: *Get rid of that paper. And if there's trouble on Monday, go to the cathedral.*

At bedtime that night, my mother, aunt, and I were in the room that I shared with Aunt Shakeh. All three of us wore the white flannel nightgowns that my mother had sewn. My mother had let her long hair down from its tight bun, and it made a dark cascade on the back of the white gown. No matter how many times I saw my mother's loose hair at night, there was always something shocking about it, as though my prim mother had turned into another woman. But her oval face remained domestic and familiar.

My mother took a seat behind me on the bed and started to brush out my long, heavy hair.

"Did the teacher give back the math exam?" my mother asked.

"Yes."

"Top of the class?"

I said, "Denise Rozenbaum was number one."

"Next time."

"This year I haven't bested her once. I need to study harder."

My mother paused the brush. "You work hard enough already, my smart girl."

Auntie Shakeh, who was sitting on the other bed, added, "Our girl is smart, and she's beautiful."

A snake of guilt lay coiled behind my ribs. They both thought I was their good, smart, beautiful, nice Armenian girl. However, not only was I jealous of Denise Rozenbaum, who was my best school friend, but I was hiding from them our plans to attend a student rally. I was becoming the *char aghchig*, the bad girl my mother had always warned me about.

At the breakfast table Monday, my father said, "I'd like you two to come by the shop this evening so I can measure you. Vahan Kacherian gave me some leather from his workshop, a little more than enough to make you boots, I think, unless your feet have doubled in size."

"Eh, Babig, today is no good," Missak said. "Tomorrow could work. Or Thursday I'll be at the shop anyways."

"And you?" my father asked me.

"Me?" I responded.

"Yes, you. Can you come by the shop after school?"

"Babig, she's going with me to the library," my brother deftly lied. "We'll come by tomorrow."

As she poured mint tea into my cup, my mother remarked, "You're being quiet this morning, *anoushig*. Are you okay?"

Missak eyed me in warning.

"I'm fine," I said.

"Are you sure you aren't coming down with something?" My mother put a wrist to my forehead and peered into my eyes.

I lifted the cup of tea, turning from her gaze. "I'm okay. I'm just tired." I was relieved and saddened that she believed me.

That afternoon when I exited the wooden portals of the lycée, Jacqueline was waiting across the street. I noticed that her wrists were sticking out of the sleeves of last year's winter coat. Jacqueline Sahadian was the eldest of five children. Their father was a manual laborer, their mother took in laundry, and there had rarely been an extra franc, even before the war. Despite her too-small coat, Jacqueline looked stylish, with a royal blue tam at an angle on her dark, wavy hair, which she had cut to a fashionable chin length.

"Beautiful hat." I fell into step beside her as we headed toward the Métro.

"I borrowed it from a girl in my typing class."

"My hat was the wrong color, so I brought this." I pulled a thick length of red ribbon from my satchel. Pausing on the sidewalk, I took off my hat, slid the ribbon under my thick, black braid, and made a bow at the top of my head.

"Let me fix that for you." Jacqueline adjusted the ribbon so the bow was just above my left ear. "That's better. But you really should cut your hair."

"Denise cut hers last week. I'm the only one in our class with long hair. My mother says a woman's hair is her crowning glory. And so on and so forth."

"Is Denise coming?"

"I didn't ask her. She's too scared for this kind of thing."

Jacqueline asked, "Are you scared?"

"If my brother and Zaven are going to be there . . ."

"Whatever the Left Shoe and the Right can do, the Right Glove and the Left can do," Jacqueline answered.

These were the nicknames my father had for the four of us. Jacqueline, who was my best friend, had been in and out of our apartment since her mother had first allowed her to cross the street. Missak and Zaven, who were inseparable, had ranged the neighborhood with a gang of local boys since they were old enough to tie their shoes.

We went down the steps into the Métro, where the platform was thick with gray-green uniforms. When the train doors opened, people quickly pressed into the car. Jacqueline and I ended up seated between two German soldiers. I inched my foot away from a well-polished black boot on the floor. We sat in silence, staring at our laps, as the train rattled from one station to the next. I could see in my peripheral vision that the soldiers on either side of us were looking us up and down and winking at each other.

Suddenly, the soldier next to Jacqueline leaned toward her and said with a heavy German accent, "*S'il vous plaît, mademoiselle.*"

Jacqueline turned away from him, grimacing at me.

I said in Armenian, "Pretend you don't understand."

"*S'il vous plaît, mademoiselle,*" he repeated. After a brief pause he said it again. "*S'il vous plaît, mademoiselle.*"

Jacqueline shook her head no and said to him in Armenian, "I don't understand."

He tried once more. *"S'il vous plaît, mademoiselle."*

Jacqueline muttered to me in Armenian, "He sounds like a parrot."

"It's probably the only sentence he knows in French. He tries it on all the French girls he sees. Let's get off."

The train pulled into the station and when the doors slid open, Jacqueline and I bolted onto the platform. We hurtled up the stairs, not pausing until we reached the street.

When I looked up at the Naval Ministry and the Hôtel de Crillon, I felt as though someone had knocked the wind out of me. The towering white facades were draped with scarlet banners scarred by black swastikas. The Germans rarely ventured into our neighborhood, and in the first months of the war, if you ignored the propaganda posters and the hunger, you could forget sometimes for a few hours that the city was occupied.

We walked along the Champs Élysées, where most shopkeepers were in the process of rolling down their metal shutters in anticipation of trouble. We saw dozens of girls walking arm in arm by twos or threes, many of them dressed in one of the colors of the tricolor flag. French police patrolled the boulevard, warning groups of young men to disperse and go home. There were also clusters of gray-green uniforms sitting in cafés and strolling along the avenue as though they were on holiday.

Jacqueline and I approached the Étoile and joined a stream of young people—thousands of lycée and university students—filing toward the Arc de Triomphe. A boy passing through the crowd with an armful of flowers wordlessly handed Jacqueline and me each a red carnation. Ahead of us, the monument dwarfed the tiny figures pausing to drop blooms at the foot of the Tomb of the Unknown Soldier.

Spying a group of German soldiers lined up on the far side of the Étoile, I told Jacqueline, "Let's stay at the edge and go around to the other side."

It was the first time since the start of the Occupation that there had been such a gathering; public assemblies of any kind were forbidden. Jacqueline and I threaded through the crowd while more and more students poured into the Étoile, flocking toward the monument. I noticed that in our vicinity the boys outnumbered the girls by at least ten to one and that Jacqueline and I were among the youngest students there. I scanned the faces streaming past us, hoping to find my brother and Zaven, but I didn't recognize anyone. More German soldiers arrived at the intersections of the broad boulevards leading to the circle, where they lined up in neat rows. As I surveyed the troops, I sensed that they were poised for action, merely awaiting the order. The tension rippling through their ranks seemed to me a warning, like the smell of ozone before a storm.

"Jacqueline," I said, "we should go to the cathedral."

She looked at me quizzically. "Now?"

Just then, German military vehicles roared into the intersection, some of them rolling onto the sidewalks, forcing pedestrians to scatter. Soldiers leaped out of their trucks and were met by others who came trotting in formation toward the crowd. Shouts of *"Les Boches!"* rose up from all sides. Within seconds students were running pell-mell away from the Germans, jostling and shoving one another in the panic. Jacqueline and I were in a cluster that moved as though pushed by invisible hands. But we were headed in the wrong direction, away from, not toward, the Armenian cathedral. Someone shouted *"Vive la France!"* and soon the call echoed around the vast roundabout. Then I thought I heard gunfire.

I grabbed Jacqueline by the hand, not wanting to lose her, and struggled mightily against the crowd that flowed around us. I pressed ahead until we made passage to a side street, where I paused to get my bearings.

"That way," I said, pointing toward the rue Vernet.

As we started running, a boy raced by carrying two long fishing poles, one of which hit me in the head as he passed. When he turned to apologize, he bumped into Jacqueline, knocking her to the ground. I tripped over her legs, twisting my ankle as I fell, and landed beside her. The boy charged ahead, calling back over his shoulder, "So sorry!"

Jacqueline leaned forward to examine her knees. "Do you know how long I saved to buy these stockings? They're ruined."

"Oh, Jacqueline, there's no time for that." I stood up and pulled her to her feet.

On my next step, I felt my ankle buckle a little, but ran on despite the pain. When we reached the courtyard of the Armenian cathedral on Jean-Goujon, we doubled over and panted for air.

Jacqueline said, "My knees are skinned and my only pair of stockings are torn. Where are those stupid boys?"

I sat heavily on the stone bench, wincing as I took the weight off my foot. My heart was pumping wildly in my chest. "I'm sure they'll be here soon."

"What if they aren't?" Jacqueline sat beside me on the bench.

"They will." I untied the ribbon in my hair with trembling hands.

"What the hell was that boy doing with those fishing poles?"

I found out later that they were a reference to General de Gaulle, the leader of the Free French movement, whose surname was a homophone for the French words meaning "two poles."

The courtyard was dark, the bench was cold, and my ankle throbbed. I had no wristwatch, and we may have been waiting only a few minutes, but it felt like hours. We could hear sirens wail in the distance. My gut was clenched like a fist. I chewed on the inside of my lip, imagining my brother and Zaven thrown into the back of an army truck with a dozen other students. In that moment it occurred to me for the first time, with all the wisdom of my fourteen years, that the Occupation might inflict more on us than inconvenience and hunger.

Jacqueline shivered. "God, I'm freezing."

"Me too." I turned up the collar on my coat.

Just then I heard the sound of churning gravel as my brother and Zaven sped into the courtyard.

Missak, puffing for air, spat angrily, "I shouldn't have let you two come. We were in the middle of the crowd when they moved in and started grabbing people. We had to circle around to avoid getting nabbed ourselves."

Zaven said, "They must have rounded up at least a couple hundred."

"Crap." Missak turned and vomited into the bushes, then wiped his mouth on his sleeve.

Zaven laughed. "Crap is right. We are up to our ears in their crap."

Jacqueline retorted, "I don't know what you think is so funny, Zaven Kacherian."

"Let's go," I said. When I tried to stand, I groaned from the pain in my ankle and sank back to the bench.

"What's the matter with you?" my brother asked.

"It's my ankle. I tripped."

"Can you stand?" Zaven asked.

"Maybe," I said.

Missak kicked the gravel and cursed under his breath. He knelt down to examine my ankle.

I winced. "Not so hard."

He said, "It's not broken. Do we have anything to bind it?"

"Give me the ribbon." Jacqueline wrapped it tightly around my ankle like a bandage.

Zaven said, "Put one arm around my neck, and one around your brother's."

We slowly made our way along the dark street. Zaven's cheek was close to mine and I could feel the muscles in his shoulders shift under my arm. But I needed to focus on keeping the weight off my ankle. I feared that we might run into a German ambush around the next corner. There were echoing footfalls on the opposite sidewalk, but we couldn't make out anything more than dark figures. Finally we filed down the Métro stairs at Alma-Marceau. The train was packed with soldiers dressed in gray-green wool uniforms with shining silver buttons, their guns in leather holsters. There were no seats available, so Jacqueline gestured at my bandaged ankle and said to one of the Boches, "*S'il vous plaît, monsieur.*"

Two of them leaped to their feet, gratified to show us a courtesy. These polite, deferential young men or ones just like them had, less than an hour earlier, charged into a crowd of unarmed students with trucks and jeeps, brandishing loaded weapons. Jacqueline and I sat while Missak and Zaven stood rigidly over us, their faces hooded with anger. Finally, when we changed train lines for the last part of the trip to Belleville, there were no more soldiers. The knot of fear in my belly released while my ankle began to pulse with pain.

We left Jacqueline at her building across the street from ours, and then Missak and I headed to our place, along with Zaven. When we reached the bottom stairs of our landing, where I could use the banister for support, Zaven said goodbye.

As we started up the flight, Missak whispered, "Don't tell them anything. I'll explain. You tripped on the curb when we were on our way home."

"Do you think I'm a fool?"

"You're not stupid, but you can't lie to save your life."

I put my hand on his arm. "Missak . . ."

"What?"

"I was afraid that you and Zavig had been arrested like all those others. What will happen to them?"

"There's nothing we can do. Come on, up the stairs." He gestured for me to go ahead.

When we entered the apartment, my mother and aunt were setting food on the table.

"Let me guess," Missak said in Armenian, sniffing the air. "Turnips?"

My mother smiled grimly. "Turnips with—"

He interrupted. "Turnips with bulgur."

I was awed that my brother could slip so easily into kitchen banter.

My mother and aunt noticed my limp, and there followed a good fifteen minutes of agitated clucking while the two of them attended to the injury with cold, damp towels. Missak explained how it had happened, and my mother and aunt were impressed at our good fortune that Zaven was on hand to help us get home.

We sat down at the table for dinner, my foot propped up on a stool, and I had a strange sensation as I listened to my father talk about the details of his day at work and heard my mother recount some bits of gossip reported by a neighbor while they were in line at the market. The words sounded as though they were coming from far away. I kept seeing the trucks rolling onto the sidewalk as students scattered in terror. *We are up to our ears in their crap*, Zaven had said. Crap, so much crap.

"Maral, I asked you a question," my mother said.

"What did you say?"

"Are you sure you're not coming down with something? You just don't seem like yourself these past few days." My mother put her hand to my forehead.

"I'm fine, Mairig, really. It's just the ankle, and it was a long day at school," I said. The second lie was easier than the first.

3

THERE WAS A SNOWSTORM that first winter of the Occupation that marked for me the last day of my childhood. I think it was a Sunday; it must have been, because my father was home, or perhaps he had decided not to open the shop because of the inclement weather. I drew back the curtain in the front room and stared out at the downy flakes dancing on currents of air. Swirls of white dust blew above the snowy sidewalk, and tall drifts were forming along the street. The snow had been falling for hours and showed no signs of stopping. A thick layer of down camouflaged the uneven cobblestones, the overflowing trash cans, and the propaganda posters.

After lunch, Zaven came to our apartment. He joined Missak and me at the table, where I was working math problems and my brother was bent over his sketchpad. My father was in his armchair reading the paper, and Zaven's presence inspired him to put down his newspaper for some verbal jousting.

In those days, my father and Zaven enjoyed a running semi-joking dialogue that ranged over the political philosophies that had cast the continent into misery: fascism, Nazism, communism, and socialism, with a detour through the various warring Armenian political parties. My father and Zaven agreed on their antipathy for Hitler, but my father loathed the Soviet leader, whom he referred to as Stalin the Assassin, just as much. My father was fond of ribbing Zaven about the pact between Stalin and Hitler, which had posed a dilemma for the Communists of France, including Zaven's father.

I wasn't following their banter, having heard it all before, but Zaven's physical proximity, with his knee barely inches from mine under the table, was more interesting than the math problems. Meanwhile, Missak finished his sketch, tore it from the pad, and held it up.

"Any takers?" he asked.

It was a drawing of Zaven and me, and while I thought it was skillfully rendered, and a handsome likeness of Zaven, I was shy about asking for it right away.

After a brief pause, Zaven said, "My mother might want that."

"I'll take it," I said.

Missak scrutinized the picture anew. "No. I like this one. I think I'll keep it."

By midafternoon, the wind had died down but the snow was still falling. Missak, Zaven, and I bundled into our winter clothes. As we raced out, my mother called after us, "Be careful that you don't slip and break your necks! And be back before dark."

We crossed the street to Jacqueline's building. Mrs. Sahadian, a small, stocky woman wearing a flowered apron over her gray coat, leaned out the door of their apartment and said in Armenian, "Your mothers let you out on a day like this?"

"It's beautiful outside, Auntie," I answered. "Please tell Jacqueline we're here."

Mrs. Sahadian asked, "You want to come in?"

"No, thanks." Missak pointed to the puddles forming around our boots.

She withdrew into the apartment, shutting the door against the draft.

Within minutes Jacqueline appeared with two of her younger siblings in tow: thirteen-year-old Paul, whose ears stuck out like handles on a sugar bowl, and twelve-year-old Alice, who was wearing a green wool hat that I had passed down to her. The three siblings had used twine to tie burlap over their school shoes.

We stopped at the Kacherians' to collect Barkev and Virginie, who was the shortest by more than a head. Next we gathered the three Meguerditchian brothers, the two Kostas girls, and Denise Rozenbaum and her older brother, Henri. Under gray skies and a curtain of thick-falling snow, we returned to the side street near our building. I started rolling a snowball, and Jacqueline helped me push it when it got big. The other girls joined in, and soon we had three big snowballs that we stacked into a human form.

I turned from our sculpture as Zaven raced by. He smiled as he scooped up some of the heavy snow and pressed it between his mittens into a fist-size ball. He pitched it at my brother, shouting, "Take that," and hit his target square in the chest.

Missak responded, "You dare attack me?" He launched a missile at Zaven, who turned to take it in the shoulder.

Soon all the boys were pursuing one another up and down the block, the snowballs whizzing by, thudding against their marks.

Henri Rozenbaum aimed at Missak. "That one is for you!" The ball flew wide and slammed into a wall.

"You need glasses, Henri. This one is for the honor of France!" Zaven hurled a ball toward Henri.

"Get out of the line of fire," my brother warned me.

I ducked too late. The snowball slammed into my nose like a hard, cold punch. When I looked down, there were bright red drops staining the snow at my feet. Suddenly I had a premonition that not all of these boys would survive the war. I was filled then with a sense of dread, as though the game the boys played was a rehearsal for things to come.

Henri said, "Let me see."

I moved my sodden mittens away from my face, tasting blood as it trickled over my lips.

Henri carefully touched my nose. "It's not broken."

Barkev said, "You should tip your head back."

Missak pulled out his handkerchief to wipe my face and then he pinched the bridge of my nose.

Zaven said, "Sorry. That wasn't meant for you."

When the bleeding stopped, Barkev picked up a handful of snow. "Hold this to your nose. I know it's cold, but it will keep the swelling down."

Henri commented, "That's going to be pretty."

Jacqueline pushed her way past the boys. "Haven't you done enough?"

Virginie sidled up behind her. "Are you all right, Maral?" I glanced at tiny Virginie and saw that her lips had gone purple from the cold.

Alice Sahadian was shivering in her thin coat. The snow had stopped falling, and as the skies darkened, the air grew colder by the minute. It was time for us to go home.

When I think back to that afternoon, I see us as though we are in a group photograph. It's black-and-white; not posed, but a moment suspended in time. My friends are clustered around me, concern etched on their features. With a black pen, someone has drawn circles around the faces of those whom we were soon to lose.

4

OUR NEIGHBORS THE LIPSKIS, who were Yiddish-speaking Jews from Poland, lived in the apartment across the landing. The father worked in a tailor's shop, and the mother did piecework at home so she could take care of their three-year-old daughter, Claire. Occasionally, I watched the little girl for a few hours while Madame Lipski did errands.

On one such afternoon, Claire and I sat on the day bed in the parlor where Missak slept at night. Between us was a circular cookie tin filled with spare buttons that my mother had amassed over her years as a seamstress. Claire thrust her hands deep into the buttons, lifted two fistfuls, and let them slip through her fingers. The buttons rained back into the box.

"Do you want to dump them out?" I asked.

Claire turned over the tin, laughing as the buttons cascaded onto the bed. We spread them out to examine them more carefully. There were buttons with two holes and those with four, plus metal and leather shank buttons. The colors were varied: shiny gold, red, all shades of white and brown, and thin disks made from shimmering mother-of-pearl. I had spent hours playing with them when I was small, sitting on the carpet near my mother's feet while she worked at the sewing machine.

When Claire tired of the buttons, I suggested that we make a doll. We searched the ragbag in the kitchen and found an old white sock. She watched as I cut and sewed, then she helped me stuff the form with bits of cloth and fluffy cotton. Claire selected yellow yarn for hair and two pearly gray buttons for eyes. I stitched on a red mouth with embroidery floss and made a simple jumper from a scrap of calico.

"Does this dolly resemble anyone you know?"

"She looks like me," Claire answered.

"What are you going to call her?"

"Her outside name is Charlotte. And her name for inside is Sheindeleh."

"Both of those are beautiful names," I told her.

I knew the system of double names. Inside I was Maral and outside Marie. Missak was Michel. Zaven was Stéphane. His brother, Barkev, was Bernard. And Jacqueline's original name was Iskouhi, but no one called her that except for the priest who had baptized her, and her mother when she was in a fit of rage. We had two languages as well—Armenian in the house and French outside. My excellent grades, neatly ironed clothes, and well-polished shoes made me popular with the teachers, but my strange surname marked me as the child of foreigners, the stateless Armenians. I glanced at

Claire, who sat playing with her doll. She was too young to be able to read the yellow signs on the park entrances saying FORBIDDEN TO JEWS.

While Claire was absorbed with Charlotte, I cleared up the materials left from our work. I slid my hand under the day bed to search for stray buttons, a few of which I retrieved and dropped into the cookie tin. Then I reached under again and pulled out a small bundle wrapped in brown paper and tied with a bit of twine. Inside were two thick sticks of white chalk. I knew immediately what they were.

As part of a campaign that was launched over the BBC and soon spread by word of mouth, Paris had been chalked with *V* for *victory*. The walls of Belleville were marked with *V*s, and I had seen them also in the Marais, near my school.

That evening, I had no chance to talk with my brother out of earshot of the family, so the next morning as Missak and I left our building, I said, "I found the chalk under your bed."

"There's no chalk under my bed," Missak answered.

"So I suppose now it's in your satchel."

"It's not your business," he snapped.

When my brother used that tone of voice, I knew better than to badger him. Sometimes, if I held my tongue, he would offer things up on his own. So we walked a few paces in silence.

"It's nothing to worry about. We do it after dark, with one person to draw and one to stand watch," he said.

"You and Zaven?"

He shrugged, and from the steely look on his face, I knew the conversation was over.

We reached the corner of the rue de Belleville where Denise Rozenbaum was waiting. Denise and I attended a lycée in the Marais, and Missak and Zaven were students at a technical school in Belleville.

"See you later," Missak said jauntily as he headed toward Zaven's building.

Denise and I turned down the hill. We walked because the buses were no longer running, due to lack of gasoline, and the Métro was too expensive to take both ways.

I ran my fingers under a row of *V*s along the wall we were passing. I looked at Denise, who had been my classmate since we were six and with whom I had gone to lycée at the age of eleven. Both of us had scholarships that helped pay for the materials we needed and for lunch at the school canteen. We both loved the Lycée Victor Hugo for its notebooks, French dictations, and even the exams, at which we excelled. I enjoyed wearing the required hat and gloves and putting on the beige smock with my name and the name of the school embroidered on it. The smock kept anyone from knowing if the dress underneath was fashionable or not or if the same dress was worn several times in one week.

The war had marred the closeness of our school community. One of the most unsettling aspects of the Occupation was the way it made you suspicious of your neighbor. How could you truly know where people's loyalties lay? When we had returned to school that fall, the noticeable absence of Mademoiselle Lévy, the beloved Latin and Greek teacher who had been dismissed because she was a Jew, had upset us all, but our dismay had been muted. We found out after the war that Mademoiselle Lévy had joined the Resistance soon after leaving us and that eventually the Nazis had decapitated her with an ax in Germany.

I was sure the Rozenbaums felt the way our family did about the Occupation, but even so, it was important to be careful about what one said.

"Seems as though there are more of these each morning." I gestured at the chalk marks on the wall.

Denise took my arm, moving her head closer to mine. "I've been counting them while we walk. I've passed eighty-six so far. Better than the stupid posters the Boches plaster on all the walls. 'Put your trust in the German soldier.' Not even Pétain believed that one."

"What would you think if you found chalk hidden under your brother's bed?"

"Or if he came home with chalk dust on his jacket cuffs? There are thousands and maybe tens of thousands of these marks. That's a lot of chalk."

I imagined an army of boys deployed in pairs, moving through the lightless streets and scrawling defiantly on walls in each neighborhood.

"You know what I dream about?" Denise asked after we crossed the boulevard.

"Chocolate?"

"I do dream about chocolate, but no—I dream about writing *traitor* on each photograph of Pétain in the lycée."

"That would be an all-day job."

"Some of the teachers admire him, you know," Denise said. "He has made of his person a gift to the nation, and so on and so forth."

"Some of them seem to admire German efficiency."

"It can't be more than a few," Denise answered.

"And it's not the concierge!"

The concierge of our lycée, the only man in the building, had lost a leg in World War I. Since school had opened in September, he had been stomping around on his wooden leg, grumbling under his breath about the Boches.

"Not him. But I wonder about Madame Bourdet," Denise said.

Madame Bourdet, our math teacher, had a razor for a tongue. No one talked out of turn or daydreamed in her class. She berated offenders in the most elegant French.

"Is it something she said?" I asked.

Denise shook her head. "It's just a feeling I have. I don't think she likes Jews."

I said, "Oh, Denise. It's not particular to Jews. She doesn't like anyone."

One night a few weeks later, Missak was uncharacteristically late for dinner. My mother insisted on waiting, but after an hour my father ordered us to the table, where I stared down at my plate without appetite. Throughout the meal my aunt and my mother exchanged glances, and at the sound of footsteps on the landing, my mother flew from her chair to the door. It was only Mr. Lipski arriving home.

My father threw down his fork. "I'll go look for him."

He returned alone an hour later. "Zaven hasn't seen him since they left school. Missak went off with a few other boys and Henri. I went to the Rozenbaums', and Henri was home. He said he had left Missak and a boy named Marcel at the Parc de Belleville some hours ago. The park was

empty. God only knows what mischief they've gotten themselves up to."

My mother slapped her forehead. "Mischief? This isn't
like when he was seven and brought home a stray goat."

At that moment there was a knock on the door, and we
all rushed to the front hall. My father opened to find Missak
and Officer Godin standing on the landing. My brother's
shoulders were slumped and he stared down at the floor, so
it was difficult to read the expression on his face.

"Good evening, Monsieur Pegorian," the officer said.
"This boy I believe belongs to you."

"Thank you so much, Officer Godin," my father said.
"Please come in."

"No, thank you. I'm here to drop him off. Some colleagues
picked him and another boy up this evening. They were
defacing the walls with antigovernment symbols. Fortu-
nately, when I arrived I recognized him and saved him from
a trip to La Santé, where people would have been much less
understanding. We let the other boy go too. But I'm afraid
you might not be so lucky next time, young man."

"Thank you, Officer," my mother said. "It will never happen again. We are so sorry for the trouble he caused."

My father asked, "How can we show our gratitude?"

Godin shrugged. "I do have a pair of shoes that could use
new heels . . ."

"Bring them," my father said, "bring them all: your wife's,
your children's. Your mother's, and your neighbors'."

The officer smiled. "Generous offer, but I have in mind
just one pair."

The minute the door shut behind Godin, my mother and aunt wept as though a great calamity had arrived rather than been narrowly averted. Their wailing exasperated my father, as did Missak's monosyllabic responses to all questions. The main emotion that played across my brother's face that night was irritation as my father harangued and my mother tearfully cajoled. It took me years to understand that anger was my brother's primary defense against the guilt that flowed through our household like an open brook. My mother managed to extract from him a promise that he would never, ever write on the walls again. It might have been wiser for her to be less specific in her demands.

5

I PEDALED QUICKLY TO keep close behind my brother as he navigated his bicycle easily through the streets. German military vehicles and a few private cars passed us on the broad boulevards. We weaved through a crowd of bicycle taxis and other cyclists. Because replacement parts for bikes were so hard to come by, a flat tire would have been a disaster, and we took special care to avoid the potholes.

Once we were outside the city's limits, Missak picked up speed and I struggled to keep up. The skies were blue and cloudless. There were colorful flowers in the window boxes of the pale stucco houses that we passed. The short plane trees were bright with new green leaves.

When we wheeled our bicycles up the drive and into the backyard at the Nazarians' house in Alfortville, the two parents and their three teenage children were outside working in their garden. Karnig Nazarian was my mother's distant cousin and the only other surviving member of the Nazarian clan from the Old Country town of Aghn. As the children of two orphans, Missak and I knew no grandparents; we had no uncles and no aunts, aside from Auntie Shakeh, so the Nazarians were our only other family.

When Cousin Satenig saw us, she dried her hands on her apron and pulled my face in for a kiss. "What a surprise!"

Cousin Karnig propped his rake against the fence, wiped his brow with a white handkerchief, and shook hands with Missak.

"Maro," sixteen-year-old Akabi exclaimed, "will you take my sandals to your father so he can fix them?"

"It's time for a break. Let me go make some tea." Cousin Satenig hurried into the house.

Karnig sat down on the bench. "Show your cousins," he told his son, gesturing toward the garden.

Vasken, who was thirteen and had a shadow above his upper lip that hadn't been there the last time I'd seen him, gave us a walking tour of the garden: tomato plants covered with yellow flowers and a few green fruits, beans growing on a trellis, onions, carrot tops, lettuces, beds of mint and parsley, green peppers, cucumbers, and eggplants.

I thought about the narrow window boxes my father had built for my mother; she was growing tomatoes and parsley on our sills. People in the city, unless they were rich enough for the black market or had relatives on farms in the countryside, ate so much worse than those who had a bit of earth to tend.

Vasken pointed to a small wooden coop in a corner of the yard. "That's where my father keeps his chickens."

"Chickens?" I asked. "Do you have eggs?" An egg was an almost unimaginable luxury.

Cousin Karnig came up behind us. "We had the first two eggs this week. The pullets are going to start laying regularly any day now. I helped the Varjabedians build a new room on their house for their son and his bride, and they gave me some fertilized eggs."

Akabi said, "He paid more attention to those eggs than he ever has to us. If he weren't afraid of crushing them, I think he would have sat on them himself."

"Go ahead and make fun of your father," Karnig said. "But it's thanks to me that every one of those eggs hatched. One will grow into a rooster and then we'll have even more. Maybe I'll give up carpentry and go into the chicken business."

Cousin Satenig carried out a tray of tea and cups that she placed on the wooden table. "Come sit down. No sugar today, but we have dried peaches. Oh, you're admiring your cousin's new business. How are we going to keep those birds alive come winter, Karnig? They're going to freeze."

Karnig answered, "I'll make a pen in a corner of the kitchen. They are my queens, and they can sleep in our bed if that's what it takes."

An hour later, as Cousin Satenig, Akabi, and I were chatting while Missak loaded a box of vegetables onto the back of his bike, Cousin Karnig approached with a pullet under one arm.

"This is for Maral."

He held the bird out to me. I took her gingerly in my arms, and the chicken cocked her head to the side and looked up at me with a beady eye.

"What's her name?" I asked.

"This one is Takouhi. She laid the first egg."

"This is too generous. I can't accept." I tried to hand Takouhi back to him, but he put his palms up and shook his head.

Cousin Satenig said, "Yes, you must. It's your birthday gift."

"No, it's really too much," I insisted.

"Don't argue," Karnig said.

"But I can't."

"Sweetheart," Karnig said, "now you've said no three times and we've said yes three times, so it's finished."

Missak used wire mesh to secure the chicken in the front basket of my bicycle.

As Missak and I pedaled back to the city, I drew up alongside him and asked, "What do you think they'll say when they see the chicken?"

"The first thing out of Babig's mouth will be 'Is that chicken going to shit all over the floor?'" He pulled out ahead and grinned at me over his shoulder.

"I'll bet he won't say that at all!" I called, pedaling quickly behind him.

We reached the rue de Belleville, dismounted, and pushed the bikes up the steep hill.

Missak said, "Tonight I'm going to tell Babig that I've found a job."

"What? You aren't going to work in the shop?" I asked.

Missak was to graduate from technical school in July, and it had been assumed that he would take a place alongside my father at the cobbler's bench.

Missak said, "I've been working in the shop since I was six and I've had enough."

"I started when I was six too," I said.

"You swept the floor and lined up the finished shoes on the shelves. But nobody ever thought you were going to be a cobbler. You're the scholar."

I winced at the tone he used for the word, as though it were at once a royal title and an insult. But he had been allowed to roam the neighborhood while I was confined to home, with my hair neatly plaited down my back, and my head bowed over my books. I was the one whose primary-school teacher had come to the apartment to speak with our parents. In preparation for the expected visit, my parents had put on their Sunday clothes and taken the dust cover off the sofa. My mother had served the teacher coffee and fresh *paklava*, and my father had seated her in his sacred armchair.

I had sat quietly in the room while they talked about me over my head as though I were a piece of furniture. The teacher said, "The child is at the top of her class. It would be a waste if she didn't continue. She must take the exam, and if she does as well as I expect, she will be admitted to a lycée for girls."

Later that night, after my aunt had fallen asleep, I tiptoed into the hall and stood listening outside my parents' bedroom door.

"If it were the boy, I could understand," my father said.

"But it's not the boy. It's your daughter."

"And what use is Latin going to be to her? No one speaks this language."

"If it's for the smart students, then why shouldn't she learn it?"

My brother wasn't much of a student. The only thing Missak had a passion for was drawing. From the time he was old enough to grip a pencil, he had filled pages and pages with sketches. He was often reprimanded for drawing across the top of his homework papers. When it was slow at the shop, he made pictures inside the lids of shoeboxes. He once used the colored pencils my mother gave him for Christmas to draw beautiful, intricate replicas of franc notes.

Now, as we walked our bikes up the hill, Missak went on, "I can't be a cobbler. It's not possible."

"But what will you do?" I asked.

"I looked for a job in mechanical drafting, but there weren't any openings. I have an offer to be an apprentice to a printer in the Eleventh. I think I'll like it. And I'll bring home some money. There's not enough work at the shop right now to support us all, even with Mairig's sewing and Auntie's knitting. You see how Babig spends hours groaning over his account books. I'm going to tell him at dinner tonight."

"You don't want to talk to him privately? You know, just you two alone."

Missak said, "Sorry. You can't get off that easily."

We reached our building, and I carried the nervous bundle of bones and feathers up the stairs while Missak lugged the baskets of vegetables and shoes behind me.

My father took one look at Takouhi and asked, "Is that chicken going to crap all over the floor?"

"Garabed, what kind of talk is that?" my mother asked.

I said, "She laid her first egg this week."

Auntie Shakeh stroked the chicken's back. "I can make her some *vardig* and it will be fine."

Within minutes my aunt had outfitted the bird with a sort of diaper held in place by a large pin. "This is just until I can sew some real ones."

Takouhi ran around the kitchen squawking, and my father observed, "She doesn't appear to like wearing panties."

"She'll get used to it," my mother said.

Before dinner, I constructed a nest in the corner of the kitchen by lining a wooden box with some rags and scraps, over which Missak hung a sign that said TAKOUHI'S THRONE.

Halfway through the meal, Missak, trying to sound casual, said, "I've found a job with a printer starting the end of July."

My mother's fork stopped in midair. There was a sharp intake of breath from my aunt. Without moving my head a centimeter, I shifted my eyes to look at my father's face. I watched as the flush crept up his neck, and the muscles in his jaw began to twitch. Even his mustache seemed to bristle.

When he spoke, it was with great restraint. "You have found a job with a printer?"

Missak said, "Not far from the Bastille. It's in an alley off Popincourt. I'll be an apprentice with a small salary. When I showed him my drawings, he thought maybe I could help with illustration too."

I watched the flush move up to my father's forehead, where the veins now stood out on his temples.

Suddenly he thundered, "Have I been training you for more than ten years so that you could go work for another man in another trade?"

Missak said nothing. None of us did. Instinctively, I lowered my head and drew up my shoulders as though reacting to a gust of cold wind.

"Azniv, did you know when you gave birth to this boy that he would grow into an ass who would kick his father in the teeth?" my father shouted. "Who would have guessed a son could be this ungrateful?"

There was a pause and I hoped for a second this was the end of the tirade. But in my heart, I knew that my father had only begun.

"It would be one thing if he had ambition to study, like his sister. Maybe if he had wanted to go to university and make something grand of himself. But he has no such ambition. Instead he wants to exchange his father's honest trade for another. Why does he think that ink under his fingernails is any better than shoe polish? I'm going to go down to the river with all my tools—the hammers, the lasts, the sewing machine, and all of it—and pitch them in the water. What good is any of it? Why have I been working so hard? What will happen to my business when I die if my son refuses to make it his own?"

I looked at my brother, wondering how his heart wasn't breaking a little at hearing, behind the bluster, my father's hurt. *Okay, Babig,* I imagined him saying, *of course I will join you at the shop, and gratefully accept the fruit of your labor when the time comes.* But Missak had decided on his path, and his face was a mask of annoyance.

"How did I end up with a son like this? I know you, boy. You will not bend. You are more difficult than a mule." Here my father paused for a moment.

My mother and aunt exchanged glances. Where could the stubbornness possibly have come from?

My father started shouting again, but I stopped listening. His words were like hailstones on a tin roof. After a while, the pelting slowed and the force of the wind waned as the storm passed over. His volume lowered. The insults stopped. He was asking, "And how much will he be paying you?"

My neck relaxed, and my head went back to its natural position. We had weathered the worst of it, although I didn't think my father would ever entirely forgive Missak for this rejection.

When I carried the supper dishes to the kitchen, I noticed that Takouhi was sitting in her nest. I set the dirty plates on the counter and leaned down to the bird. Takouhi clucked with irritation as I slid my hand under her. She objected loudly as I withdrew our first brown speckled egg.

6

THAT FALL MY MOTHER'S sewing machine broke down, and a family emergency was declared. My father, who was generally skilled at mending his own machines and tools, had worked on it for several hours before giving up.

Missak assured my mother, "Don't worry. Zaven can fix it."

"Do you really think so?" she asked, grimacing with anxiety. My aunt was at my mother's elbow, mirroring her pained expression. There was no money for a new machine, and without my mother's work, there would be a substantial hole in our household budget.

Missak said, "He can fix anything."

The next day, Zaven leaned over the wounded machine in our front room, Missak behind him, as I knit sweater sleeves for my aunt. I observed from nearby as he deftly tinkered among its innards.

"How does it look? Do you think you can make it work?" My mother was hovering over him. My father sat in his armchair reading the newspaper.

Zaven lifted his head and smiled at her. "Don't worry, Auntie. It doesn't need any new parts—there's just a jam in one spot, and some fiddling that needs doing in a couple of others. Missak, can you pass me the rest of my tools?"

Missak handed Zavig a leather satchel that opened to reveal an array of screwdrivers, pliers, wrenches, and mysterious implements. When Zaven was nine years old, he had taken apart the family bicycle, saving his skin by putting it back together the same afternoon. He had finished school at the end of July, and at the same time that Missak had taken up his position at the print shop, Zavig had started as an assistant at an appliance-repair shop. His father and brother both worked in the shoe trade, but as Zavig was the second son, there had been no objection to his choosing another line. The shop was on the rue du Faubourg-du-Temple, and there, under his boss's supervision, Zavig was honing his natural skills.

My father dropped his newspaper. "Would you women move away and let the boy do his work? How is he supposed to get anything done with you breathing down the back of his neck like that? My boy, you have the steady hands of a jewel cutter. Too bad your father couldn't have arranged for you to work in the diamond district. Doesn't someone you know have a cousin down there?"

Zaven laughed. "What I do is more useful than that, I hope."

"As long as the Germans don't find any use for you with their machines." Here my father lifted his newspaper and then commented from behind it, "For each German soldier the Resistance kills, the Germans shoot fifty or a hundred hostages. And the hostages are all Communists or Jews. They like it best when they are Communist Jews."

"Missak," Zaven asked, "can you hold this for me?"

Missak moved forward, almost tripping over Takouhi, who squawked as he tossed her toward the kitchen. "That stupid bird of yours is always underfoot."

I replied, "This stupid bird of mine laid the eggs that went into the cake I baked."

As though he hadn't heard any of this commotion, my father said dryly, "Well, since Hitler invaded Russia, the Communists have changed their tune, eh, Zaven?"

Zaven said, "My father was always clear about who the enemy was, Uncle."

My father dropped his paper to his lap again. "Yes, well, now Stalin also understands quite well who the enemy is. You can only guess what's going on by reading between the lines of this lie-filled rag. But the Soviets won't fold like a house of cards the way the French did. Stalin will make every man and boy fight the Germans to his last breath. If they can hold them off until winter, the Germans will be buried up to their frosted eyebrows in snow. With England on one side and Russia on the other, two cats will strangle one dog."

Zaven stood up and closed his tool bag. "It's done, Auntie."

My mother sat at her chair before the machine and clamped a length of scrap fabric under the silver foot. When she pumped the pedal, the machine produced a rapid ratcheting sound as the needle darted up and down.

My mother's face brightened. "Bless you, my boy. I don't know how we can repay you."

He grinned. "No need for payment, Auntie. I'm planning to eat half the cake Maral made."

I dropped a finished sleeve into my aunt's basket. "So we can go now?"

"Please be home before dark. Remember, they moved the curfew again," my mother said.

Missak, Zaven, and I collected Jacqueline, Barkev, Hagop Meguerditchian, and Hagop's girlfriend, Alice Balian. We headed toward the Buttes Chaumont, and Alice, Jacqueline, and I strolled ahead.

Jacqueline asked, "What do you have in that basket?"

"My mother packed a bottle of pickles, two tomatoes, and cheese. I also made a spice cake. What did you bring?" I asked.

Alice said, "My mother made some string cheese and *lavash*. Hagop brought a bottle of wine."

Jacqueline shrugged. "Sorry. I'm a freeloader."

"Don't worry about it, Jacqueline," I said. "We have plenty."

We arrived in the park and spread the blue-checked table-cloth over a boulder near the waterfall. Jacqueline, Alice, and I laid out the food, using Zaven's knife to slice the cheese, the fruit, and the vegetables.

Barkev said, "It's a feast."

Missak said, "Before the war, this would have been barely enough; now it's a feast."

Jacqueline said, "Don't be so sour. My belly is full for once."

"Thanks to Maro for the delicious cake," said Barkev, holding up a jam jar and nodding at me.

"Our thanks to Takouhi, who laid the eggs." I looked up to see Zaven staring at me. I blushed and turned my eyes away.

Hagop opened the instrument case he had borrowed from his father, pulled out a pear-shaped oud, and started playing. His fingers moved quickly over the strings.

"Don't you know the words to any of those tunes, brother?" Missak asked.

"I can play, but I have no voice. Hey, Alice, my little canary, will you sing for us?" He played the first chords of the song "Maro Jan."

Alice knew the verses, and at the chorus we all joined her.

> *For your red blouse I will die,*
> *for your long blouse I will die.*
> *I shall die for the blouse that Maro sews . . .*

At the end of the song, Jacqueline asked, "Hagop, can you play 'Bel Ami'?"

"I can play anything you want." Hagop strummed the first chords of the song.

As Jacqueline and Alice sang, I leaned back on the bench staring up at the tall beech trees that surrounded us. The sun was low in the sky, and its late-afternoon rays were amber. The trees cast long shadows across the lawn. I shaded my eyes with my hand and glanced around at my brother and my friends, their features sharply defined by the golden light. The scene was briefly suspended, like a single frame from a moving picture.

I would find out later that by this time, Missak was already forging documents for a Resistance network, making false identity cards for those who had gone underground. Zaven and Barkev disseminated leaflets that were printed on a mimeograph machine in the basement of the building adjacent to the shoemaking atelier where Barkev and his father worked. Our customary values had been turned upside down by the war; lies and secrecy were the highest good, while openness and honesty led to betrayal. The boys protected us by keeping us ignorant of what they were doing, and we turned our faces away from any clues.

As the shadows lengthened, I studied Zaven's profile, his face seeming pensive and remote. He had never looked so handsome, and I longed to put my hand to his cheek. When I was a little girl playing house with a doll and a miniature tea set, Zaven was always my imaginary husband. He arrived home from work in the evening and after supper read his newspaper while I bathed the baby in the sink. My parents never held hands or embraced. I had never heard them say that they loved each other, so marriage seemed to me an amicable living arrangement designed for the rearing of children. But at fifteen, infused with images of romantic love from movies and books, and with the war heightening the drama of daily life, I no longer saw it as a game. Now when his eyes rested on me for a few seconds longer than they had in the past, a thrill raced under my skin.

I sat up, suddenly noticing that the sun had dropped to the horizon. "We should go. We promised we'd be home before dark." I started stacking the plates in my basket.

Hagop stopped playing and placed the instrument into its case. "Okay, little mother."

"Isn't she, though?" said Jacqueline. "She always makes sure you take an umbrella when it might rain. She used to correct my homework on the way to school."

Missak said, "Do you know how hard it is to have a sister like that?"

"What's so hard about it?" Zaven asked.

"She's been making me look bad from the minute she started talking," Missak answered. "When I said *bird*, she said *starling*. I couldn't figure out where she learned half the stuff she knew."

"Would you please stop talking about me as though I weren't here? I need some help," I said.

After we retrieved the remains of the picnic, I picked up the tablecloth and stood to shake off the crumbs.

"Let me help." Barkev moved forward.

"No, brother, it's my turn." Zaven stepped in front of him.

I held two corners, Zaven took the two others, and we folded the cloth in half by bringing the corners together, and then in half again. When we folded it a third time, it brought us close, our knuckles brushing and his face inches above mine. I looked into his dark eyes for a few dizzy seconds.

"I have it," I said, tugging the folded cloth from his hands and turning quickly to hide my embarrassment. I knelt down to put the fabric in the basket and then closed the lid.

Barkev was suddenly standing over me solicitously. "Let me carry that for you."

"There's no need," I answered, glancing up at him and his brother. "It's not heavy."

"I'll carry it," said Zaven.

I looked from one to the other. I imagined that both of them would lay hold of the wicker basket and yank it back and forth until the handles broke off.

I told them, "I appreciate your chivalry, boys, but I'll carry it myself."

7

WHEN I TRIED ON my green woolen dress in November, I found I needed to cinch the belt two notches tighter than I had the previous winter. I hadn't grown any taller, so the length was fine, but something was wrong about the way the dress now hung. I studied my figure in the oval mirror on the bedroom wall. We all had grown thinner and there was nothing to be done about it.

Turning from the mirror, I glanced at my aunt, who I had forgotten was in the room. Auntie Shakeh sat quietly on the bed, dressed as usual in a shapeless, dun-colored dress with a brown sweater over it, winding her long hair into a bun. It suddenly struck me how gaunt she had become.

"Auntie, what has happened to you?" I asked. "You are melting away."

Auntie Shakeh finished inserting the long black hairpins that held the bun in place. "I don't know, honey. I don't have much appetite."

"Maybe if we had something other than turnips, you would eat more."

"Maybe," my aunt said. She stood and plucked a few pieces of lint from the front of her sweater. Her skirt belled around her spindly legs.

"We're all suffering from rutabaga-itis," I said.

My aunt gave a wan smile.

At dinner that evening, my father made reference to the new notices that had been plastered to the walls along the rue de Belleville. They listed the names of the latest supposed criminals executed by the Germans. Auntie Shakeh grew pale and she put down her fork.

"Shakeh," my mother scolded, "you have to eat something. You are turning into skin and bones. Garabed, why do you have to talk like that at the table?"

My father said, "Shakeh, stop dwelling on the past. The Turks didn't manage to kill us, and the Germans won't either. Now eat your food."

"It's not for myself that I fear," Aunt Shakeh replied, glancing at Missak. She picked up her fork and dutifully moved some bulgur to her mouth.

My mother and I decided that Auntie Shakeh should no longer help with the grocery shopping. Terrible stories and rumors circulated up and down the long queues outside the shops. Auntie Shakeh arrived home trembling and distraught after her trips to the market.

Madame Auger's son had been caught out after curfew and was held in the Cherche-Midi prison for two days, although no one knew where he had been until he arrived home and told them. Madame Moutsakis's son had almost been arrested at the cinema when people booed the news-reel; the Germans cleared the auditorium and arrested every fiftieth person. God must have been watching because he was number forty-nine and missed being taken by a hair.

My aunt wasn't the only one in the family who was suffer-ing. Takouhi was looking skinny and bedraggled as well. Her feathers were falling out in clumps. She had stopped laying eggs. I didn't know anything about chickens and suspected that she was ill with a disease particular to barnyard fowl. One day I took her down to the courtyard for fresh air and a change of scenery, but the weather had turned cold, so we soon retreated to the apartment.

After two weeks with no eggs, Missak began to lobby for chicken soup.

"That bird is on her way out, Maral. Anyone can see that. Why let good chicken meat go to waste?"

"You ingrate. That bird has given this family about a hun-dred eggs we wouldn't otherwise have had," I said.

"Well, if you're counting, she hasn't laid one in fifteen days," Missak pointed out.

"The boy makes some sense," my father interjected. "And this is the perfect weather for chicken soup."

"I have two onions left. You know what they say. Eat lamb in the spring and chicken in the fall," my mother said.

I wasn't surprised that my father had sided with my brother, but I knew that without my mother's support, poor Takouhi would soon be in the pot.

I argued, "We didn't have lamb in the spring, so why should we have chicken in the fall?"

Missak replied, "Because we're hungry, that's why."

"You think one meal of chicken soup is going to fix that?" I asked. "What if she starts laying eggs again?"

"What are we going to do with that bird in this freezing apartment all winter, Maral? The poor thing will be shivering in the corner, all her feathers fallen out, getting skinnier by the day so in the end there won't be an ounce of meat on her bones," my mother reasoned.

"She can sleep in my bed," I said.

"You are not taking a filthy bird into your bed," my mother said.

"It sounds like we know the menu for tomorrow's dinner," my father concluded.

Aunt Shakeh stared at me dolefully. I looked down at Takouhi, who was pecking at the rug under the table. She cocked her head and peered up at me with one eye.

When I arrived home from school the next evening, I smelled chicken soup. My mouth watered despite my resolve, and I took the bowl my mother offered me. But when I dipped the spoon in and pulled up a half-formed egg, I dropped it in disgust.

"If only we had waited two more days." I jumped up from the table and ran out of the room.

"Maral," my father called after me. "Come back here. Your mother worked hard to clean that chicken and make this soup."

"I'm not hungry," I shouted, and slammed the bedroom door behind me.

The following evening, Missak placed a set of forged ration tickets on the table. My parents exchanged tense glances but asked no questions. My father laid our authentic tickets on the table alongside the fake ones.

After scrutinizing them carefully, he announced, "They look the same to me."

"Of course they do," Missak said. "The only way you could see any difference is with a magnifying glass, and even then you'd have to know what you were looking for."

"Bread is expensive, and death is cheap," my father said.

"I wouldn't dare use them," my mother said.

"Maral will go," said Missak. "Right?"

I pretended more courage than I felt. "It's my turn to do the shopping."

"Oh, sweetie, I don't like the idea. What if you get caught?" my mother asked.

"She won't get caught," Missak said.

The next day I walked quickly up the hill away from our immediate neighborhood. I had not considered going to Donabedian's Market; I headed to shops where my face was unknown. I wouldn't do all the shopping in one place—I planned to go to several different stores for our supplies. If we had been less hungry, Missak wouldn't have brought home fake tickets, and my father would never have allowed me to use them. I stood in the first line, trembling from the cold and shifting from foot to foot.

When I reached the counter, I fought an impulse to bow my head and lower my eyes, forcing myself to look up at the grocer's long, graying mustache and smile.

After I walked out of the shop with a sack full of apples, I exhaled hard. It was a little easier in the next shop, and easier still in the third. When my basket was full, I crossed the threshold of the last shop, stepped onto the street, and sped down the hill toward home as though the Devil himself were trying to step on the backs of my shoes.

"Thank God," Auntie Shakeh cried as I walked in the front door.

My brother took the heavy basket and carried it to the kitchen.

"Was there any trouble?" My mother followed behind me.

"No one noticed a thing," I said.

"I told you," Missak said.

As my mother unpacked the basket, she started to laugh.

"What's so funny?" I asked.

My mother shook her head and smiled. "It was silly of me, but I thought because we had black-market tickets, there would be black-market food. I imagined butter and meat, isn't that crazy? But it's the same root vegetables . . ."

"Only more of them," Missak said tersely.

8

"LIKE CARTHAGE, ENGLAND WILL be destroyed." The radio commentator made the same pronouncement at the end of each of his nightly broadcasts. I braced myself for my father's reaction—he snapped off the radio and shouted, "That fool will be the first one shot as a traitor when this cursed war is over."

My mother said, "Not so loud. If he bothers you so much, why do you listen?"

"Don't you think I'd rather hear 'This is the French speaking to the French'? But the Germans have the BBC so jammed I can't make out anything they're saying," my father replied.

"We could just keep the radio turned off. After all, Maral is trying to do her homework."

"Don't worry about me," I said.

My mother said, "Between that man's foolishness and your father's bellowing, I don't know how you can work."

My father snorted. "Speaking of fools, where is that son of yours?"

My mother answered, "He's out with Zaven. I think they went to the cinema. They should be back soon."

I glanced up from my book and smoothed my eyebrows with the tips of my fingers. The mention of Zaven made me worry about my appearance. I had developed an unfortunate habit of pulling at my brows when I studied. I went to the bedroom to check in the mirror that I hadn't plucked out half an eyebrow without realizing.

I took a moment to straighten my sweater, and then I picked up my brush from the top of the dresser. I was sure my hair would wave nicely if it was cut to chin length, the way all the other girls wore theirs, but because my mother disapproved, I was stuck with hair that fell to my waist. I turned sideways to the mirror to examine the part of my figure I could see without climbing onto the bed.

"Are you expecting company?" my aunt asked.

I jumped. "Auntie, you scared me."

"I didn't mean to scare you, *yavrum*. I thought you knew I was here. I'm not feeling well, so I came to knit in bed."

I heard voices in the front hall.

"Missak is home," observed Auntie Shakeh. "And is that Zaven with him?"

"It sounds like it."

"Will you make my excuses, honey? I'm too tired to say hello. Can I ask you a favor? Would you get me an extra blanket? It's not even so cold outside, but there's a chill in my bones."

I pulled a wool blanket from the dresser's bottom drawer, spread it over the bed, and tucked it around my aunt.

"Is that good, Auntie?"

"Is there maybe another one?"

I looked in the drawers of the bureau and found a large woolen shawl, which I held up. "How about this?"

"That's good."

"I hope this keeps you warm." I laid the shawl on top of the blankets.

"Thank you, *yavrum*. I'm going to sleep now."

"Good night, Auntie," I said, leaving and closing the bedroom door behind me.

I went into the front room, where my brother was sitting at the table with his sketchpad.

"Where's Zaven?" I asked.

"He stopped in to say hello. We thought you had gone to bed."

I suppressed a sigh. "No, I still have more work to do."

For a few minutes, the marks on the page of my math notebook were stick figures gesturing at me with tiny raised fists.

It had been three weeks since I had seen Zaven. He and I hardly ever crossed paths, and when we did, my brother, if not a whole crowd, was always there too. The few times I'd noticed him looking at me, I had felt too shy to meet his gaze. Once, I was briefly alone with him in the courtyard while he was waiting for Missak, and we had stood in excruciating silence. Or at least *I* was uncomfortable; maybe he was just distracted.

I wanted to blame my awkwardness on my parents' Old World ways, but Jacqueline's parents were much like mine, and she had boys and even men trailing behind her. Some of the older lycée girls met their boyfriends after school around the corner and out of sight of the street monitors. I noted with envy the effortless way couples laughed and chatted together at café tables and sat with their arms around each other on park benches. One afternoon when Denise and I were heading home, I saw a girl in the class ahead of ours kissing a German soldier full on the mouth. They were half hidden behind a tree in a small, fenced garden not far from school, but it wasn't as private a spot as she assumed. I stopped, unable to tear my eyes away, and when Denise tapped my arm to get my attention, my face burned with shame.

Now I glanced back at the notebook on the table before me. The numerals were legible again, and I worked for another hour before going to bed.

In the middle of the night, the sounds of distant blasts and the drone of airplanes overhead awakened me. Air raids near Paris had started a few months earlier, and outings to the designated shelter had become part of our routine. That night, pilots of the Royal Air Force were dropping bombs somewhere on the outskirts of the city. The air-raid sirens had failed to give advance warning, so we stayed in our apartment, standing by the windows with the lights out and the curtains opened. We listened to the explosions and watched far-off flashes above the building across the way. Giving up on getting any sleep, we closed the curtains, turned on the lights, and took our usual places in the front room. I distractedly flipped through an old movie magazine Jacqueline had loaned me.

Auntie Shakeh, tightly wrapped in the shawl, rocked from side to side in her chair. "Lord have mercy," she whispered, closing her eyes.

Missak jumped up from where he was perched on the side of his bed. "I can't stand it anymore. You can probably see the whole thing from the park. I'm sure Zaven and Barkev are already there."

"What kind of an onion head are you?" my mother asked.

"They've been dropping bombs for over an hour; they're all in the same place, and it's miles from here," Missak said.

My father said, "I think it's Boulogne. The English must be hitting the Renault factory."

"Can I go?" Missak asked.

"I'll come with you," my father said.

They hurried to the front hall and took their coats from the hooks.

"What about me?" I leaped from my chair.

My mother said, "Maral Pegorian, you are not leaving this apartment. If your father and brother are crazy enough to think there is some kind of show to watch, I won't stop them. But my daughter is not going into the street at this hour of the night while bombs are falling. And what about the curfew?"

Missak said, "The Germans almost never come this far out, and who would be patrolling during a bombing raid?"

"Good point, my boy," my father said.

My mother threw up her hands. "Impossible."

After they left, I sat back down near my mother, who

began sewing buttons on one of the vests she had run up earlier on the machine. She stabbed the needle through the cloth as though it were an enemy. My aunt picked up her knitting needles, and the sound of them competed with the clock that noisily ticked the minutes. Was this to be my lot? Stuck in an apartment knitting or sewing or cooking while waiting for the men to come back from some adventure? It made me want to take the kitchen plates and throw them out the window just to hear them smash into a thousand pieces on the cobblestones below.

I sighed heavily.

My mother said, "Why should you want to be out there watching bombs fall? It's not like fireworks, you know."

"Maybe because it's more interesting than sitting like a hen in a coop."

"You think war is interesting? I saw a war once and there was nothing interesting about it. Better a hen in a coop than a bloody pile of feathers by the side of the road." My mother drew her eyebrows together and pressed her lips thin, jabbing the needle through the hole of a button.

Auntie Shakeh said, "May the good Lord watch over us and protect us from ever seeing such things again."

It was strange that I knew so little about what they had gone through, especially as it seemed to loom like a vast, amorphous shadow over our lives. My mother and my aunt referred vaguely and ominously to what they called the Massacres or the Deportations. If I asked a question about that period in the Old Country, my mother would say darkly, "It's better not to talk about those times." Auntie Shakeh would go pale and invoke God. So after a while, I stopped asking, and it was all I could do to keep from rolling my eyes when they made their dire, cryptic references.

My father and brother returned a half an hour later, saying they hadn't seen anything but bright flashes along the skyline. But the Kacherians had been there, as well as other neighbors. Once the British planes had flown off, people dispersed.

"No one complained about the English going after Renault," my father said.

Missak laughed. "You might even say they were happy."

My mother said, "I promise you, the people of Boulogne are not happy tonight. And all I'm feeling is exhausted."

The night was almost over as we wearily returned to our beds.

I lay in the dark listening to the soft wheezing of my aunt, who had fallen asleep immediately. I was unhappy because I had missed seeing Zaven twice in one night. I wished it didn't matter so much to me, but there were so few chances for romance in my life, and I had pegged my heart on this particular boy.

When finally I fell asleep, I dreamed that I was walking along the lake in the Buttes Chaumont. Zaven strolled beside me. It was a beautiful afternoon, the skies clear and the trees adorned with flowers. He slipped his arm through mine as though we had walked like this a thousand times, and he smiled into my eyes. My heart beat its feathered wings. I looked down at our feet. There were ducks and swans lying at the edge of the water. They were lifeless, their necks twisted at awful angles, their eyes staring up without seeing. Shuddering, I hid my face against Zavig's shoulder.

9

I STOOD ON THE STOOL in my bedroom while my mother pinned the hem of a new dress. The fabric was ruby taffeta, and my mother had managed to hide the discolored folds in such a way that no one would guess the dress was made from a pair of flea-market curtains.

"Hold still," my mother mumbled through a mouthful of pins. "If you keep moving, it's going to be crooked."

I glanced at myself in the mirror. The dress had three-quarter-length sleeves, a tight bodice, and a full skirt that made my waist look tiny. I wished that I had someplace special to go, and someone to take me there.

"Done," my mother said. "Give it to me so I can hem it."

"Can I wear it to Sunday dinner at the Kacherians', or do you think it's too fancy?" I undid the buttons and pulled off the dress.

My mother draped the dress over her arm. "You can wear this to church, to Sunday dinner . . . Speaking of Sunday dinner, I promised Shushan that your aunt and I would help her make *manti* on Saturday. So we might not be here when you get home from school."

"*Manti?*" I could almost smell the meat dumplings swimming in broth. "She can get lamb?"

"Chicken, but you'll hardly be able to tell the difference," my mother said. "In times like these, you make do. In the Old Country, no one ever made *manti* alone. The whole neighborhood gathered, and we each brought a rolling pin. You didn't have to sit alone in your kitchen and do it all by yourself. You should have seen the times when they made phyllo dough for *paklava*. My mother could roll it out so it was thinner than a sheet of paper."

Saturday was my sixteenth birthday, but there was no cake that evening at supper. My gifts were the dress from my mother, a pair of leather-soled black pumps from my father, and a hand-knit summer sweater from Auntie Shakeh.

"Babig, where did you get the leather?" I asked my father.

"From Vahan. No wooden soles on my daughter's birthday shoes."

The last and best gift was a bar of lavender soap that Missak gave me.

I held the smooth bar cupped in my hands and put it to my nose, breathing in. "It smells beautiful. Where did you manage to find it?"

My brother just smiled.

On Sunday morning after the breakfast dishes were done, I barricaded myself in the kitchen and boiled water for a bath in the large zinc tub we kept under the sink. Using the soap, I lathered my hair and then, with a rough washcloth, scrubbed my skin until it was pink. Wrapped in a towel, I rinsed my hair under the cold tap so that it would shine.

I spent the rest of the morning sequestered in the bedroom. First I filed my fingernails, and then, using a pair of tweezers, I carefully shaped my eyebrows, making them narrow and sleek. I studied my face in the mirror, smiling and pouting and frowning, then sticking out my tongue at my vanity.

When I finally emerged from the bedroom wearing my new red dress, my family were all sitting in the front room, except for Auntie Shakeh, who had gone to church right after breakfast.

"Are we ready to go?" I asked.

"*Meghah!*" my mother said. "What did you do to your eyebrows?"

"What about her eyebrows?" My father peered over the top of his newspaper.

"Do they look bad?" I put my hand to my face.

"Ridiculous," Missak said.

This was not at all the reaction I had been hoping for. We were going to the Kacherians' for Sunday dinner. I hadn't seen Zaven in weeks, and I wanted him to think I looked elegant and mature.

My mother clucked her tongue. "I don't know why you'd do something like that. They are hardly wider than a thread."

Missak said, "Jacqueline did the same thing. It looks silly."

I retorted, "I don't care what you think. You don't know anything about fashion."

"If it were the fashion to shave your head, would you do that as well?" my father asked.

I turned on my heel and headed to the door.

When we reached the Kacherians', we found that Auntie Shakeh had arrived ahead of us and was already seated on the parlor couch with Virginie and Vahan Kacherian.

Missak asked, "Where are the guys?"

Vahan said, "Any minute they'll be here."

Zaven and Barkev arrived just then, and we all took seats around the dinner table. I ended up with my mother on my right and Virginie on my left, far from Zaven's place between his mother and my brother. Auntie Shushan ladled out the *manti* soup, and the bowls were passed around. The steam rising from my bowl smelled so wonderfully of chicken and onions that I said before I even tasted it, "Auntie, this is heavenly."

My father said, "In lean times, heaven is a full belly."

Missak imitated my father with fake solemnity. "Heaven, my friends, is a bowl of chicken dumplings."

Vahan laughed. "Enough proverbs, my friends. Time to eat."

With such a crowd, there was no chance for anything interesting to pass between Zaven and me: no meaningful glances, no words whispered on the stairs. When the men retired to the front room to talk politics and the women repaired to the kitchen, I fantasized that Zaven and I headed to the park, where the roses were just starting to bloom. He used his penknife to cut a rose from a bush and presented it to me with a flourish. But, of course, I was actually in the crowded kitchen with a damp dishtowel in my hand. Much later, I realized that all he was waiting for was a small gesture from me—going a few steps out of my way to cross his path or slipping a note into his jacket pocket—but for me at that age, even a small act seemed impossibly bold.

The next morning when I met Denise on the corner of the rue de Belleville on the way to school, she was wearing a yellow fabric star sewn to her jacket. The law had gone into effect a few days before, and it was the first I had seen of this new insult.

Denise avoided my eyes. "Did you see Z.K. this weekend?"

I followed her lead, slipping into conversation without comment about the ignominious star. "We had Sunday dinner with his family yesterday."

"Did you get to talk with him alone?"

"Nothing. Not even an elbow next to mine on the table."

"At this rate, you could be eighteen before he says anything," Denise said.

"Maybe he never will. Maybe he's not interested in me."

"You know that's not true."

Just then, a mother and a little blond boy of about five years old walked by. The boy pointed at the star on Denise's jacket and said, "Mama, look, a Jew." The mother leaned down and whispered something into his ear as she hurried him past.

Denise flushed. "I was pretending there was nothing different today. But this is our life now. So one might as well get used to it. The first morning will be the most difficult."

"It's like something out of the Middle Ages. How can this be happening in the twentieth century?"

Denise shrugged. "The irony, if you can call anything about it ironic, is that we're required by law to wear them but we have to pay for the fabric with our ration tickets."

"What would happen if you didn't wear them?"

"They would put us in jail, I suppose, if they caught us."

As we continued down the hill, we saw others wearing yellow stars, and Denise exchanged empathetic glances with them. It was as though they were acknowledging their membership in a no-longer-secret society. We walked in glum silence toward the lycée. When we were a few blocks from our destination, a young man we crossed paths with noticed Denise's star and with a smile pointed to his own. In the center, instead of *Jew*, he had written *Buddhist* in black letters.

"Do you think he's really a Buddhist?" I asked.

"Well, he's not a Jew. My brother says we're crazy to do what they tell us. We registered as Jews, and Henri says they have our address any time they want to come find us. Now my mother has sewn these stars on our clothes. Henri ripped his off this morning, threw it on the floor, and ground it under his heel. My mother was weeping, he was yelling at her, and my father started shouting at Henri. Henri's angry they didn't listen to him two years ago when he wanted us to go to America. We have cousins in Baltimore. But my parents trusted in the French Republic. They are French citizens, or at least they were until recently. What about your parents?"

"They have Nansen passports, the ones for stateless people. That's what most Armenians have."

"My parents' citizenship was revoked. They have no country now either."

I thought of an Armenian maxim my father used in his darker moods: If they send two baskets of shit to our city, one will come to our house. The Occupation was baskets of shit, that was sure, and the largest one had been delivered to the Jews.

When Denise and I reached the school, I noticed other classmates wearing yellow stars on their jackets. One girl had let her long hair hang down so it obscured most of the yellow, and another had turned back her jacket lapel to cover hers. Thankfully, when we all entered the lycée and exchanged our outerwear for the school's democratizing smocks, the Jewish girls looked like everyone else.

Denise and I went together to our first-period mathematics class. The teacher, Madame Bourdet, had a bonnet of short, gray curls and a long, pointed nose. She was a rigid and demanding instructor, but on this morning she seemed flustered whenever she turned from the board to face the class. She dropped her chalk several times and pulled out the hankie tucked into her sweater cuff to wipe her perspiring face.

Just before the class came to an end, Madame Bourdet declared, in her formal manner, "My dear girls, this has nothing whatsoever to do with algebra, but I cannot restrain myself from sharing with you the profound regret I experienced this morning as I witnessed the latest affront to the values of the French Republic. And to those of you who are subject to this indignity, I can only say that I offer you my sincerest apology on behalf of the vast majority of the French people. Class is dismissed."

As we soberly filed out of the classroom, I turned back to see Madame Bourdet dabbing at her eyes with the white hankie.

Denise took my arm and whispered, "She forgot to assign homework."

10

I WAS AWAKENED BY the sounds of muffled shouting and pounding. Pulling back the curtain, I glanced at the clock on the windowsill. It was just after six in the morning, but it seemed earlier because the skies were gray.

Auntie Shakeh sat up in bed. "What is it?"

I slid my feet into my slippers. "I don't know."

We pulled on our robes and went to the front hall. My mother leaned her head out the doorway while my father stood on the landing.

"What's happening?" I asked.

"They're taking the Jews," my father answered. "The police are in the next stairwell. They'll probably be coming here in a few minutes. They're taking them all, even the women and children."

I noticed that my brother was missing. "Where's Missak?"

"He went down to the street to see what's going on," my father said.

"What about the Lipskis?" I asked.

"They are packing their bags." My father shook his head. "I told them to hide on the roof, but it would be no use. The police are searching from top to bottom."

My mother's face was ashen. "Joseph is concerned about Sara. He's afraid all this will make the baby come early."

"What about Claire?" I asked.

"Children are to go with their parents," my father answered.

I said, "They should leave her with us."

"*Yavrum*, why didn't I think of that?" my mother exclaimed. "Go get her, Garabed. Bring her here and tell them we'll keep her until they come back."

"What should we do with this yellow-haired baby?" my father asked. "Think a minute. Who knows where they're taking them or when they'll be back?"

"Garabed, enough. Maral, go get the child." My mother motioned me toward the doorway.

I looked at my father questioningly, and he nodded.

I quietly rapped on the door, and Joseph Lipski opened it, his face grimly set.

"Please come in." He waved me into the apartment.

Two valises were sitting by the front door. In the kitchen, Sara was folding Claire's clothes and putting them into a small cardboard suitcase. Claire was sitting on a straight-backed kitchen chair, holding Charlotte in her lap.

I said, "Mr. Lipski, my mother has offered to keep Claire until you come back. But we have to hurry. The police will be here soon."

"It is a kind offer, but I must ask my wife."

He spoke to his wife in Yiddish. She glanced quickly from

Claire to her husband and finally to me. Her large eyes were bright with tears when she nodded yes.

Sara Lipski snapped shut the suitcase and said something into Claire's ear, embracing the child tightly before pushing her toward me.

I picked up the suitcase and took the child's hand, feeling as though the two of us were starting on a long journey. "Let's go play some games, okay?"

Claire looked up at her mother and her father, both of whom nodded yes, and then she nodded as well.

"Go quickly." Joseph Lipski escorted us to the door.

Sara said something urgently in Yiddish. I didn't understand the words, but I heard panic in her voice and knew she was having second thoughts about letting Claire go. I imagined that her heart must feel like a piece of cloth caught on a jagged nail.

Quieting his wife with a firm word, Joseph herded Claire and me into the hall and closed the door behind us.

The door to our apartment opened a crack and then wider to let us in.

"Hello, little one," said my mother. "We're so glad you are coming to stay with us for a while."

Just then Missak returned. "What's she doing here?" he asked in Armenian.

My mother said, "We're keeping her until they come back."

He slapped his forehead. "Have you all lost your minds?"

"What else should we do?" My mother glanced down at Claire.

Claire, who didn't understand what we were saying, looked with large gray eyes from one face to another.

Missak said through gritted teeth, "Do you not understand

how dangerous this is? They're filling buses they have lined up out on the rue de Belleville. There are some of Doriot's blue-shirt Fascists in the courtyard watching the entrances. The police have lists of names with addresses and apartment numbers."

"And you think we should send her with them?" my father asked.

Missak groaned. "It's done. But keep in mind that if they find her here, we'll be on our way to prison. I'll tell the Lipskis what to say if the police ask for her. Then I'm going out."

I took Claire to my bedroom, and after I shut the door behind us, we opened the tin and spread the buttons on the bed and began to sort them by size and color. When the sounds of loud voices and slamming doors filtered in from the stairwell, I took Claire in my lap and sang her a French lullaby and then an Armenian one. Mercifully, she dozed for a while.

After the building grew still, I led Claire to the kitchen to find some breakfast.

"We have no milk," I said to my mother. "What should I give her to eat?"

My mother shrugged. "Margarine and toast. I'll make some tisane."

I put Claire's plate on the table, and we perched her atop several folded blankets on a chair so she could reach her food. Auntie Shakeh, whose eyes were rimmed with red, sat in her armchair rocking back and forth, muttering to herself. I caught the words *orphan*, *desert*, and *shame*, this last repeated again and again.

My mother said, "Shakeh, you're going to frighten the child. Maybe you should go lie down."

Auntie Shakeh went to the bedroom, still mumbling under her breath.

When Missak returned, he reported, "Those are municipal buses they are using. I talked with one of the drivers who said he'd made the trip twice already. They're taking them across town to the Vélodrome d'Hiver.

"You know who's in charge of this, don't you? It's not the Boches. The local cops, city bus drivers, and those creeps in their blue shirts are doing the dirty business," Missak said with disgust. "Zavig told me they took the Rozenbaums too, but Henri wasn't home last night so they didn't get him. He tried to warn them, but it was too late."

"Denise?" I asked.

He nodded.

I felt sick, and tears smarted in my eyes.

Claire, who didn't understand Armenian, tapped my arm and asked in French, "What's he saying?"

"He just told me that your parents are going on a bus," I explained.

"Where will they go on the bus?" she wanted to know.

"They are going to the Vélodrome d'Hiver," I said.

"When are they coming back?" Claire asked.

My mother said, "We're not sure, but you can stay with us until they come home."

I asked my brother in Armenian, "Do you know where Henri is?"

"Don't ask for information you don't need. And you have to keep that kid quiet and out of sight until I figure out what to do with her."

Claire pulled on my wrist. "What's he saying?"

I smoothed her hair. "We're just talking about some other friends who were on the bus with your parents."

When I went out to the shops a few hours later, the skies were overcast and the mood somber. In front of the grocer's, people passed stories of the morning's roundup up and down the line. Some families had been alerted the night before and had gone into hiding. A few people had managed to sneak off the buses and disappear down side streets. A mother on the rue Piat had thrown her children out the sixth-floor window and jumped out behind them rather than be taken by the police.

As I passed through the courtyard of our building on my way home, Madame Girard, the concierge, stopped me at the foot of the stairs. She told me that in our building alone, six families had been rounded up.

Madame Girard said, "It's a disgrace that they took the Lipski woman in her condition. Those messieurs have no decency, no decency at all."

I said, "It's a wretched business."

"And even the little ones, they took them also. But I didn't see Claire with her parents." Madame Girard looked at me. "I wonder what happened to her."

Our concierge, who was up and down the landings with her mop and bucket, had eyes like a bird of prey and ears as sharp as a dog's. No matter what her sympathies, we couldn't afford to let anyone know we had the child. A secret told to one person is a secret no more.

"Maybe they left Claire with their cousins," I suggested.

Madame Girard eyed me. "They have cousins? Funny, they never mentioned it. You know hiding a Jew is now against the law."

"That's too bad. I thought that for a Jew as small as Claire, too young even for the yellow star, they wouldn't care so much."

"Even as small a Jew as Claire." The concierge shook her head and clucked her tongue. "But in this building, the only one who might make a problem is Monsieur Delattre, on the third floor at the back. The rest mind their own business, but that one would sell his own mother if someone offered him five francs."

When I reached the landing, my father and brother were carrying a mattress out of the Lipskis' apartment. My mother followed them with a few framed photos and more of Claire's clothes.

At dinner that evening, we spoke French in deference to Claire. She watched us intently but didn't say anything unless addressed directly. When we took up our work in the front room after dinner, Claire sat at the table with a pencil and some parcel paper drawing stick figures that had large round heads and fingers like sausages.

My mother said in Armenian, "Look at that little face. It's searing my heart."

It was decided that Claire should sleep with Auntie Shakeh and me in our bedroom. It was a hot, breezeless night, so I spread a sheet loosely across Claire and Charlotte. I sat on the end of Claire's mattress on the floor with my back against the wall, singing the same two lullabies—one in French and one in Armenian. With the hall light falling into the room at an angle across the floor, I waited for Claire to ask an impossible question or to start crying. Soon, though, the sound of deep, rhythmic breathing told me that she had fallen asleep.

The next afternoon, after a family consultation, I rode the bicycle to the Vél d'Hiv, taking a basket of provisions for the Lipskis. I was red-faced and sweaty by the time I arrived, my white cotton blouse sodden and sticking to my back. There were dozens of police officers on the street guarding the entrance to the stadium. After walking up and down the sidewalk a few times, studying the face of each policeman in turn, I sidled up to a young officer whose open expression seemed the most sympathetic.

"Pardon me, sir, but would it be possible to get in touch with someone who is inside?" I asked.

He looked me over carefully. "A relative?"

"Oh, no," I told him. "I have brought this basket for our neighbors."

"There are thousands of Jews in there," he said. "It's hellishly hot."

I nodded.

"What's in the basket?" he asked.

"Bread, cheese, some pickles, and a bit of sausage. The sausage is for you."

The young officer took the basket and an envelope with Joseph Lipski's name on it. "Stay here. I'll be back to tell you if I manage to find them."

I stood rooted to the assigned spot for what seemed like a long time, but finally the sun was too much for me. Sweat trickled down my neck, and I wished I had money to buy a drink from the café on the corner. I positioned myself across the street in the shade so I could watch and be seen from the entrance into which he had disappeared. I wondered if he would really return as he'd promised or if he had made off with the whole basket and was having a jolly picnic by himself. I wondered if it was even possible to find Joseph and Sara Lipski among all the thousands inside that stadium. I leaned heavily against the wall behind me. I imagined that Denise Rozenbaum and her parents were in there as well. I wished we had been able to send some food for the Rozenbaums, but it had been difficult enough to scrape together the basket for the Lipskis.

Finally the police officer returned with the envelope I had given him. On the back, there were words hastily scribbled in pencil.

Dear Maral, Thanks to you and your family a thousand times for this food and all other assistance. When it is possible please send the package we left with you to my sister, Myriam, in Nice. You will find money for postage in the small suitcase. S. Lipski

A name and address were printed beneath.

"Even if the money they left in the child's suitcase covers the fare, I don't see how it is possible," my father said that night after Claire had been tucked into bed. "How can we get that child to the Free Zone? And even if we got her over the demarcation line, how would we get her all the way to Nice?"

Missak said, "There are people who can help. It may take some time to arrange, but it can be done."

My mother and father exchanged apprehensive glances but didn't ask Missak who these people might be. I knew no details, but it was clear to me that Missak felt Claire's being with us put more than his own personal safety at risk. He was angry because that risk was shared with these unknown associates.

The next day, I tried to keep Claire entertained with buttons, spools, and scraps of cloth. When she tired of these, I tied a half apron around her waist and let her help wash the dishes. My mother ran up a few small dresses for the doll Charlotte, and Auntie Shakeh knit Charlotte a sweater. In the afternoon, before I went to the shoe-repair shop to help my father, we put a sheet over the table in the front room so Claire could play house. She sat under the table changing the doll's clothes and whispering to her. But it was difficult keeping a child cooped up in the small apartment in the summer heat. And I started to think it was unnatural how polite and cooperative Claire was. She didn't cry and she didn't complain; she just stared up at us with round eyes.

The next night, after Claire was asleep, Missak relayed the news that the stadium had been emptied. He heard the Jews had been sent to Drancy, and from there they were being put on trains heading to work camps in the east.

My mother paled when she heard this. "But what work is Sara Lipski fit to do in her condition? She's going to have a baby in two months."

Auntie Shakeh said, "Thank God they left Claire with us."

Even though Claire made little noise, we were painfully aware of any sound or sign that might betray her presence. When my mother washed the child's clothes, she never put them outside on the drying line. Instead she tied a rope across our bedroom and pinned them up inside. Claire was not allowed in the hall to use the toilet; we had a chamber

pot for her in our apartment. When the concierge was outside sweeping and mopping the stairs, we made Claire take
off her shoes and told her to pretend to be a little mouse.
We didn't want to scare her, but Missak thought she should
understand what to do if anyone knocked on the door: she
must immediately go to the bedroom, and if we didn't call
her out within minutes, she should hide under my bed.
She should never speak Yiddish when anyone might hear.
I taught her some Armenian, which she picked up quickly,
and I realized we soon wouldn't be able to count on her not
understanding our conversations.

I barely knew Monsieur Delattre, the tenant the concierge had warned me about, but passing him in the courtyard I forced myself to say good day. He was a mild, balding middle-aged man who replied with a polite nod of the
head, and it was hard for me to imagine that he was capable
of the craven behavior the concierge attributed to him. We
found out after the war that Delattre had indeed been sending denunciatory letters about people in the neighborhood
whom he deemed suspicious or whom he disliked, including
the concierge, and he sent them to not only the prefecture
but also various Nazi offices. Madame Girard was so infuri-
ated when she learned of his treachery that she managed to
get him evicted.

One evening after Claire had been with us for several
weeks, the child broke her characteristic silence at dinner,
saying, "Mama told me that when the baby comes, she would
wrap it in a blanket and let me hold it in my lap if I sit in the
big chair. Papa said when the baby comes, I will help Mama
like a big girl."

"You are a very good girl," I replied.

"When do you think they will come get me?" Claire asked.

We all looked uneasily at one another.

Finally Missak said, "Your mama and papa have gone on a long trip by train. It may take them a while to get back to Paris. But they asked us to send you for a visit to your aunt Myriam in Nice."

"Aunt Myriam?" she asked. "I've never met her. But I have a picture of her. May I go get it?"

"Of course you may," my mother answered.

While the child was in the other room, my mother said in Armenian, "The poor child is upset enough about her parents and now you're talking about sending her someplace else."

My father said, "Azniv, we can't keep her locked up in this apartment for months on end. We don't have ration tickets for the milk and food she needs. We're not her family. Her parents want us to send her to her aunt in Nice."

Claire returned with a framed photograph of her mother and her aunt. "Aren't they pretty?" she asked, holding out the picture to me.

"Beautiful," I said. "And you know, you look a lot like your aunt Myriam."

"Mama said so too," Claire answered. "Will my parents be able to find me in Nice?"

My father said, "Of course they will."

Claire asked, "Will you go with me, Maral?"

Missak answered, "Maral can't take you, but I have a friend named Juliette who will go on the train with you. You'll like her."

"May Charlotte go?" she asked.

My mother nodded emphatically. "Of course you can take Charlotte. And I'll make you and Charlotte matching dresses."

That night I expected to hear the child crying in her bed, but instead it was Auntie Shakeh who turned to the wall and dampened her pillow with tears. After a while, Shakeh left the room. I slipped out behind her and hid in the entrance hall listening to my mother and aunt whispering in the kitchen.

"*Vahkh, vahkh, vahkh,*" Shakeh moaned.

"Shakeh, shh! You'll wake Missak."

"What will become of them? Scattered to the winds like seeds. The parents sent one way and the child another. And what if they should decide to come for us?"

"Don't talk like that. We aren't on the Germans' list. The only Armenians they have arrested are Communists. Don't you think we did right in keeping the child? What would one as small as that do in a work camp?"

"Of course we did the right thing. But I don't believe they are ever coming back."

"We don't know that," my mother protested feebly.

"The child is an orphan," my aunt said bitterly. "The same as we were. Except we saw it all. Our parents dead before our eyes. Bodies in the dirt. Children with big bellies and heads, arms and legs skinny like spiders. It is the same thing again, Azniv, the way they sent us to die in the desert. They are driving them out of their homes with nothing but a suitcase, sending them to who knows where, to do God knows what. Shame, it's a terrible, terrible shame."

My mother patted her sister's shoulder while Shakeh wept.

Early in the morning, Madame Girard was across the hall in the Lipskis' apartment, so we told Claire it was mouse time and set her up with the buttons and Charlotte in the bedroom. I went to check on the concierge.

She paused her mop. "Well, the landlord told me the Jews aren't coming back, so I'm to clean their apartments for rental."

The next evening, Missak, speaking in Armenian over Claire's head, told us the arrangements had been made with his friend Juliette. He was close-mouthed about the details, saying nothing beyond the fact that Claire would be relayed to Juliette on the platform at the Gare de Lyon the following morning.

"But I won't have time to wash her things," my mother protested. "How can we send the child with dirty clothes?"

"Did you finish the dresses?" Auntie Shakeh asked.

"Almost. I can hem them tonight. And Maral, you must give Claire a bath. At least the child will be clean, even if her clothes aren't. And pack her suitcase."

"What about my suitcase?" Claire asked me in French.

"You are going to your aunt tomorrow. And my mother wants me to give you a bath," I explained.

Claire's eyes were solemn, but she didn't say anything. It was unnerving how cooperative she was, and it made me want to pitch myself onto the floor and kick and scream.

After dinner I filled the zinc tub with water. I used a washcloth and the last slip of the lavender birthday soap to wash Claire's arms and legs, taking special care to rub clean the knees dirtied from playing on the floor. She tipped back her head while I poured water from a battered pot over the curls that stretched and streamed down her back. The nails were trimmed, the ears were swabbed, and then I dried her with a clean, rough towel before helping her put on a yellow nightgown.

I folded her thin cotton dresses and underclothes, and Claire mimicked my gestures as she prepared Charlotte's clothes to go into the suitcase. Once the lid was latched shut, I sat down on the edge of the bed behind Claire, running the brush through the damp, honey-colored curls.

"You have beautiful hair, Claire," I said.

"I like yours better."

"Why?"

"When you let it down at night, you look like a princess."

"You're the one who looks like a fairy princess," I said.

After she was asleep I went to the front room. Auntie Shakeh was knitting a tiny sweater for Charlotte that matched one she had already made for Claire. And my mother was hemming a new dress for the girl. Missak told us that he would be leaving with her in the morning while it was still dark, because the two of them would be less likely to be seen by neighbors at that hour.

Before dawn the next morning, Missak tapped me on the shoulder, waking me from a fitful sleep. He put his finger to his lips and motioned for me to follow him out of the room.

"You have to take her," he said.

"Me?" I felt as though he had dashed a bucket of cold water in my face.

"I'm sorry. If I could have thought of a different way, I

would have. It's too risky otherwise. The first train to Lyon is at six fifteen, and you're to meet Juliette near the ticket window at six."

Not wanting him to think me a coward, I ignored the electric panic rising inside me. "How will I recognize her?"

"She'll be wearing a red hat and a plaid jacket and carrying a copy of *Le Petit Parisien* under her arm."

I silently gathered up the clothes we had laid out for Claire the night before, and I grabbed some for myself and deposited them outside the bedroom door. I lifted the sleeping child from her bed. Auntie Shakeh roused briefly, but I told her that I was just getting Claire some water, and she went back to sleep. The suitcase was already waiting in the front hall. Claire sat on a stool in the parlor as I helped her on with her dress and socks.

I whispered to Missak, "Should I give her something to eat?"

He shook his head. "Juliette will take care of that. The important thing is to get her out of the building now without anyone seeing. And you have to be calm, or at least pretend to be. No looking over your shoulder. No handwringing. The more jumpy you are, the more attention you'll attract."

My heart was thumping against my ribs, and my nerves were jangling like a noisy key ring as Claire and I slipped down the stairs and through the courtyard. To keep myself steady, I imagined that I was walking with a book balanced on the top of my head: eyes straight forward and spine erect. Luck was with us and we crossed paths with no one until we were around the corner. On the rue de Belleville, we walked past peddlers setting up their carts and early-shift workers heading to the factories. We passed unnoticed as we descended the steps to the Métro. While the train rattled through the tunnel, I explained to Claire where we were going and how Juliette would be waiting for us in the station. She held Charlotte curled against her chest, listening attentively without responding. Here she was, about to be handed off to someone she didn't know to be taken on a journey to see an aunt she had never met who lived hundreds of miles from the only home she had ever had. I couldn't imagine how her five-year-old mind made sense of all this—starting with her parents' disappearance—as she bobbed like a tiny cork in the rough, dark sea.

When we arrived, the tower clock outside the Gare de Lyon showed ten minutes to six. I steered Claire by a cluster of German soldiers, my blood beating high in my neck. I gripped the suitcase tighter and tried not to squeeze Claire's hand too hard. Only the imaginary book on the top of my head kept me from turning to see if we were being followed. When we reached the ticket window, I scanned for a red hat and a plaid jacket, but Juliette was not there. The clock on the interior tower read two minutes to six. We waited to one side of the queue of ticket buyers. I had no idea what I should do if Juliette didn't turn up. What would I do with Claire? I couldn't bring her home in broad daylight. I felt jittery just thinking about it. Suddenly, a woman appeared beside us—requisite hat, jacket, and a newspaper tucked under one arm. She was pretty, blond, and appeared to be in her late twenties.

"Good morning, you two," she said cheerfully, bestowing a kiss on each of my cheeks as though we were old friends. She leaned down to Claire and kissed her as well. "We don't have much time. I purchased the tickets already and went to buy some breakfast rolls. So, Claire, it's time for you to come with your aunt Juliette. That's a pretty dolly you have there. What's her name?"

Claire, who hadn't spoken a word all morning, answered, "Charlotte."

"That's a beautiful name. If anyone asks, I am your father's sister, okay, *chérie*? Say goodbye to Maral now."

I sensed Juliette's competence under her breezy chatter. She emanated natural warmth that Claire responded to immediately.

When I leaned down to embrace Claire, she whispered in my ear, "Charlotte says she is going to miss you."

"I'll miss both of you, little mouse," I whispered back.

And with that, Juliette whisked Claire and her suitcase toward the quay where the train was boarding. After they disappeared onto the crowded platform, I turned toward home with a heavy heart.

Missak was waiting for me in the courtyard of our building.

"They made the train," I said.

He nodded. "She's good."

I suddenly envied Juliette her usefulness and her courage. She wasn't just sitting by while people were being rounded up like sheep. "Can I help? There must be something I can do."

"You're not cut out for it, Maral. You're too nervous, and

your thoughts show on your face. And besides, only one of us can do it. Your parents have just two children."

Ten days later we received a postcard from Myriam Galinski, one of the preprinted variety that was used to communicate between the occupied and unoccupied zones. She had checked off the box for WE ARE IN GOOD HEALTH and written in pencil beneath: *The package arrived safely. Many thanks.*

11

As the autumn slipped by, I grew used to the fact that Denise was not waiting on the corner on weekday mornings. We had heard nothing from either the Rozenbaums or the Lipskis since July. I asked my brother several times about Henri, but Missak maintained that he'd had no news.

When the English teacher, Mrs. Collin, handed back the first composition of the academic year, I saw that I had received the highest mark. I knew that I was first in the class only because Denise was no longer there. Several other Jewish girls in our group were also gone, but it was unclear whether they had been taken in the July roundup or had managed to make their way to the Free Zone in the south.

There were other changes in my family's routine that fall. Missak started staying later at his job, and sometimes, when he worked past curfew, he didn't come home at all. He said his boss had set up a cot in the back of the shop where he could spend the night. My mother agreed it was safer for him to sleep there than to try to make his way home on dark streets and risk being picked up by a patrol.

When the leaves began to fall and the air grew chill, Auntie Shakeh came down with a ragged cough. Within a few weeks, she had taken to spending most of her time in bed, weak and pale. Despite her illness, Auntie Shakeh continued knitting, propped up with pillows. I delivered her finished work to the boss's atelier, where I also picked up skeins of wool and patterns for new sweaters.

In November, Radio Paris announced that the Germans had crossed the demarcation line. At the same time, the Italians extended their occupation zone to include Nice, Toulon, and Corsica. Missak said it was good that Claire was in Nice because the Italians were not so interested in rounding up Jews as the Germans were.

My father was glad to see Vichy overrun. "Now they can't pretend anymore. I wonder who'll end up stringing that old goat up by the neck, the Boches or the Allies. With the Allies in Africa, it's only a matter of time until the bear gets caught in its own trap."

Winter was upon us, so my mother and I pulled out the woolens, which emerged from the cupboards reeking of naphthalene. We soaked them with some ersatz soap flakes in the zinc tub in the kitchen before rinsing them and then draping them on the sills to dry. With the apartment smelling of wet wool, I shredded an old sheet and stuffed rags in the cracks around the window frames.

As the weather turned bitter, Auntie Shakeh's coughing grew worse. She was distraught when she was unable to make her weekly pilgrimage to the cathedral on Jean-Goujon—it was the first time she had missed Sunday services in years. I offered to accompany her, but my aunt said she didn't have the strength. At my mother's insistence, Auntie Shakeh finally agreed to go see the doctor. My mother and I bundled her up, each of us taking one of her arms as we led her slowly down the steps to the Métro. Climbing the flight of stairs at the other end of the trip was a long process with many pauses for my aunt to catch her breath.

Dr. Odabashian listened to her lungs and thumped her back with his fingers. In response, Auntie Shakeh coughed and coughed, doubling over and spitting into her hankie. After she finished her fit of coughing, her eyes were ringed with red and her face was ashen. She looked haggard and suddenly ten years older.

When Auntie Shakeh went to the WC, the doctor informed my mother that her sister was suffering from tuberculosis.

"She's likely been sick for a year or more. I've been seeing many of these cases. It's the lack of nutrition and the miserable cold. No heat, no nourishment; it's a wonder we're all not half dead. If we could send her to the south, where there is sun and plenty of fresh air, and make sure she had lamb stew and fresh fruit, she would improve." He shook his head.

"There isn't anything you can do?" my mother asked.

"They have been experimenting with new treatments, but nothing I can yet recommend. I'll give you some pain pills in case she needs them. They are hard to come by in the pharmacy."

"How long?" my mother asked.

"It could be months; it could be weeks. It's in God's hands."

My mother said nothing.

"Does she share a room with anyone?" he asked.

My mother nodded toward me. "She and Maral . . ."

"Is there someplace else the girl could sleep? I wouldn't like to see Maral or anyone else in the family get sick with this. Be careful how you handle her linens."

My mother made me promise not to tell Auntie Shakeh. "It's better that she doesn't know."

On the way home, my mother told her that Dr. Odabashian thought everyone would sleep better if she had her own room. "All that coughing is so noisy and he doesn't want you to worry about keeping Maral awake," she explained.

We pulled out Claire's mattress from where it had been rolled up under my bed and moved it to the front room. On the weeknights that Missak stayed at his job, I slept in his bed, and when he was home I slept on Claire's mattress on the floor. But no matter where I lay, I could still hear my aunt's coughing through the bedroom door. In the morning, Auntie Shakeh's sheets were soaked with sweat, even though the apartment was stone cold.

My mother and I washed and washed—soiled sheets, pillowcases, hankies, and nightclothes. My hands were soon red and chafed. We hung wet laundry outside from the balconies and shutters, where they froze. Then we strung up the stiff forms in the kitchen, where they slowly thawed and dried during the hours the stove was hot. Finally my mother ironed them.

One Sunday afternoon when my parents went out to visit

some friends in the neighborhood, and Missak was off with the Meguerditchian brothers, I sat in the bedroom on my old bed with books and notebooks spread around me while Auntie Shakeh lay nearby in her bed. I thought my aunt was asleep until I heard a small voice say, "Maral?"

"Yes, Auntie?"

Auntie Shakeh said, "It is not for man to talk about the day of his death. That is for only God to know. But I'm not afraid, Maral. I just worry about your mother. We have never been apart, not for one day in all our lives. We lost everything, but we had each other. I don't know what she will do without me. You and Missak will watch over her, won't you, sweetheart?"

Her pale, thin face was expectant. There were dark rings under her eyes.

"We will take care of her all the days of her life, Auntie. But you shouldn't talk like that. We can't do without you. Who will knit me new underwear?"

A tattered cough of a laugh came from her throat. "When this war is over, *anoushig*, you will have had enough of woolen *vardig*. You tell your mother I said she should buy you some satin ones with lace trim."

As the winter progressed, my mother attended to her sister like a nurse. She made tisane and toast. She contrived to get a bit of meat for her, but Auntie had no appetite. My mother moved her sewing machine into the bedroom so the two of them could work together, and when Shakeh slept, my mother switched to hand sewing so as not to disturb her.

With my mother and aunt sequestered in the sickroom and Missak staying late at the print shop, I sat in the cold front room with my stacks of books and papers. At the end of the year, I would be taking the first part of the baccalaureate exams, and I had already begun to prepare. My father was ensconced in his armchair reading the newspaper, withholding his commentary in deference to my studies. He couldn't stop himself from sighing and snorting in exasperation, but I ignored him. As hours went by, the wall clock dosed out the minutes like medicine.

Auntie Shakeh grew worse with each passing day. Soon she was coughing up blood, then she was unable to leave her bed without assistance, and she was even too weak to knit. Ignoring the doctor's advice, my mother began to sleep in Auntie Shakeh's room. From behind the door came intermittent sounds of the sewing machine and the long murmuring of their talk. It was as though the two sisters had gone together to a far-off country, leaving the rest of us behind.

In order to give my mother a little break and a few moments of fresh air, I sat with my aunt as she rested on her pillows. Her face was strained and tired, but she smiled wanly at me when I asked if she wanted to hear some neighborhood gossip.

So I started. "Madame Dupuy threw all her husband's clothes out the window onto the street, pretty much on top of his head as he stood below. And she was yelling at him that he was a drunk and an animal and she was going to have the locksmith come and change the locks on the apartment. He shouted up at her that she wasn't fit to be a wife to a dog and that he was going to throw her out and change all the locks himself. The whole neighborhood stopped on the sidewalk to watch."

"You too?" Auntie Shakeh asked weakly.

I nodded. "A woman stuck her head out the window from the floor above Madame Dupuy and told them to shut up. Then the husband started cursing at the neighbor, telling her to mind her own business. The neighbor yelled that Dupuy should be locked up, and then Madame Dupuy told her she had no right to speak that way to her husband. Monsieur Dupuy gathered up his shirts, underwear, pants, and shoes and went back upstairs."

"It's not the first time," Auntie Shakeh said, her breathing suddenly slow and labored. "Would you read to me, *anoushig*?" she whispered.

"What should I read?"

"Psalms," she said. "Number Twenty-Three."

I went to the dresser and found my aunt's worn copy of the Armenian Bible. The spine was cracked, and the cover was held in place by a thick rubber band. On the black cardboard, there were traces of gold decorative flowers and scrolls that had been worn away by years of daily use. This was the book my aunt had used to teach me to read and write Armenian when I was a little girl. I pulled off the rubber band and opened the book, turned leaves that were as thin and brittle as onion skins. The pages were crowded with small spiky letters and punctuated by my aunt's marginal notations in blue ink. I found the requested psalm and began to read.

It was a short passage, but before I reached the end, my aunt's eyes were closed. I watched Auntie Shakeh sleep until my mother returned.

A few days later I opened the front door to Father Avedis, a priest I had known since my aunt first took me to the cathedral, when I was five years old. He was a kind man with a white beard, a large hooked nose, and eyes the color of Greek olives.

He said in his deep, raspy voice, "Don't look at me like that, my girl. I'm not the Angel of Death. I've come to visit your aunt. And when will we be seeing you again on a Sunday?"

"I have so much schoolwork these days . . ."

He shook his head from side to side. "Excuses, excuses. I'll be looking for you. Now let me go see how this young lady is doing."

A half an hour later he and my mother came out of the room, both of them with somber faces. Once the door was shut, he said to my mother, "It is in the Lord's hands."

Later that week, early in the morning, my mother came to the kitchen, where my father, Missak, and I were taking breakfast. She said simply, "She has gone to her Maker."

I began to cry, Missak's face crumpled, and my father's eyes brimmed with tears, but my mother stood before us with her eyes dull and empty. She turned and walked slowly to the bedroom she shared with my father. Without looking back, she closed the door behind her.

Dr. Odabashian arrived at midmorning and went into the bedroom, where he threw open the windows to the frigid air. After the doctor left, Father Avedis appeared and performed the house rite. It was decided that because of wartime scarcity and expense of transport, the body should be kept at home and not be transferred to the church before burial. My father, without telling anyone, had already purchased a small plot in the cemetery. Jacqueline's mother and Zaven's mother came to dress the body.

The next morning, Father Avedis, who was wearing stiff black robes and a black peaked hood, intoned the ritual prayers at the graveside. The trees were bare, the skies were gray, and our family stood there with the Kacherians, the Sahadians, and other friends as the snow began to slowly filter down over us. Father Avedis sang, *"The time has come for me to enter the womb of the earth . . ."*

It occurred to me that Auntie Shakeh would think that the shawl of bright snow falling over the dark wood of the casket was beautiful. The pattern was as intricate as some of her handiwork. I imagined her looking down at us from heaven, where it was always springtime. The flowering trees were in bloom, and lambs gamboled across a sunny meadow. Auntie sat at Jesus's right hand at a long table spread with a feast for the angels.

She had left us behind, and we were far from heaven. I thought about the chill apartment, the cold classrooms at school, the gnawing hunger that wasn't sated by parsnips and rutabagas. Everything seemed dismal after Auntie's death, and the war itself seemed like a dark and interminable winter. Every day, I walked to school past posters on the walls of Belleville and the Marais that announced the latest "criminals" shot in front of a stone wall outside a prison on the edge of the city, and the most recent bit of neighborhood treachery was that of a locksmith on the boulevard de Belleville who had turned in a Jewish family that had been hiding in the attic of his building.

I knew from looking at my father's newspapers that life in Paris was easier than in London, or Warsaw, or any of the other cities where the war was more brutal in its daily habits.

But what did any of this have to do with my aunt? Instead of grieving her loss, I was feeling sorry for myself.

After the service at the graveside, when the mourners filed down the icy stone steps to leave the cemetery, my foot slipped and I stumbled. Zaven, who I hadn't realized was just behind me, caught me by the elbow and helped me regain my balance. I turned toward him.

For the few seconds that our eyes met, I forgot everything except for the pressure of his fingers on my arm. I saw the warmth in his eyes, his black hair flecked with snow, and the collar of his thin coat turned up so it grazed the sides of his face. A few bright snowflakes had caught on his dark lashes.

"Thank you" was all I said.

Amid a cluster of mourners, we walked down the hill as shovelfuls of frozen earth thudded onto my aunt's casket.

Armenian women from the neighborhood arrived at our apartment carrying cloth-covered plates and steaming casseroles. They moaned and sighed in the front room while their men wandered in and out during the day as their vocations allowed.

It was left to me to go through Auntie Shakeh's scant possessions. She had lived lightly on the earth, like a sparrow. I folded her clothes—a few plain dresses, some underclothes, two worn pairs of shoes made for her by my father before the war, the hand-knit sweaters, and a frayed cloth coat. She had never married or had children. I wondered if she had ever been kissed, if she had ever wanted more from life than being our spinster aunt. As I went through her belongings, I could see her sitting in the corner watching, her knitting needles busy as always. I heard her voice: *Don't forget,* anoushig, *to put some mothballs in with the woolens when the spring comes. You don't want to find them later full of holes.*

I gathered up the items on the top of the dresser my aunt and I had shared, among them a hairbrush, a comb, a hand mirror, some hairpins, and the Bible. I put everything except the book in a suitcase and slid it under the empty bed. The Bible I placed in my own dresser drawer. Then I sifted through the knitting baskets, putting the small balls of left-over yarn into one bag and sorting the knitting needles into pairs. I stowed all this in the bottom of the small armoire in the front room, where my mother sat in silence.

For the forty days of mourning, my mother, dressed in black and with her hair pulled severely back from her face, sat in the parlor, her hands folded in her lap and her eyes straight ahead. She barely spoke and when she did, it was hardly above a whisper. When my father leaned toward her and said words into her ear, her face remained immobile. She made me think of a bell with no clapper.

One evening soon after the formal mourning period had ended and when my mother had gone early to her bed, my father sat in his armchair staring into the air. Missak hadn't come home that night. I was, as usual, bent over my books, an old blanket my aunt had knit over my shoulders for warmth.

"Babig," I said. "Can I ask you something?"

My father nodded.

"Do you think she'll come back to us?"

"Give her time," he said. "No one can sigh for forty years."

He continued, "My brother also died of this disease, when we first came to Camp Oddo in Marseille. He was all the family I had. The rest had been killed in the Massacres. Just like your mother and Shakeh, my brother and I had been the only two left from our family.

"The two of us were sent to an orphanage in Jbail, where they trained us to make shoes. That's where we met Vahan Kacherian. Then my brother and I took the ship to Marseille so we could find work and make a new life for ourselves. At Camp Oddo, he got sick, like your aunt. He was in the hospital, where he wasted to nothing, and there was nothing I could do for him. I visited him in the evening after work each day. One night when I came, he wasn't in his bed, and the nurse told me he had died.

"Food tasted like ash in my mouth and everything was dim. Then I found your mother. When we were married, the whole camp celebrated with us like they were our cousins. Because we had no real family—no parents, no grandparents, no aunts, no uncles. We were orphans, but most everyone there had lost as much as us, and some a little more. Azniv and Shakeh were my new family. It was my job to take care of them. Little by little, the sun came back. And when your brother was born, we named him for my brother.

"This world is made of dark and light, my girl, and in the darkest times you have to believe the sun will come again, even if you yourself don't live to see it."

I asked, "Is that an Armenian proverb?"

My father smiled faintly. "I made that one up myself."

12

ON A SUNDAY AFTERNOON in January, I layered on my warmest clothes and left the apartment carrying a bouquet of fabric flowers. I had made them from scraps of material, with a large white button sewn into the center of each. They were bound to a knitting needle wrapped with green yarn to resemble a stem. It was a homely tribute to Auntie Shakeh, whose absence I had been feeling keenly.

As I approached the rue de Belleville, I saw Zaven leaning against the wall on our corner. It seemed like an odd place to be loitering on such a cold morning.

I waved to him. "So nice to see you. You never visit us anymore."

"I'm a workingman. You don't see your brother much either, do you?"

"Only on Sunday."

"Where are you off to?" he asked.

"Père-Lachaise."

"If you don't mind, I'll join you."

He fell into step beside me. He was wearing his gray cloth coat with the collar turned up and no scarf, no hat, no gloves.

"Aren't you cold?" I asked him.

"It's good for the circulation," he said.

"And hunger stimulates the appetite."

"Of course. And when the well runs dry, you appreciate the water."

I laughed. "Now you sound like my father."

The skies were clear and blue. The smell of wood smoke hung on the air as we made our way up the hill. Walking with Zaven dispelled the melancholy of my pilgrimage. Now the cold air and the exertion of the climb were exhilarating.

"How's your mother?" Zaven asked.

"She's working, eating, sleeping. But she doesn't smile, and she hardly talks."

"I should come spar with your father to liven things up."

"You should. He worships the Americans these days. And he's happy that the Russians are holding out against the Germans. But he still thinks—"

He completed my sentence: "—that Stalin's an assassin."

After reaching the cemetery, we made our way past rows of marble mausoleums to the divisions far up the hill where the Armenians were buried. We passed in front of the tomb of General Antranik and then the ornate marble mausoleum of Boghos Nubar Pasha. Finally we arrived in a corner and stood before the smallest, simplest stone: SHAKEH NAZARIAN, 1907–1942.

As I knelt down and pushed the knitting needle into the frozen earth near her name, the sadness welled up inside me again. Zavig sat down on the stone border and gestured to a spot next to him, where I came over and settled.

"You managed to bring your aunt flowers in the dead of winter," he said.

"We manage to find something to eat, even if it's turnips. We manage to stay warm, even if it's by burning crates or hiding in our beds."

"You shouldn't be so bitter, young lady."

"You sound like Missak. He acts like he's sixty years old and I'm his granddaughter."

"Your brother was born an old man."

"And how were you born?" I asked.

"Me?" He grinned. "Tell me what you think."

"You were born smiling. And what about me?" I asked.

"You're complicated."

"You've known me since I was born. I'm as plain as bread."

"Look," he said, almost abruptly, "your lips are blue, and this stone has frozen my backside. Let's get a hot drink."

On the way down the hill we stopped at a café—fake coffee for Zaven, and for me a weedy imitation tea, no milk, no sugar. But it was hot. And I enjoyed sitting at a table with him as if we were on a date, even though we didn't say much. In the Old Country, families arranged marriages for their children, so girls didn't go about in public with boys who were not their relatives. It occurred to me that if this was a date, it was the first one I had ever been on, and that it was a date with the boy that I had long desired.

Zaven interrupted my reverie. "What are you smiling about?"

"Nothing. How's your sister?"

"She's skinny and nervous, but she's okay. I promised I would help with her math homework this afternoon."

"What time?"

He smiled and shrugged. "A while ago."

When we reached my corner, Zaven asked, "Should I walk you to your door?"

"No need," I said.

He paused. "You want to do this again next Sunday?"

"Go to the cemetery?"

"Or someplace else. Whatever you like."

I wondered what my brother would think. "Maybe I should check with Missak . . ."

"Don't worry," Zaven said. "I already talked to him. It's okay."

I was suddenly annoyed, imagining the two of them discussing me as though I were a piece of livestock. "Oh, it is, is it? You two already talked about me and decided it was okay? What if it wasn't okay with me? What if I didn't like the idea?"

He winced, ducking his head. "That's the risk, isn't it? But I hoped you would."

My anger quickly burned out because I had, in fact, been waiting a long time for him to ask me.

"So, what do you think?" he asked.

"Come by our house next Sunday in the early afternoon. But no cemetery . . ."

He grinned, took my hand, and kissed the rough wool of my mitten.

I floated the rest of the way home. He had kissed my hand. What a romantic thing to do. I paused at the bottom of the stairwell to run the scene through my mind again, sighing happily. Then I ran up the stairs two at a time, out of breath as I reached our landing.

When I walked in the door, Missak was in the front hall.

"So, how was Zavig?" he asked.

I said, "Stay out of my business."

"You think it was a coincidence he ran into you this afternoon?"

"Thanks, but we won't need any more help from you."

"We?" He laughed. "Already you're a *we*?"

"What are you two fighting about?" my father called from the front room.

"Nothing," we said in unison.

That night I pulled a bag of yarn from the armoire and sorted through the remnants. There was almost enough black yarn for a hat, but any scarf from it would have to be striped. I went to the bedroom and dragged the suitcase of Auntie's clothes from under the bed. Inside was a thick black sweater.

I hesitantly approached my mother with the sweater as she stood over the sink in the kitchen peeling rutabagas.

"Mairig, would it be okay if I took this apart and used the yarn?" I asked.

My mother paused in her work. "It's easy to unravel a life. What will you make?"

I said, "A scarf, a hat, and mittens."

"And who will wear them?"

I tried to sound natural, as though this were nothing out of the ordinary, but I felt a thrill of excitement when I said, "Zaven."

"We all love that boy, don't we?" My mother looked at me knowingly.

An hour later I had two fat balls of black yarn in my lap. Sitting in Auntie's chair in the front room, I quickly cast on the stitches and began to knit.

When Zaven knocked at our door the following Sunday, I pointedly ignored Missak's raised eyebrows and smirk. I pretended there was nothing unusual about this visit. But as Zaven entered the front room, my father clapped him on the back and said, "If it were anyone but you, I would chase him off with a pitchfork, but I will accept you as a suitor for our Maral."

I glared at my brother, who gestured that it wasn't his doing. I turned accusingly to my mother, who pointedly avoided my eyes.

Zavig laughed. "Such a formal word, Uncle! We are good friends."

"Don't be a fox sneaking into my barnyard," my father replied.

I said, "And I suppose that makes me a chicken."

My mother asked, "Do you two have plans?"

Zaven replied, "I thought we'd go for a walk at the Buttes Chaumont."

My mother said, "On a cold day like this? Ah, but you're young. Just make sure you bundle up."

In the front hall as we were putting on our coats, I said, "I have something for you."

I handed the new woolens to him, and he turned them over admiringly. "Nice work, Maral."

"What are you waiting for?" I asked. "Put them on."

He pulled the cap over his ears, wound the scarf around his neck, and slid his hands into the mittens.

"How do I look?" he asked.

Of course he looked terribly handsome. "Are you fishing for compliments?"

"Who me?" He laughed.

As we walked toward the park he said, "I'm sorry I couldn't think of anything else to do today. I'm short of cash."

"Don't apologize. It's more cheerful than Père-Lachaise. And I like to walk."

"I'm glad you feel that way. I'm happy to spend the afternoon with you no matter where we are."

I blushed at this and then he took my hand, his black mitten clasping my gray one.

We reached the shallow pond in the middle of the park and saw it was frozen over. I stood leaning against a tree trunk watching as Zaven began to slide on the ice at the edge of the pond. When he was halfway around, he gingerly stepped toward the middle to see if it would hold. He inched his way farther onto the sheet of ice.

"It's solid," he shouted. "Come on."

I shouted back, "It's too dangerous."

He had made his way to the middle of the pond. "I promise you, it's solid. Watch." He jumped up and down on the ice.

"Stop that! You're crazy!"

"No, I'm not. Don't be a coward."

"Who are you calling a coward?"

"Then come out here."

I slid my boot onto the icy edge, excited and fearful. He took a step toward me and waved for me to come closer. I took another step toward him. I inched to the center, pausing with each step to check that no fissures appeared beneath my feet. There were no signs or sounds of cracking ice. It was solid, as he had promised.

When I reached him, we stood facing each other, our breath making clouds on the air.

"Now what do we do?" I asked him.

"This," he said, breaking into a run and skidding across the pond.

I chased after him and slid a few feet.

"Come on, you can go faster than that." He flew over the ice.

I followed suit but lost my balance and landed in a spill at his feet. He pulled me to standing. Then we zipped back and forth across the ice until we were panting.

"It's getting late," he finally said. "We should head back."

He put his arm around me as we strolled down the path leading to the park exit. It wasn't exactly comfortable, the way his arm weighed on my shoulder, but I was afraid to say anything or pull away. All of this was new to me, but I saw him after school once walking with his arm around a girl on the rue St. Antoine. I had also passed him when he was sitting in a café with a girl on the place de la Bastille. He hadn't seen me either time. Neither of the girls was Armenian. They both had short, stylish hair. One of them wore red lipstick. It made me feel drab and old-fashioned to remember it.

When we reached my corner, he asked, "Can I walk you home?"

"You don't need to," I said.

"I'd like to."

When we entered the dim stairwell of our building, Zaven paused before the bottom step.

"Maral," he said.

My heart beat faster.

He asked, "Would you mind if I kissed you?"

"I wouldn't mind at all," I said.

I closed my eyes, he put his lips to mine, and it was like a match set to dry leaves. When we separated, I was breathless.

"Oh," I said. "I had better go now."

"Until next week," he called.

As I flew up the stairs, my feet barely skimming the treads, I thought, *So what that my hair is long and I still wear knee socks to school—he has chosen me.*

13

THE END-OF-YEAR EXAMS LOOMED ahead of me like a tall mountain range. I had no time for anything except preparing to scale them. In the one bit of good luck the war had brought, at the request of the Agriculture Department oral examinations were canceled for all students because people were needed in the fields. Our teachers were appalled at this interference with the regular program, but I was relieved we had to contend with only the written tests, which would be difficult enough. Each lunchtime, I went to the school library to prepare study guides, and in the evening, I pored over these outlines until my vision was blurred. I woke up early to study before school. I recited mathematical formulas while brushing my teeth.

My father muttered, "This girl's going to ruin her eyesight and her health." But it was said with pride.

My mother shooed me out of the kitchen. "I don't need help with the dishes, girl. Go, go to your books."

I set aside a few hours every Sunday afternoon for Zaven. Sometimes we had midday Sunday dinner with my family and sometimes with his. Our mothers always found something special for the meal, whether it was dumpling stew made from the meat of two squirrels Missak had hit with his slingshot or Auntie Shushan's cabbage leaves stuffed with rice and minced black-market sausage.

Zaven's mother taught me how to crochet doilies. His sister wanted to show me her schoolwork. One afternoon, his father offered to make me a pair of pumps, and he asked Zaven's brother, Barkev, to take the measurements. Barkev and I went to the front hall, where I climbed onto a low stool and stood barefoot on a piece of cardboard. Barkev knelt on the floor in front of me running the stub of a yellow pencil around the edge of my foot. I looked down at the top of his dark head as he brushed his fingertips and the point of the pencil along my bare skin.

"That tickles."

"Don't move," Barkev said.

"Sorry," I said.

"Lift your foot."

I followed his instructions, and he wrapped the tape measure around the ball of my foot, his fingers warm on my skin. Then he made notations on the side of the cardboard.

"Done," he said. "I don't know why your boyfriend didn't do this."

When Zaven and I left the apartment a few minutes later, I said, "I don't think Barkev likes me."

"Either you're joking or you're blind," Zaven said.

"What?"

Zaven shook his head. "As smart as you are, you can be pretty slow. You want to go to the park?"

The weather had warmed, and our favorite place had become the Buttes Chaumont. That spring we spent hours exploring the park—its artificial lake and waterfalls, the grottoes and the hanging bridge. Each Sunday we went, another kind of flower had burst forth: daffodils gave way to hyacinths, which were followed by scarlet tulips. The ornamental fruit trees put on their show, the bright petals drifting down like confetti onto the lawns and sidewalks. I hated to leave as dusk approached. At that hour, the trees were alive with birds calling to one another while the sky moved through darker and darker hues.

One Sunday afternoon it started to rain, and we took refuge under an enormous beech tree with deep purple leaves, sitting with our backs against its smooth gray trunk. Zavig put his arm around me and I leaned into him, resting my head on his shoulder and watching the rain falling beyond the sheltering canopy of the tree.

I said, "It's like a house under here. This is our parlor. We need some chairs and a table."

"Where would we plug in the radio?" he asked.

"No radio. We don't want any bad news in this house."

"What will we eat?"

"The kiosk will be our dining room, and the servers will bring us trays of ice cream and tall glasses of mineral water with almond syrup."

"Sounds too sweet."

"Do you want a beer?"

"Sure."

"Okay, a beer, then, and a cheese sandwich."

"Ham and cheese."

I added, "And chocolate cake for dessert."

"Don't talk about food. My stomach is rumbling," he said.

"You know," I said, rubbing my cheek against the softness of his worn cotton shirt, "you smell good. Like damp leaves in a garden on a rainy day."

He laughed. "That's the dirt we're sitting on."

"You're so romantic," I said.

"And yet you like me anyway."

I looked up at him. "When I was little I decided that I was going to marry you, but I knew that if I told Missak, he would laugh at me. And I thought maybe you would laugh at me too, and so in my head I told you off."

"You had a fight with me that I didn't know about."

"Yes, but then we made up. And I still wanted to marry you."

"Well, let's get married then."

My heart swooped inside my chest.

"How does that sound?" he asked.

I answered carefully, "It sounds perfect. But I won't be seventeen until next month. And I have another year of school and another round of exams . . ."

"There's no rush," he said. "Your education is important."

"You know, since I started lycée, when I was eleven, I've always felt proud to be working toward my bac. But I've never been able to imagine what I might do after."

"No idea?" he asked.

"I've always wanted to get married and have children. And sometimes I thought I might go to the *école normale* and become a teacher."

"I can see you at the front of the classroom. Mademoiselle Pegorian. Or Madame Kacherian.

"Look," he continued, turning to pat the tree, "see all the lovers who have been here before us."

The silver trunk was scarred with initials. He pulled a penknife from his pocket and carefully carved in the bark *M.P. + Z.K.*, surrounded by a heart.

I ran my fingers over the rough edges of the letters. "These trees can live for hundreds of years."

"And our initials will still be right there, and you'll still be mine."

In the days that followed, as I sat in the classroom, my mind strayed to this moment under the tree. In the back of my English notebook I wrote a list of names: *Maral Kacherian, Madame Maral Kacherian, Madame Zaven Kacherian,* and *Maral Pegorian Kacherian.* I copied them in long columns from the top to the bottom of the page. In the margins, I drew hearts around our initials, like the image Zaven had carved into the tree. Then I decorated the empty spaces with birds and flowers.

I was staring dreamily at this page in class when my English teacher tapped me on the shoulder. "I don't believe that will be of any use to you on the examination you will take in a few short weeks."

I quickly closed the notebook, my face flushed with embarrassment. "I am sorry, Mrs. Collin."

"Girls your age often find it difficult to strike a balance between study and romance. But I would suggest for the next few weeks you focus on the former. You are an excellent student and it would be unfortunate if you didn't perform as well as you ought."

When I got home that evening, I carefully tore the thin page out of the back of my notebook and slipped it beneath the stack of cards and mementos I stored in my bureau's top drawer. Then I went to the table in the front room, where I spread out my study guides and notebooks and got back to work.

14

Zaven and I sat on a bench under a plane tree in the Parc de Belleville. The sprawl of city buildings shimmered in the bright summer sun.

"I can't believe exams are over," I said.

"How does it feel?" he asked.

"Like I've been walking around for months with a sack of bricks over my shoulder, and now that it's gone, I might just float up to the clouds." I shaded my eyes to look into the sky. "Except today there are no clouds. And it won't really be over until the results are posted."

"You're at the top of the class."

"Denise was always first. If she were still here, her name would be above mine on the list. I wonder where she is right now, and her parents, and Henri. And the Lipskis."

Zaven frowned. "This war is crap. And now with Barkev called up for the STO . . ."

Barkev was scheduled to take a train from the Gare de l'Est; he was in the Germans' new mandatory work program, the *service du travail obligatoire*, or the STO. All Frenchmen aged twenty to twenty-two were required to go to Germany. Exceptions were made only for those involved in agriculture and other essential industries, although the wealthy and the well connected would surely manage to find ways around it for their sons. Thankfully, Zaven and Missak were too young to be called up.

"Barkev won't go," Zavig said flatly.

"What will he do?" I asked.

"Disappear. I'm thinking of doing the same."

I knew as soon as he said it that the decision had been made. The ground beneath my feet dropped away. "Where would you go?"

"Out of the city. Or into hiding."

"You've been considering this for a while?"

He rubbed his forehead. "Yes."

I didn't say anything.

He said, "It wouldn't be for long. The Germans are losing. It's only a matter of time."

"You and my father are optimists."

"You think Barkev should make guns for the Nazis?"

"No. But that doesn't mean you have to run off with him."

"It doesn't feel like a choice," he said.

"I saw in the paper the other day—on the same page as the questions from this year's bac—a message from the editor about the STO. His recommendation, of course, was to obey the call. According to him, murderous Communists run the

Resistance. One day they will turn their arms against France as part of the international Communist revolution. It's odd that they printed that. I would think they would worry it might put ideas into people's heads."

He said nothing.

I asked, "Are you going underground?"

His silence was an answer.

"You promise you won't leave without saying goodbye?" I asked.

"This is goodbye," he said.

I stiffened as he put his hand on top of mine.

"What does your mother think?"

"My parents agree that Barkev shouldn't go to Germany. I haven't told them about myself. I probably shouldn't have told you, but how could I not tell my fiancée?"

"I never said I would marry you."

"Yes you did!"

"Well, if I did, I'm having second thoughts."

"Don't be like that, Maro," he said. "Don't make it harder than it already is."

That night I couldn't fall asleep. I lay twisting in my bed thinking about the terrible fates that might await Zaven and Barkev. Finally I sat up, turned on the lamp, and found my fountain pen. I didn't want to use the cheap wartime paper that filled my notebooks. Thin and gray, it ripped easily under the nib, and the ink bled so that the letters blurred. I rifled through the cards and notes in my top drawer and plucked out an old sketch of me that Missak had made on sturdy drawing paper. On the back I wrote:

Dear Zavig,

   Please forgive me for being so disagreeable. Please come back soon. I'm waiting for you.

   Maro

Feeling a little foolish, I drew a heart with our initials in it at the bottom of the page, and I put the message into an envelope that I slid in the Kacherians' letterbox the next morning.

When Missak came home the next Sunday, I asked if he knew where Zaven and Barkev were.

He answered, "They're gone."

"Are they still in the city?"

He shrugged.

"I wish I could throttle all of you! Then I wouldn't have to worry about the Germans doing it first."

"I have something I've been meaning to give you," he said.

I trailed behind my brother to the front room. He pulled out his sketchbook and opened it to the back, where there were several loose sheets. He sorted through them, selected one, and handed it to me.

I looked down at the drawing Missak had made of Zaven and me at the kitchen table during the afternoon of the snowstorm. Zavig's face was handsome and full of life. I remembered the details of that afternoon—the downy feathers falling from the sky, the troop of neighborhood friends, the snowball fight, and drops of red blood in the snow. It seemed a world away.

"Remember how you both wanted the picture?" Missak asked. "You both blushed."

"We were so young," I said.

"You're still young, sister. It's just the war that's old."

15

THE REST OF THE SUMMER was like a dry crust of bread too hard and stale for a sparrow. I took up knitting for Auntie Shakeh's old boss, sitting in the stuffy apartment making fine-gauge wool sweaters. My mother was in the same room running up vests on her sewing machine and doing the finishing by hand, still wrapped in wordless sadness. For the months that I had been focused on Zaven and exams, I had not felt the full weight of my mother's gloom. Now that we worked in a shared space for hours each afternoon, it was almost crushing. If I asked a question, my mother would give a monosyllabic answer, and then the room would again fall silent except for the sound of the machine and the clicking of the needles. During the month of August, the front room felt like an airless tomb.

One afternoon, I wanted to escape, so I told my mother I

was going to see if my father needed any help. She nodded and turned back to her work.

When I arrived at the shop, the front counter, where a jumbled pile of shoes had accumulated, was untended. My father was visible in the back at his workbench hammering at a heel. Paul Sahadian, Jacqueline's fifteen-year-old brother who had started as an apprentice when school let out, was at the finisher polishing shoes.

"Anything I can do to help?" I called over the whirring of the motor.

My father paused in his work and pointed with the hammer toward the broom standing in the corner.

I swept the floor in the front of the shop. There was no more talk here than there was at home with my mother, but at least it was alive with noise and industry. I worked my way to the back and, careful to stay out of the way of my father and Paul, swept up the sawdust, bits of wood, scraps of leather, and bent nails. Paul looked at me and grinned as he grabbed another pair of shoes to polish. He had grown tall and thin, but his ears were still like sugar-bowl handles.

"So now you're a cobbler?" I asked him.

"I'm learning. He's a good teacher," he said, gesturing toward my father with his head.

My father, who heard nothing, put down the hammer to run his thumb around a wooden heel, making sure the fit was tight. I glanced at my father's hands, callused and stained with shoe polish in the fingers' cracks and creases. It occurred to me that they were Armenian hands: whether repairing shoes, sewing, knitting, or drawing, our hands were deft and industrious. It was a national attribute. In Zaven's case, his intelligent hands gave him an almost magical ability to repair any machine.

It seemed that every stream of thought led back to Zaven. I wondered where he was and what he was doing in the shadowy world I could only half envision. How long would I have to wait for him? Would he be back before the holidays? The tide had turned against the Germans—my father was jubilant when the Americans invaded Sicily, and he was sure that in Kursk on the eastern front, the Soviets were poised to defeat the Germans. But it didn't seem to me that the war was anywhere near its end. I was already dreading another frigid, starving winter, and the idea of facing it without Zaven made it even worse.

When it was time to close the shop, Paul turned off the finisher. He and my father carefully wiped their hands with rags dampened with witch hazel. After they hung their aprons on hooks on the wall, my father switched off the lights. Standing on the sidewalk, I watched Paul use his full weight to drag the iron shutter down over the store window.

"Tell Jacqueline I said hello," I told him as he turned into his building.

"You should come visit," Paul said, smiling, his large ears turning red.

"Maybe on Sunday," I told him.

"Good night, Maral. Good night, sir," Paul said respectfully.

As my father and I headed into the courtyard of our building, he said, "That boy is a hard worker. He's not yet as skilled as your brother, but he'll learn."

"It's good of you to teach him," I said.

"It works out for everybody. Your brother didn't want

what I had to offer, and Paul is eager to learn," he said. "I
need the help. With new shoes so hard to come by, I'm putting patches on patches."

In September, food rations were decreased again. The grumbling on the food lines grew louder. The German potato
bugs were stealing our food. The black-marketers were getting fat while the rest of us wasted away. When I arrived
home from the store, my mother peered into the half-empty
sack and shook her head.

"*Meghah!* This was once the land of baguettes and butter.
Now it's the land of turnips," she said.

"The Germans are trying to starve us into submission,"
my father responded. "But they forget the French Revolution was started over loaves of bread. An eating dog is silent,
but a hungry dog bares its teeth."

Our family continued to scrape by, our official tickets sup-
plemented by the ones Missak brought home from time to
time. Through the autumn, the windowsill garden, the plot
in the courtyard, and my mother's bartering skills added to
our meager fare. Still, I often went to bed hungry, glad to
forget my gnawing stomach in sleep.

But when I slept, my dreams were a theater of yearning,
and Zaven was the elusive star in each scene. I would catch
a glimpse of him as he disappeared into the gloom of a dark
alley. I would run after him, but he was always around the
next corner and just out of reach. I would wake with my
heart pounding as though I had been chased up the hill by a
pack of dogs. Then I'd lie in bed and catalog all the catastro-
phes that might have befallen him.

Over the objections of my mother, one Sunday I rode alone to Alfortville on the old bicycle. I was even more careful about the potholes, because at this point the bicycle's fender was held together with bits of twisted wire, and the tires were balding. Since the last time I had visited, the Nazarians had expanded their backyard chicken coop, and now it took up half their garden. Their thriving poultry business kept them well fed, and Cousin Karnig, almost discomfited, said that he was making a better living now than he had as a carpenter before the war. I arrived home with a chicken—not a live one, but one ready to go straight into the pot—and a dozen freshly laid brown speckled eggs.

"Thanks to Cousin Karnig, king of the henhouse," my father said at dinner.

"Thank God," my mother said as she passed around the bowls of thick soup. "These children are looking like scarecrows."

"We're not children anymore," Missak corrected her. "And we have more to eat than a lot of other people."

"Thank you, Grandfather," I said.

That evening, feeling lonely for Zaven, I unraveled a gray throw blanket Auntie Shakeh had made and used the yarn to begin a V-neck sweater for him. The knitting became a ritual for ensuring his safety. Each stitch was a prayer; each hour we had spent together was a bead on a string of remembrance. I didn't ask myself how I would manage to get the sweater to him once it was finished.

• • •

In October, school started, and I donned my smock for the final year at Victor Hugo. The animated faces of my classmates, the crowded corridors, and the heavy books in my satchel were a relief after my lonely summer. In the middle of the morning, we all lined up to get our government-issued vitamin biscuits. I tried not to gag as the biscuit turned into a grainy paste in my mouth. At least it helped quiet my stomach until lunch.

In English class we were reading *Jane Eyre*, and I escaped into its dramatic landscape. I sighed over the book's dark and difficult hero. Against all logic, Rochester reminded me of Zaven, but then, everything reminded me of him.

One afternoon in early November as I rounded the corner toward home, Zaven fell into step beside me.

I gasped. "What are you doing here?"

"Don't make a fuss." He slipped his arm through mine. "Let's go."

"Where?" I asked. "How long can you stay?"

"For a walk." He put his face into my hair. "You smell good."

"Not here," I told him, looking over my shoulder. "The school monitor is on patrol."

He laughed. "You're worried about the school monitor."

I glanced around again. "Is someone following you?"

"No," he said. "It's okay."

He led me toward the place de la République, but we skirted the square where German troops were garrisoned, taking back streets instead.

I said, "I'm so happy to see you. I want to ask you a million questions . . ."

"Don't ask me a million questions," he said.

"Are you going to visit your parents?"

"So you're going to ask anyway? I'm not going to visit my parents. Have you seen them?"

"Your father finished the shoes he was making for me and I went to pick them up."

He glanced down at my feet.

"They're too nice to wear every day," I told him. "I wore them on Sunday when I went to church with your mother."

"You went to church with my mother? That's new. What for?"

"She goes to pray for you and Barkev. I went to light a candle for Auntie Shakeh."

"You're not getting religious, are you?"

"Don't worry, you godless Communist."

"I'm more of an agnostic."

"Oh, Zaven, I've missed you so much."

"Four months is a long time."

"You look thin," I said.

He shrugged.

"We're not far from our house. Can I get you something to eat?"

"Can't risk it," he answered.

"Let me go and bring something back."

"I have only a short time and I want to spend it all with you. I have a proposal."

"Yes?"

"There's an apartment nearby. If you want, we could go there."

Even though he didn't put it into words, I knew what he was asking. I paused for a moment to consider.

He said, "Don't worry. If you don't want to . . ."

"Let's go." I took his hand. My mother, my father, my teachers, my dead aunt, even Jane Eyre—none of them would have approved, but I didn't care.

We weaved our way through narrow streets that were unfamiliar to me but that he navigated easily. The wind picked up, rustling the last of autumn's leaves on the sidewalks and in the gutters. I noticed the way his eyes inspected the street as we rounded each corner, and how he checked behind to make sure no one was trailing us. We entered a modest building on a small side street and took the back staircase to the top floor. Zaven felt around above the door frame and lifted a piece of wood to retrieve a key.

It was a small room, furnished with washbasin, a narrow bed, a table, and a single wooden chair. The white walls were bare, and there was no rug on the red-tiled floor. The casement window gave out onto the roof, and cold white light cut like a knife across the facing rooftops.

He pointed out the location's advantages. "There are two staircases. The roof is connected to the one on that building, which also has a front and a back entrance."

"That's good to know."

"The electricity is off." He dragged the blackout curtains across the window and then struck a match in the dark to light a candle. Its flame flickered in a draft that stirred the curtain.

Zaven sat down on the bed and I sat beside him on the scratchy wool blanket, leaving a little space between us. He slid closer.

"This is okay?" he asked.

I nodded.

"You know, if you don't want to be here, we can leave," he said.

I shook my head.

"Do you have any yarn with you?" he asked.

It seemed like an odd request. "In my satchel, I have a piece I'm working. There's some in there."

"Can I have it?" he asked.

I opened my bag and pulled out the ball. "How long?"

With his pocketknife he cut two red strands. After handing back the ball and putting away the blade, he faced me holding up the yarn.

"Will you marry me?" he asked.

"I will," I said.

"Give me your left hand." He took one piece of yarn, wound it around my ring finger twice, and carefully made a small bow. "You are now my wife."

He handed me the other piece of yarn, and I tied it around his ring finger.

"You say it," he instructed.

"You are now my husband."

He leaned to blow out the flame, and the room went black.

No one had ever talked with me about what to expect or what to do. That was the way it was for us then. Armenian modesty and shame—the word for it was *amot*—shrouded these things in silence. And while I never spoke of that afternoon, in my heart I never was ashamed.

By the time we stepped out onto the street, night had fallen, and moonlight angled between the buildings. Zaven insisted on accompanying me partway home. We walked in silence until we reached the edge of our neighborhood.

I asked, "Will you let me bring you something to eat?"

"I'll wait at the park. But you have to be quick. And you can't say a word."

"You promise you'll be there?"

"Of course," he said.

I was breathless as I entered the apartment and slammed the door behind me.

"Maral? Is that you?" my mother called from the front room.

"*Parev*, Mairig," I answered as I headed to my bedroom. I rolled up the sweater I had made Zaven, tucked it under my arm, and sped to the kitchen. "I'm starving and I have to run out for a few minutes. May I take this bread and cheese?" Without waiting for a response I grabbed both and dashed to the front door.

My mother called after me, "Girl, where are you going?"

But I was already trotting down the stairs. I sped toward the park and had a stitch in my side as I collapsed onto the bench beside Zaven.

"That was fast," he said as I handed him the food.

"You're starving," I said, watching him wolf down the bread and cheese.

He grunted in response as he swallowed the last bites.

"I wish I had brought more," I said.

"No, that was plenty."

"Don't lie. That wasn't enough at all. Try this on." I held out the sweater.

He stood up, took off his jacket, and pulled the sweater over his head. "It's beautiful. And just in time for the cold weather."

I said, "It's a little big."

"It's perfect." He sat down beside me, taking hold of my hand. "After the war, when we have plenty of food, it will fit me the way you imagined."

"After the war," I repeated. "I'm afraid it's never going to end."

"Fear is like hunger. It gnaws at you, but you have to ignore it. You find other things to think about, like this new sweater and the smell of your skin." He leaned into my neck and inhaled deeply.

I put my arms around him. "Please don't go."

"I have to."

I pulled back to look at him. "What if they catch you? We won't know a thing. I'll be walking down the rue de Belleville and I'll see your name on a poster. 'Zaven Kacherian, shot by firing squad,' it will say. Each time they put up a new one, I read the list to make sure you're not there."

"Maral, please don't cry."

I wiped the tears from my face, but the words came in gasps. "Can't you stay? Each night I stare at the sketch tacked on the wall, the picture Missak made of us, and I try to imagine where you are. Sometimes I feel as though we're connected by an invisible thread, and other times all I feel is that something dreadful has happened to you."

"I'm sorry. But I have to go." There was flint in his voice.

I took a deep breath. It didn't seem that any amount of pleading would dissuade him. "I understand. Well, I don't understand, but I won't make this more difficult."

"I love you," he said.

"I love you too."

We left the park together, and when we reached the corner, he disappeared down a side street. As I trudged home, I slid the yarn off my finger, wound it into a tiny ball, and put it in my coat pocket.

By the time I arrived at the apartment, my father was in his chair in the front room with the newspaper. My mother told me there was food waiting for me on the counter. In the kitchen, I lifted the cover off the plate—bulgur with stewed green beans, onions, and tomatoes that smelled faintly of butter. I had no appetite and wished I could have given it to Zaven.

My mother came into the room behind me. "Did he like the sweater?"

"It was a little big, but he liked it."

So she had guessed that I had seen him. But it didn't seem that her intuitions went deeper than that. Now I had a new secret. It was getting hard for me to distinguish between the lies the war required and those necessary for growing up.

16

ONE SUNDAY AFTERNOON IN late November, Jacqueline, who was working as a secretary in an Armenian lawyer's office, came over with a bunch of her boss's castoff magazines and the latest news from the center of the community. She and I sequestered ourselves in my room flipping through pages; I sat on my bed while she lay on what had been Auntie Shakeh's.

Jacqueline said, "Can you imagine? Armenians in the Wehrmacht. They were in the Soviet army and were captured by the Germans. They had a choice between rotting in POW camps or joining the Boches."

"And clearly, these men made the noble choice," I said.

"Oh, don't be harsh. You don't know what you would do. What's so noble about starving to death?"

"And what exactly are they doing here in France?"

"They're working on the Atlantic wall. Some of them are on leave now, and some of them are passing through on their way to the coast. There's going to be a cultural evening with them next Saturday. We have to go."

"You are welcome to go, but I don't have to go anywhere," I said.

"It's a chance to have a little fun. You can't study and knit all the time. You're turning into your aunt, God rest her soul, and you're only seventeen."

I turned a page.

Jacqueline persisted. "When was the last time you got dressed up?"

"I don't have any stockings."

Jacqueline rolled her eyes at me. "You don't need stockings. We'll just draw black lines down the backs of your legs."

"Bare legs in this weather?"

"So go ahead and wear wool tights, no one will notice."

"It doesn't seem right, going to a party when . . ." I said.

"It's not a party. It's a patriotic evening. Don't you have any national feeling? They're Armenian, after all."

When Jacqueline and I entered the noisy hall, it was already packed with what seemed to be half the Armenians of Paris. Among them were dark-haired young Armenian men dressed in the gray-green of the German army.

"Look at those uniforms," I whispered to Jacqueline.

"I told you they were in the Wehrmacht. What did you think they were going to wear? Look at their faces."

It was true that they shared the features of our neighbors and cousins, but it made me uneasy to see them in those uniforms; it blurred the lines between who was the enemy and who was not and where our allegiances should be.

Jacqueline and I squeezed our way to the front, stopping briefly to exchange greetings with people we knew, and found two seats. A few minutes later, men from Soviet Armenia took the stage and sang a series of folk tunes in beautiful harmony. A mournful song about lost love and longing for the homeland set a flock of white hankies aflutter. The singing was followed by high-stepping Russian dances that heated up the room and brought the crowd roaring to its feet.

After the show, Jacqueline and I talked with a small circle of the performers, most of whom spoke only Eastern Armenian. One of them, though, was fluent in Western Armenian. His way of talking was formal almost to the point of being stilted, but warmth emanated from his dark eyes, and his smile was incandescent.

After a while I asked him, "How do you know Western Armenian?"

He said, "My parents hail from Moush. During the Deportations they fled to Leninakan. We conversed in Western Armenian at home; I picked up Eastern Armenian on the street, and Russian at school. Now I am learning French."

"My father's family was from Moush as well," I told him.

"Perhaps our families were known to each other. What is your surname?" he asked.

"Pegorian."

"And your first name?"

"Maral."

He smiled. "Maral Pegorian. That is a beautiful name—"

Jacqueline interrupted. "I'm Jacqueline Sahadian. And what's your name?"

"Andon Shirvanian, at your service," he said with a nod. "May I bring you young ladies something to drink?"

As we watched him thread his way across the crowded room, Jacqueline said, "He's handsome, don't you think?"

"He's very polite."

He soon returned, deftly balancing three cups of tea. After handing us each a cup, he pulled a folded napkin from his uniform's pocket. Inside were three cookies, which he offered to us.

He said, "It is kind of the community here to host us so generously. I had not eaten a homemade pastry in more than two years."

"Believe me," Jacqueline said, "our cookies tasted much better before the Boches stole all the butter."

Andon laughed. "Well, let me promise you that you are eating better here than most of Eastern Europe. When we were in the POW camp, they fed us a half a loaf of bread each day with a thin vegetable soup. Once a week, they doled out a teaspoon of jam and a teaspoon of salt. Of course, now they feed us well. The German army cannot do its job on an empty stomach. I fear that we are eating all your butter."

"Our butter, our bread, our meat, our potatoes, our milk . . ." Jacqueline enumerated on her fingers.

He bowed his head. "Please forgive me."

Jacqueline smiled. "I don't blame you. I know that under that German uniform, there beats an Armenian heart. Is it all Armenians in your unit?"

"There is an Armenian legion, but our company is mixed. In addition to Armenians, we have Ukrainians, Georgians, and an odd assortment of others."

I asked, "What work are you doing?"

"We are helping build a wall along the Atlantic coast. To my mind, France is preferable to Poland, although there is certainly no honor in this effort."

"For the moment, you seem to have better fortune than many," I said stiffly, thinking of Zaven and Barkev, who were likely half starved in some tiny, cold garret.

"I detect a note of disapproval in your voice, but I agree that a lucky star is shining down on me tonight." He smiled, looking into my eyes.

Flushing, I glanced at the clock on the wall. Curfew was approaching.

I said, "We have to catch the last Métro."

Jacqueline sighed. "You're right, as usual. Just when we were having a little fun."

Andon Shirvanian said, "I am so happy to have met you. I would hope to have the pleasure of seeing you again when I return to Paris. Miss Pegorian, may I call on your family at that time?"

I sputtered, "Well . . . we really must go now. It was nice to meet you."

As we walked to the Métro, Jacqueline said, "You weren't so friendly to him at the end. If you wanted to give him the idea that you'd like to see him again, I think you failed."

"First off, I already have a boyfriend. Second, speaking of not nice, you were the one accusing him of stealing all our butter. Third, even though he is Armenian, he is wearing a German uniform. Can you imagine the scandal it would cause if he strolled down our street?"

"It would be different if he were an officer, don't you

think? And anyway, he would have died in that camp if he hadn't joined the German army. What choice did he have?"

"Go ahead and make excuses, but Zaven and Missak would never put on German uniforms no matter how hungry they were."

"Would you rather have a dead hero or a live man?" Jacqueline countered.

"If you think he's so wonderful, why don't you chase after him?"

"He wasn't interested in me, or didn't you notice?"

When I didn't answer she added, "There's no accounting for tastes. Some men prefer the boring intellectual ones."

I laughed. "And others prefer—"

"Don't say something you're going to regret!"

I took Jacqueline's arm. "I was going to say, 'And others prefer the sassy ones with short hair.'"

17

AT BREAKFAST, MY FATHER read aloud in his heavily accented French from a newspaper article announcing the arrest of Missak Manouchian. Manouchian, an Armenian poet, former factory worker, and Communist, was accused of being the ringleader of a terrorist network that had assassinated several high-ranking German officers, including a close personal friend of Hitler. According to the report, the members of this criminal gang had also blown up munitions trains and assaulted German troops in Paris and its suburbs, all within the space of seven months.

When he finished reading, my father commented in Armenian, "If an Armenian in France does something dishonorable, the French say he's a dirty immigrant. If he does something good, the French take the credit and say he's French. Whatever they decide to say about this one, the Armenian people have another martyr."

We didn't know Manouchian, but his wife, Melinée, who

had lived in Belleville before the war, was friendly with Zaven's parents. The Kacherians had met the husband several times at social events.

Soon after the arrests, my father's mortal enemy, the radio commentator Jean Hérold-Paquis, began devoting his daily radio show to what was called the Manouchian affair. My mother and I often left the room during his broadcasts, which my father insisted on listening to despite the toll it took on his blood pressure. But during these episodes about Manouchian, I was glued to the radio as well—it was a rarity for Armenians to be referred to over the airwaves, and certainly never before had there been a mention of someone who was in our circle. My mother sat mutely in her corner as Hérold-Paquis filled the front room with insults about the dirty foreigner, the murderer without scruples, and the dark-skinned half-breed who had spit in the face of the country that had given him refuge. Death was too good for the subhuman *métèque* who had murdered the führer's friend. Then Hérold-Paquis turned his hatred more broadly, railing against Manouchian's gang of filthy Red and kike criminals and terrorists. In his opinion, they all had rotten faces and unpronounceable names and were a pox on the French nation. It was really quite a performance, I had to admit, but his venom and race-baiting made me feel ill. Clearly we Armenians were barely human, and it was only owing to a stroke of luck or a bit of oversight that we weren't being subjected to the same grim regimen as the Jews and Communists.

My father's face grew red as the litany of abuse went on until finally he burst out, "You mark my words, that Nazi puppet is going to end up in front of a firing squad or on the gallows. He talks shit, he will eat shit, and he will rot in shit by the time this is all over."

I looked to my mother, expecting her to reprimand him, but she was staring ahead vacantly. It was unclear whether she had even registered either the radio tirade or my father's scathing response.

The next night, as the puppet launched again into his catalog of insults but before my father had had a chance to work himself into a rage, I said, "I can't stomach any more of this."

I removed my books and myself to the frigid bedroom. But even there I had difficulty focusing, and it wasn't because of the temperature. All I could think of was Zaven. I knew nothing about where he and Barkev were and what they were up to, but I suspected enough to panic for their safety. The worse the war went for the Germans, the more brutal they became. Black-clad SS officers were now seen on the streets of central Paris, and rumors of the tortures practiced at the Cherche-Midi prison circulated in our neighborhood. By this point in the war, every one of us knew someone who had been arrested or deported.

The next day, after school, I stopped by the Kacherians' apartment to see if they had had any news. I knocked, and a solemn-faced Virginie opened the door.

She brightened when she saw me. "Oh, Maral. Come in. My mother will be happy you're here."

Zavig's mother, whose face was pale and drawn, invited me to stay for tea. "It's so nice of you to visit, sweetie. We haven't seen you in a while. I've been fretting about the boys, but it cheers me up to look at your pretty face."

"Have you heard anything?" I asked.

Auntie Shushan pulled a note from her pocket and handed it to me. "Someone slid this under the door last night."

Written on the card were the words *Don't worry. We are fine. B & Z.*

"That's not Zaven's handwriting."

"It's Barkev's. Telling a mother not to worry is like telling her not to breathe. Lately I can't sleep for more than a few hours at a time. I'm up in the middle of the night imagining awful things that could be happening to my boys. But I'm glad to know they are not in jail. I can't stand to think of what poor Melinée must be going through. *Vahkh, vahkh,* the agony."

The melancholy in our own apartment deepened as the anniversary of Auntie Shakeh's passing approached. That week, my mother and I went to the church to make arrangements with the priest for the service for the repose of Auntie Shakeh's soul.

Auntie Shakeh's soul may have been in heaven, but it was my mother's soul that had no rest. When I looked at my mother, I noticed that she was smaller and more fragile than she had been only a few months before.

My father shook his head when I asked him about it. "If you know a way to call her back," he said, "I would be grateful. Nothing I say or do seems to help."

In the evenings, as we prepared the meal and set the table, I told stories from my day, essentially pelting her with words. My father and I chatted through the meal, and I would tell more anecdotes while my mother and I washed dishes. I relayed gossip from the grocery lines, and tidbits about our neighbors that I had heard from the concierge. And when I couldn't think of anything else, I talked about the weather. I almost wished my mother would admonish me to be quiet, but she passively allowed this torrent to pour over her with only an occasional perfunctory murmur of agreement or cluck of disapproval.

Most of the time, my mother seemed entirely engrossed in her own thoughts, and I assumed that the most likely subject of her brooding was her sister. I avoided mentioning Auntie Shakeh for fear of provoking deeper despair, but I started to think that maybe this subject was the only one that might help.

One Saturday afternoon my mother and I were alone in the front room doing our handwork, and I forced myself to broach the topic directly.

"It's almost one year since Auntie Shakeh passed away. It feels like a part of you went with her when she died."

My mother sighed.

"I miss you."

My mother put her hand to her face and turned aside, casting her eyes down.

I tried again. "You hardly talk. You never laugh. You must be lonely."

She said nothing. I stopped knitting, she stopped sewing, and the space was leaden with silence. I noticed her exhalations and the sound of the ticking clock.

"Lonely," my mother said finally, "it was lonely in the desert. They were all dead except for Shakeh and me. There were so many thousands of ways to die. Dying was the easy thing. You could refuse to move when they told you to move and they would whip you until you bled. You could throw yourself in the river where bloated corpses passed by like rotting logs. You could not fight back when someone tried to steal your bread. You could lie down by the road and wait for death to come for you like the vultures.

"What was harder was staying alive. How should you stay alive when you had lost your humanness? Because after a while, you felt nothing when you saw them dead and dying, nothing at all. It was as though you were made of stone. There was no longer any need to turn your face from the suffering. Your heart was smaller and harder than a stone.

"But in that place I found a way to live, and there was only one. I lived in order to keep my younger sister alive. She would have died without me, you see."

When she said those words—*you see*—she wasn't looking at me. She was looking beyond me at something that was more real to her than the room we were in.

"But now she's dead," she continued, "and I have lost my reason to stay alive. Those times were unspeakable. They were unthinkable. And since Shakeh died, it's all I think about, or fight not to think about. I believed I had kept her from dying, but in the end, I failed. She lay in that bed getting smaller and smaller until she was again a child. She was a small, sick orphan. And I failed her."

I said, "You didn't fail her. It was the war and disease that killed her. There was nothing you could have done."

My mother stared down at her hands.

I spoke louder. "Please don't ignore me. I'm listening. Talk to me."

My mother said nothing, her face a mask of grief.

"Mairig, I need you to come back. I need you. Do you hear that? And before she died, Auntie Shakeh made me promise that I would take care of you. You won't let me help you and you are pushing me away. Don't make me break my promise to Auntie Shakeh. That would be failing her again."

My mother's eyes moved almost imperceptibly. I could tell that she had heard me.

"Let me take care of you," I repeated. I left my chair and moved closer to her. I stretched out my arm and put my hand over hers.

My mother's face fell and she began to cry. Once she started crying, it seemed that she would never stop. She sobbed with the force of her whole being, and I held her tightly, as though she were my own child.

18

MY PARENTS AND I traveled by Métro to the cathedral for Auntie Shakeh's *bokehankisd*. Jacqueline and her family joined us, as did the Kacherians and some other neighbors, the same group that had been at the cemetery one year before. Only Zaven and Barkev were missing.

The priest and the deacon recited their parts of the ritual for the dead. As the swinging gold censer filled the room with incense, we intoned our lines in response, calling on God to grant rest and mercy for the departed. *Der voghormia*, Lord have mercy, Lord have mercy. Have pity on the soul of Thy departed servant Shakeh Nazarian. Have pity on us all, and forgive the sins of the living.

As I repeated the words of the liturgy, I understood that one of the sins of the living was to be still alive when the loved one was no longer walking the earth. The priest sang to us that Aunt Shakeh was in the Heavenly Jerusalem, the dwelling place of angels. I wasn't sure I believed in heaven, or in God for that matter. My father was an anticlerical atheist, as were Missak and Mr. Kacherian. They were at the church service out of deference to my mother. And with all my doubts, I came to the cathedral fueled by nostalgia for the childhood hours spent there with my aunt, who had been a devout parishioner.

In the days after the service, my mother seemed calmer and less burdened. For hours at a time, she was back to her old self. After that afternoon when the story and its grief poured out of her, she never spoke again of the ordeal in the desert. But I now recognized the expression that came over her face when she was thinking of it.

I started preparing for the exams I would face at the end of the school year, and, as my parents relied on my contribution to the household income, I continued knitting. I even grew used to Zaven's absence. At first it had felt like running my tongue over the space where a tooth had been—always a little sore, always a little bit of a surprise to find the lack. But then the pain receded, and the gap was no longer unusual. Still, at night I lay in bed remembering our first kiss in the dark stairwell, or the rainy hour under the tree, or that last meeting in the bare attic room.

On Saturday afternoons, I often went to help my father and Paul close up shop. I washed the front window, swept the floor, and helped sort the shoes into their places on the shelves where they awaited repair or pickup. We pulled the iron shutter down over the storefront. When I was small, I had imagined that the minute that my father, brother, and I walked away from the shop, all the shoes sprang to life on the shelves. They talked to one another, their tongues wagging like busy gossips' in the market. The kids' shoes spoke in high, childish voices, the old-lady shoes had quavers, and the large men's boots were gruff and loud. Now the shoes were still—silent as the city without cars, and dark as the streets in the middle of the war.

When Missak came home one Saturday a few weeks later, his expression was so grim that I could tell something calamitous had happened.

"What is it?"

"Zaven and Barkev have been arrested," he said.

"How do you know?" I asked.

"I heard this afternoon. I just stopped by the Kacherians' and they had received word as well."

"Where are Zaven and Barkev?"

"They were at La Santé, but they've been moved to the prison at Fresnes."

"What can we do?"

Missak said, "Visitors aren't allowed, but I told the Kacherians I would take food and clothes to them early next week."

"I'm going too," I said.

"I'll borrow the Kacherians' bicycle, and you can take ours. It's going to be a long, cold ride. And you'll have to miss school."

"Should we tell the parents?" I asked.

"We don't need to tell them we're going out there. Mairig is jittery enough."

When my mother heard the news, she put her hand over her eyes and began to rock from side to side in her chair. "Our boys, our boys, they have taken our boys. What will become of them? What will become of us all?"

My father said, "They're holding Manouchian at Fresnes as well."

My mother turned to Missak. "You stay out of trouble, okay, my boy? Don't do anything that would give them the idea to arrest you. Poor Shushan. Both of her boys."

When Missak and I went to the Kacherians' early on Monday morning to pick up the basket, Auntie Shushan was red-eyed from crying, as was Virginie. Mr. Kacherian was more stoic, but his face was ashen.

Auntie Shushan and I went into the kitchen so I could collect the wicker hamper they had packed: a jar of jam, a loaf of bread, a wedge of cheese, some long underwear, and two clean shirts.

"I wish we had more for them," she said. "Do you think I should put in combs and toothbrushes?"

"They could use those," I said. Then I pulled from my school bag two pairs of hand-knit socks: a dark green pair for Barkev and gray for Zaven. "I made these. And my mother sent pickles. Auntie, we didn't tell my mother that we're going, so please don't say anything."

Shushan Kacherian nodded in assent. She took the socks, rolling them carefully before adding them to the hamper. "You are such a good girl, Maral. I hope that you and Zavig . . ." Her eyes filled with tears. "Do you think they'll let them go? Why both of them? Can you imagine what it has been like these past months, not knowing anything? But why am I saying this to you? Of course you know. He loves you, sweetie. He isn't one to talk much about that kind of thing. But I know. I put a small note in the basket telling my sons that I love them. It's in French so the police will know it is nothing bad. Virginie helped with the spelling. You should write something for Zaven too."

Before Missak headed off to the printing shop with the basket and the Kacherians' bicycle, we made plans to meet early the next morning. That evening I wrote and tore up a dozen notes to Zaven, imagining other people reading my words. Finally I settled on a simple message: *Dear Zavig, I think of you often and when I do, I can feel your thoughts are turned toward me as well. I send you a pair of warm socks and much love. Your Maro.*

The next day, Missak and I set off on our bicycles to Fresnes. I wore long woolen stockings under my skirt, but the cold wind still bit at my skin. After a few miles of pedaling, I was hot with exertion, except for my fingers, which were numbed by the bike's icy handles. We sped through the Porte d'Orléans and took the Nationale 20 to the town of Fresnes. We stopped at a café in the town's center to ask for directions to the prison.

The prison itself was like a huge medieval fortress, with a high wall around it and rows of tall stone and concrete buildings within. We approached the front entrance and talked with a guard through a small window.

"We're looking for Barkev and Zaven Kacherian," Missak said. "We brought them a package from their family."

"Kacherian?" The guard opened a large leather ledger and ran his finger down a page. "Ah yes, Kacherian. You can leave that package with me."

"Is it possible to see them?" I asked.

He shook his head. "No visitors."

We walked our bicycles toward the road.

"I just have to see him," I said.

Missak didn't reply.

"How can we come all the way out here without at least trying? I'm going to walk around the other side. Maybe it's possible to glimpse something from the back," I said.

"There are sentries in the watchtowers."

"You wait here with the bikes." I dumped my bike against his and took off at a trot before he could tell me no.

"Maral! Get back here!" he called.

I jogged the perimeter of the prison ten feet back from the high fortress walls so I could see over them, gazing up at the rows of windows along the buildings inside. They were covered with wire mesh and bars, and many of them were darkened so no one could see in or out. There must have been a thousand men in there, and among them Zaven and his brother. I sensed that it was a dreadful place, full of fear and hunger and suffering.

I paused for a moment and closed my eyes, conjuring up Zaven's face. Not the lean, haggard countenance that was hidden away in the prison, but the face that he had turned to me as we sat under the tree in the park. He was close by—I could feel it.

So without even thinking, I shouted as loudly as I could, "Zaven! Zaven! It's me, Maral. I'm here. I'm here. Zaven! Zaven!"

"You! Shut up!" a gruff voice barked from the tower above. The sentry was pointing a rifle at me. I took off at a gallop to where Missak was waiting.

I reached my brother and stopped to catch my breath. "Okay, we can go now."

"That was the stupidest thing I've ever seen you do. You're lucky he didn't shoot you." Missak swung his leg over his bike and pushed off for the long ride back.

That night I told my parents about the journey, and neither of them reproached me. For the week after that trip to Fresnes, I hardly slept, and when I did my dreams were nightmares set in the prison. I wandered up and down the dark halls, knocking on doors of cells that rang hollow. There were coughs and cries, but I never saw anyone. I heard weeping behind a door, but when I called, there was no response.

Now it was my mother's turn to fuss over me, clucking her tongue and admonishing me to eat. She insisted that I drink hot tisane before bed so I could get some rest.

Several weeks later we heard on the puppet's broadcast that Manouchian had appeared before a military tribunal at the Hôtel Continental. The headline of the paper on February 22 was "23 Terrorists, Almost All Foreigners, Condemned to Death." We found out later from Zaven's father that Manouchian and his men had been shot the previous day at Mont-Valérien. Manouchian had made a brave final speech that we were told had been broadcast on Radio Alger and repeated later on the BBC.

My father said, "With his last breath, he spoke like a free man. He died a hero and a patriot."

Small consolation for his wife that he died a hero, I thought.

There had been no word from Zaven and Barkev. As far as the Kacherians could determine, their sons were accused of disseminating forbidden tracts, but at that point in the war, even being in the wrong place at the wrong time could result in deportation.

A few weeks later, one morning on my way to school, I saw red posters plastered on the walls of Belleville. Across the top was the question LIBERATORS? I stood in front of one of them, scanning the faces in the medallions on the poster: Manouchian, Alfonso, Rayman, Elek, Fontanot, Grzywacz, Wasjbrot, and the rest. There was a caption beneath each man describing him in terms of the despised group he had belonged to—an Armenian, a Red Spaniard, a Hungarian Jew, a Polish Jew, an Italian Communist, and so on—and noting how many attacks he had committed. Their faces were shadowed and puffy, probably from the beatings they had suffered at the hands of their jailers, and it made me sick with fear that Zaven and Barkev were being mistreated. Across the bottom of the poster it said LIBERATION BY THE ARMY OF CRIME. I knew the Germans wanted us to loathe them, these foreigners, immigrants, and Communists who had taken up arms against the Occupation.

But I didn't despise them. They were our cousins and our martyrs. At the end of the day, as I was on my way home from school, I saw that there were pyramids of flowers dropped at the foot of the wall under the posters. And the next morning I saw that on each red poster along the rue de Belleville, someone, in the dark of the night, had scrawled *Mort pour la France.*

19

IN THE SPRING, THE ALLIES flew many bombing raids over France, but out of respect for Paris's monuments, the targets were in the suburbs. Several times that season, the warning sirens blared in Paris, and we tumbled out of bed and headed to the air-raid shelter. The Sahadians were there, and Jacqueline and I spent the time whispering in a corner. One night in April, the sirens didn't sound the alert until the bombs were already dropping, so my parents and I didn't have time to go to the shelter; we stayed in the front room of our apartment while explosions thundered only a few miles away.

My father cocked his head to one side. "Sounds like it's near La Chapelle."

The next day, the newspaper reported a grisly 651 dead and 461 wounded. The factories at La Chapelle were damaged, and some bombs had gone astray and hit Montmartre.

My father grumbled, "You'd think with the modern equipment the Americans have, they could be a little more precise."

Missak and I consulted with the Kacherians and planned another bicycle trip to Fresnes. My mother and I scraped together the ingredients to make some bread sticks to add to the basket. The tires on our old bicycle had become progressively thinner, but we decided to take our chances.

On a warm, sunny day in May, Missak and I pedaled through the suburbs, where the window boxes on the houses we passed were filled with primroses and hyacinths. Plane trees along the road had unfurled their bright new leaves, and the chestnuts were in bloom. Wildflowers had sprung up alongside ditches and in the fields. Despite the grimness of our destination, I was buoyed by the sunny skies and the wind in my hair. It was hard to believe on such a beautiful spring day that the war could last much longer.

"Hey," I called over my shoulder to my brother. "Look at the poppies!" I pointed to a field of grasses dotted with red.

We arrived at the prison entrance, and the guard searched his ledger. He went through the pages twice, finally shaking his head.

"They're not here," he said.

"Where have they gone?" Missak asked.

The guard pulled out another ledger and flipped through the pages, pausing when he found their names. He replied, "They went to Compiègne over two weeks ago. From there, they would have gone to a work camp in the east."

Missak pressed him for more details; the guard said he wasn't certain, but he thought they might have been headed for a camp in Germany called Buchenwald, where most of the political prisoners were sent.

We turned and wheeled our bicycles away from the prison.

My mind felt sluggish, and I was glad that for once my imagination had stalled. "What do we do now?" I asked Missak.

"We go home."

My brother and I didn't speak on the long ride back to Paris. As we neared Belleville, our pace slowed, until at the end we walked the bicycles up the hill.

"How far is Compiègne?" I asked.

"Too far," he said.

"How long would it take?"

"About twice as long as Fresnes. It would be almost impossible to do in one day. And these bicycles wouldn't make it. Zaven and Barkev are probably not even there anymore. You heard him."

I said, "Oh, Missak, I'm sorry to be such a coward, but I don't think I can face Auntie Shushan."

"You go home," he told me.

I slowly wheeled the bicycle along the narrow street, stopping to wipe tears with my sleeve. I entered the courtyard and left the bike behind the steps in the bottom of the stairwell.

My mother came running into the hall as I entered the apartment. "*Yavrum!* You look like a sheet. What happened? Tell me what is the matter. Where is your brother?"

"Missak went to tell the Kacherians that Zaven and Barkev have been deported," I said. "They've been sent to a camp in Germany."

My mother raised her palms and eyes to heaven. "*Yaman,*
yaman. Dear God, is death the only end to this suffering?"

That night I lay in bed studying the drawing on the wall.
Missak had captured Zavig's nature in that sketch: the high
forehead; the large, soulful eyes; the open smile. I tried
every ritual I knew to fall asleep—turning to my habitual
position on my side with a hand slipped beneath the pillow,
and counting to a thousand in French and then in Armenian. I switched on the bedside lamp and tried reading from
Auntie Shakeh's Bible. But nothing helped, and I lay in the
dark as the infernal machine of my imagination began to
work: Zaven was in a grimy factory where unwashed, rail-
thin men in tattered clothes trundled misfortune around in
wheelbarrows. I must have fallen asleep at some point, but
when the alarm went off in the morning I felt as though it
had been only ten minutes since I shut my eyes.

The news of Zaven and Barkev's deportation cast a pall
over our household for many weeks. I continued having
difficulty sleeping and stumbled wearily through the day.
My mother's hands were either frantic with work or still as
dead birds. On Saturday evening when Missak was a half an
hour late for dinner, my mother wept into her apron while
my father scolded her. When Missak finally arrived, no one
reprimanded him. We sat at the table and ate dinner to the
sounds of cutlery against plates.

One morning at the breakfast table, my father announced
with forced cheerfulness that the Germans were in a tough
spot and it was only a matter of time before Hitler was
defeated. He predicted that the Kacherian boys would be

back before the holidays and that life would return to normal soon thereafter.

He said, "The Americans and the British will land on the coast any day now. They'll break through that wall and roll across France."

My mother eyed him skeptically. "Did Saint Sarkis tell you all this in a dream?"

"There are rumors going up and down the hill, and I can feel it in my bones," he said.

"Maybe what you're feeling in your bones is old age," she said. "Or maybe it's going to rain."

As sad as we were, we returned to the routine of our lives. I studied for my exams. My mother set my father to building several more window boxes out of old crates. She sent Missak out to the park to collect dirt to fill them. I helped her plant tomatoes, peppers, and parsley in the boxes. Then my mother worked her magic on the grocer and came home with another sack of bulgur.

One Sunday, I was dispatched by bicycle to the cousins in Alfortville. My father sent newly made sandals with wooden soles that I traded for onions, eggplant seedlings, and another beady-eyed laying hen. Since the bird would eventually land in a pot, I christened her Havabour—Chicken Soup. On my way back, the bicycle finally suffered a flat tire and I had to walk the last mile home.

I took my exit exams in early June, and days later, as I was standing in line at the market, I heard the long-anticipated news. It was Tuesday, June 6, and the street was buzzing: the Americans and English had launched their attack on

Normandy. The Allies had landed on French soil and would soon be heading east.

With the news of the Allied landing, our daily lives felt provisional and petty. But still, the shopping had to be done, the meals prepared, and the table set for dinner. My mother sewed, my father repaired shoes, and I completed my last days at the lycée. We brushed our teeth at night and slept as best we could. I woke in the middle of the night thinking of Zavig and Barkev somewhere deep in Germany, where the war might go on for many months. I tried not to think about how awful it was that they had been deported only weeks before the Americans arrived.

All the girls in my class were concerned that their exam results would disappear into the war's chaos, but even here, the routine was maintained; French bureaucracy held sway, and the marks were posted on the wall.

My English teacher, Mrs. Collin, pulled me aside. "Marie, what are your plans for next year?"

"I don't know. I have a knitting job this summer. In the fall, I thought I would look for an office job of some kind—"

Mrs. Collin interrupted. "Young lady, it would be unfortunate if you didn't continue your education. Would you like me to put in a word for you with the English Literature Department at the Sorbonne?"

As much as I was flattered by my teacher's concern, and as deeply as I would have loved to study more, the disorder of the war, the closure of the teacher's colleges, and my family's strained finances had made me wonder if going to the university made any sense. I hadn't even brought it up with my parents, and truthfully, I felt that my life was on hold until Zaven returned.

Mrs. Collin peered into my face. "Look, you should at least apply. There is a chance for a scholarship, and the English Department's library hires part-time assistants. Who knows where we will all be in October. Let me help you so you may at least have a choice."

So she lobbied on my behalf, and a place and the funds were found. My father grumbled about higher education being wasted on a girl. Studying literature seemed frivolous to him; if I had been studying for something practical, like a teaching or a nursing degree, he might have responded with more enthusiasm. My mother told me not to pay any attention, and in the end he grudgingly gave me his gnomic blessing: "Reading is a golden bracelet."

20

CARRYING A HEAVY BAG full of yarn one hot evening, I plodded up the rue de Belleville from the Métro; three boys on bicycles whizzed down the hill, tossing leaflets behind them like confetti. Several of the papers fluttered to the sidewalk at my feet. I picked one up and saw it was a call to action for Bastille Day.

Rise up, rise up, citizens, on the 14th of July, take to the streets of Belleville and show your defiance of the Nazi Occupier.

Since the Allies had landed in Normandy, the atmosphere in the city was electric and mercurial. In our neighborhood, with its history of working-class revolt, each day there was some new act of defiance: Métros were purposely stalled in the tunnels, factory workers walked out on strike, and underground newspapers were openly distributed on corners. The quiet muttering against the Germans turned into a loud discourse in the market lines.

When Bastille Day arrived I was unable to convince my

mother to join Jacqueline and me on the streets, but she didn't attempt to stop us. At the first sign of trouble, I promised her, we would scuttle home. We passed by the shoe-repair shop to pick up my father and Paul, and the four of us made our way to the corner. The Kacherians were already there, as were Jacqueline's parents and siblings.

Boys were moving along the sidewalks of the rue de Belleville selling miniature paper tricolor flags. The profits were for the benefit of the Resistance, so the boys soon sold all their wares. The street quickly filled—the crowds went up and down the rue de Belleville as far as I could see. People had gathered on one side of the street, while on the opposite sidewalk the police had lined up. But marching down the middle of the street were members of the armed Resistance—the Francs-Tireurs et Partisans—openly carrying their weapons for the first time.

At the sight of the Partisan Snipers, Shushan Kacherian exclaimed, "*Meghah!* If those boys aren't afraid, it must be true that the Germans are losing!"

My father laughed. "Maybe now you'll believe me."

Just then a young man waving a full-size tricolor ran to join the gun-toting irregulars. Suddenly the crowd was singing "La Marseillaise"—singing, bellowing, and shouting with all the rage and joy of believing that the Occupation would soon be over.

My father slapped Vahan Kacherian on the back and yelled over the roar of the crowd, "Those are our men! If only your sons were here to see this. But they'll be back. The Soviets are headed west and the Americans are headed east. Soon they will crush the Boches in the middle."

Turning to me, Zaven's father said happily, "You'll be pleased to see Zaven when he comes home, won't you, young lady?"

Everything seemed possible in that moment. As the raucous chorus continued, I imagined that any minute Zaven would round the corner to join us.

There were no Germans to be seen, only the French police. At one point, orders must have been given to disperse the crowds, and police vans started to move in. They attempted to drive down the street, but no one moved. Men shouted, "The police are with us! The police are with us!" And it appeared that they were. The vans retreated and some of the officers themselves joined in singing another round of "La Marseillaise."

My father grinned. "Too bad your mother and brother aren't here to see this."

Missak suddenly bobbed up beside us. "I'm here!"

My father clapped him on the shoulder. "Where have you been?"

"Down on the boulevard de Belleville. It's a wild party. Everyone's singing and dancing. It was so jammed it took me a half an hour to get through."

After a while the police vans arrived again, but people had already started dispersing, leaving the street littered with paper flags, trampled leaflets, and crushed flowers.

Jacqueline, Missak, and I sat on the bench in the courtyard of our building watching Havabour peck and scratch at the weeds growing between the cobblestones.

"Your mother invited me to stay for dinner," Jacqueline

said, eyeing the hen. "Too bad that chicken isn't in the pot."

I said, "My mother saved eggs to cook with the bulgur. I think there's even butter to fry the onions."

"You're so lucky. We're eating badly at my house, or we're hardly eating. The kids look skinnier every day. All I earn I spend on black-market food, but I can't buy much. A kilo of butter costs a thousand francs. Can you imagine that? Who has a thousand francs to spend on butter?"

Missak reached into his pocket. "Here," he said, handing her two fake ration cards.

"Oh, Missak, I could kiss you!" Jacqueline said.

He flushed. "Just because you have the tickets doesn't mean you'll be able to find the food."

I studied Missak out of the corner of my eye. He wasn't one to embarrass easily. Then I noticed the way we were sitting—with Jacqueline in the middle between my brother and me. I wondered how long their romance had been going on without my noticing.

Jacqueline put her hand on Missak's arm. "But still, we should be able to get something with these, and something is better than nothing."

I stood up. "Time to set the table."

"Do you want me to come with you?" Jacqueline asked, withdrawing her hand from Missak's arm.

"No need," I said, scooping up the bird and nestling it in the crook of my elbow. "I'll come down and let you know when it's ready. And Jacqueline, will you do me a favor?"

"Sure. What do you want?" Jacqueline asked.

"Will you cut my hair?"

"You want a trim?"

I pointed at my jaw line. "I want it cut to here."

"Your mother will have a fit," Jacqueline said.

"So we'll do it at your place."

The next day, I went to the Sahadians' carrying in my bag a purloined pair of my mother's sharpest shears.

As the first long tress fell to the kitchen floor, Jacqueline's mother said, "Are you two crazy? Why are you cutting it so short? Maral, your mother's going to cry when she sees what you've done."

"It's the style," Jacqueline said. With a snip of the scissors, another lock of hair dropped, and then another.

When it was done I shook my head, surprised by how weightless it felt. I put my hand to the ends.

"I knew it," Jacqueline said triumphantly. "See how nicely it curls? Think about all those girls who have to put waves into their hair. Do you like it?"

I examined myself in the hand mirror. "Do you think it looks good?"

Jacqueline said, "It's perfect. What do you think, Mairig?"

Auntie Sophie said, "Okay. So it's nice. Maybe your mother won't be too sad."

21

By early august, rumor had it that General Leclerc and the Americans were just over the horizon. The whole city was waiting, and when people got tired of waiting, they took action. First the police went on strike, disappearing from the streets and slipping out of their uniforms. The next day our letterbox was empty because the postal workers had walked off the job. The following day my father was thrilled to hear static where Radio Paris was usually found. There were no newspapers, electricity was cut, and gas was suspended. The Métro was shut down, and with the tires on our bicycle flat and beyond repair, we had no way to move around the city except on foot. Out of habit my father went to his shop, but customers were rare. I strayed only a few blocks from home, and my mother went no farther than our courtyard. One morning I ventured out to discover that posters had been plastered all over the walls of Belleville calling for a general strike and insurrection. We had heard nothing from Missak, who was, as far as we knew, living at the print shop.

The following Sunday morning Missak showed up at home looking as though he hadn't slept in days. His voice hoarse and taut with excitement, he reported that the battle for Paris had begun the day before, with street fighting in the Latin Quarter and around the Gare de la Villette.

"Finally," he said, "Paris is rising up."

That afternoon a truce was announced via loudspeakers on cars that cruised the neighborhood. Missak and I went out to see what was going on, joining the jubilant crowds who had poured into the streets to celebrate. But a neighbor reported that the fighting was continuing in small pockets around town, despite the official announcement.

Vahan Kacherian waved to us from the corner, and we went over to say hello. Just then a column of German army trucks sped up the hill and people scattered in fear. Missak, Vahan, and I dashed into the Kacherians' courtyard.

Once inside, Vahan beamed. "The Boches didn't stop, and they probably won't stop until they get to Berlin. With any luck, my boys will be home by Christmas." He patted my arm. "Then we'll have some raki to celebrate!"

I remembered the day four years earlier when we had watched from behind the slatted shutters in the Kacherians' apartment as the German troops marched down the hill toward the heart of Paris. It seemed unreal that the long night was almost over.

On Monday morning, Missak was up early, claiming he had to return to work at the print shop.

My mother pleaded, "Oh no, Missak. Stay home. It's too dangerous."

"My boss needs me."

My mother retorted, "I'm your mother, and I need you. Why should you roam the streets when there are bullets flying in all directions?"

My father interjected, "Azniv, he's a man now. And he's not stupid, are you, boy? You will keep your wits about you and your head down."

"You are actually going to let him go?" my mother asked.

"It's his decision, Azniv. And as they say, if disaster is on its way, it can strike you even while you sleep in your bed."

When my mother was in the other room, I took hold of Missak's hand and examined his fingernails.

"Brother, there isn't any ink here. It doesn't look like you've been doing any printing at all."

"There's other work to do."

"With guns?" I asked.

"Guns, grenades, Molotov cocktails," he said, laughing and miming the tossing of a flaming bottle.

"I'm glad you think that's funny. Missak, please don't be an idiot and get yourself killed now."

"I'm coordinating the printing and distribution of leaflets. Dull, I know, but someone has to do it."

He left, and we had no word from him for days. With no newspaper and no radio, we relied on street gossip and Resistance handbills for news. There were gun battles on the quays along the Seine, and random shootings of passersby by enraged German soldiers as they fled. My mother was panic-stricken about Missak's whereabouts and safety.

Meanwhile, a few blocks up the hill from us on the rue de Belleville, men had pulled up the cobblestones and built a barricade. When my mother heard about it, she asked my father to go see if Missak was there.

"All the white hairs on my head have Missak's name written on them. If you find him, Garabed, you grab him by the scruff of the neck and bring him home."

When my mother's back was turned, I slipped out the door behind my father.

"What are you doing, girl?" my father asked as I caught up with him at the foot of the stairs.

"I want to see what's happening."

"Your mother's going to be angry at both of us," he said.

"So maybe now there will be a white hair with my name on it."

The barricade was assembled of paving stones and whatever else the men had been able to lay their hands on, including broken shutters, an old baby carriage, and metal bed frames. Trees had been cut down and tossed on top of the pile. The boys and men of Belleville stood around the barricade armed with ancient pistols, their grandfathers' hunting rifles, and iron rods. Missak was nowhere to be seen.

From the men on the barricade we heard there was heavy fighting in the Latin Quarter and around the Hôtel de Ville. Even though many Germans were leaving Paris under orders, the remaining troops were well armed and battling in the streets against poorly equipped Resistance men. There were also German snipers on rooftops around the city, which made moving from place to place hazardous.

"We're not going to just sit and wait for Leclerc's guys

and the Americans, you know. We're fighting to liberate Paris," one boy said. He looked to be about fourteen and was holding a rusty sword.

Another man added, "Yes, well, we haven't seen a Boche here yet. But if they do show up in Belleville, we'll damn well liberate ourselves."

The waiting game continued, with most stores closed and people cooped up in their apartments. My father's shop was near enough that he still went there each day, primarily as an escape from my mother's anxious handwringing and groaning, which were getting on my nerves as well. Jacqueline came by to find out if we had heard anything from Missak, which we hadn't. Then Jacqueline and I went to see if Donabedian would let her use his phone to contact Baron Hovanessian at the law office. She had been unable to get to work for almost a week, and when she called, her boss told her that the Germans had used tanks against some of the Resistance barricades in the city center, but he thought the worst of it was over.

Finally, on Thursday evening, the electricity came on again, and my father turned on the radio and twisted the dial until he found a voice. We heard an announcement from something calling itself the Radio of the French Nation saying that the first French troops led by General Leclerc had entered the capital. Missak came home late on Saturday, and instead of greeting him with joy, my mother collapsed into sobs. By Saturday evening, the liberation had been accomplished. That night all the churches of the city set their bells ringing. My father, Missak, and I headed to join a crowd at the Parc de Belleville, where we watched celebratory fireworks showering over the Hôtel de Ville.

The following day we heard on the radio that General de Gaulle was on the Champs Élysées, and then the American soldiers, who would soon be on their way to their next battle, streamed into Paris.

Jacqueline came by to invite Missak and me to a gathering in honor of the Armenians in the American army who were passing through town. The next afternoon, taking the Métro for the first time in weeks, I met Jacqueline and Missak at her office and then the three of us walked the few blocks to an Armenian restaurant in the diamond district that was already crowded with revelers. Just inside the door, I was almost bowled over by the heady smells of lamb, butter, and spices.

Jacqueline said, "Look at that food! Who cares about the Americans? Come on. I want something to eat."

The side table was spread with a royal banquet. As we held out our plates to be served, I whispered into Jacqueline's ear, "How in the world did they get all this food?"

The Armenian American soldiers were jolly and round-cheeked while most of us were thin and pale from a four-year regimen of root vegetables. But it felt as though they were our cousins, and, as often happened with Armenians, some of them *were* in fact distant cousins. The patron of the restaurant broke out bottles of raki he had been holding in reserve for this occasion. Soon a troupe of Armenian musicians started to play, and everyone, fueled by food and raki, began singing.

I was pulled into a line of dancers snaking around the room. When I glanced back to find my brother and Jacqueline, I saw that they were in the corner talking, their heads so close together they almost touched. The look on Missak's face was earnest and bashful. The usually sardonic Jacqueline was gazing at him adoringly.

When the line broke up at the end of the song, I went in search of something to drink. As I was standing in a dark alcove of the room sipping a glass of water, a tall young man in an American uniform approached me and said in Armenian, "I hope you won't think this is rude and I'll understand if you say no, but we're leaving tomorrow to join the fighting in the east. I'd like to be able to say that I kissed a girl in Paris. What do you think?"

The earnest look on his face charmed me.

"Where are you from?" I asked.

"New York City," he said. "The Bronx."

"What's your name?"

"Hrant. But they call me Harry. What's your name?"

"Maral. Where are your people from?"

"The mountains of Zeitoun," he said.

"That's why you're so tall." I tipped my head back to stare up at him.

"You're very pretty, Maral," he said. "You remind me of a girl I know back home."

"Your girlfriend?" I asked.

"Just a girl from church. You know what, Maral? I think we need a drink!" he said. He raced off and returned with two glasses of raki.

"*Genatz!*" I held up my glass.

"*Vive la France.*" He saluted and then threw back the drink in one gulp.

I followed his example and drained mine as well. The raki

burned going down, starting a small internal fire. I felt lap-
ping flames travel under my skin from my head to my toes.
Suddenly life was clean and bright and easy.

"So what do you say?" he asked.

"What do I say about what?" I asked, feigning ignorance.

He said with enthusiasm, "The kiss! What else?"

Here was a brave American soldier who had helped liberate Paris. He was about to march off into battle and anything
might happen to him. Even with my mother's horrified face
flickering in my mind, how could I have told him no? I
pushed my mother aside, and there behind her was Zaven, a
tiny forlorn figure in an oversize sweater. But I wasn't feeling
any pity at that moment.

I looked up at the tall Zeitountsi and answered, "Why
not?"

We moved deeper into the alcove so we were out of sight.
He quickly leaned down and put his mouth to mine. It was
an exuberant and celebratory kiss—nothing romantic or
passionate—and when we broke apart, both of us started
laughing.

"So now you can say you kissed a girl in Paris," I told him.

"Would you mind trying that again?"

"Oh, not at all," I replied, smiling.

He put his arms around me and kissed me. But this time,
I was pulled down into a whirlpool of dark water. I shut my
eyes and forgot where we were. My head was spinning so
fast that I was dizzy and breathless when we separated.

"Wow!" he said in English.

Just then my brother appeared beside us. "Maral, what do
you think you're doing?"

I said, "Harry, this is my brother, Missak. Missak, this is Harry. He's from New York. The Bronx, in fact, right, Harry?"

Missak took hold of my elbow. "That's enough, Maral. If you'll excuse us, Harry, we're going home now."

As Missak led me away, I called back over my shoulder, "Good luck, Harry! May victory be ours."

Missak said, "Is it the short hair that makes you act like a fool?"

"Oh, don't be such an old goat," I said. "It's the raki."

22

IN THE WEEKS FOLLOWING the liberation of Paris, known
and suspected collaborators were arrested. Women who had
consorted with German soldiers in what was called hori-
zontal collaboration had their heads shaved in public. Food
was still rationed and hard to procure. The Occupation may
have been over, but the war was not.

In October, I started classes at the Sorbonne and a part-
time job in the English library. I loved the university—from
the notebooks, to the lectures, to the marble and wooden
staircases worn smooth by the thousands of students who
had trod them before me.

Most of the other girls had an array of pretty dresses
that they wore with matching sweaters and brightly colored scarves. I missed Victor Hugo's democratizing smock,
which had disguised the shabbiness of my clothes. After
carefully eyeing the sweaters of the other girls, I knit myself
an approximate replica. When I mentioned to my mother
that I had only three presentable dresses, she sewed me two

white blouses out of a flea-market tablecloth, a blue wool skirt out of a remnant her boss had given her, and a brown dress from a length of cheap cotton. The new clothes were almost hopelessly out of fashion, but I said thank you and convinced myself that intelligence was a more important attribute than style.

Missak moved back into the apartment, and despite his long hours of work at the printer, we saw more of him now that he and Jacqueline were keeping company. My parents couldn't have been more pleased—they thought of Jacqueline as a second daughter. As for me, my pangs of jealousy were less frequent and less sharp.

"You don't mind?" Jacqueline asked me one night when she and I were washing dishes after dinner.

"Now that I'm used to the idea, I think it's a good arrangement. You've always been a part of the family. Lately I get to see you more often. Do you think you're going to marry him?"

Jacqueline smiled ruefully. "He hasn't asked me yet."

"Don't worry, he will. My mother is pestering him about it. She's even talking about grandchildren. If he doesn't ask you soon, my mother will do it on his behalf."

Jacqueline laughed. "Oh, I should be able to wrangle it out of him before she has to do that."

We started another winter season with fuel rationed and harder still to come by. I stuffed the cracks around the windows with rags and pulled out the woolens so my mother and I could wash the smell of naphthalene out of them. The rituals reminded me of Auntie Shakeh.

Havabour started to lose her feathers, and this time I knew that the bird was molting and would lay eggs again if we gave her the chance. But I didn't argue against my father's suggestion of a nice chicken stew. When the war was over—and that day was on the near horizon—there would be other eggs and other chickens. I was also hoping for chocolate, meat, and cheese in large quantities. I longed for abundant hot water, scented soap, silk stockings, and reams of fine paper. But it seemed frivolous to covet luxuries while there were still tens of thousands of prisoners of war in Germany and hundreds of thousands of soldiers battling across the continent.

When we gathered at the table on Sunday afternoon, the steaming chicken soup in our chipped white bowls, I couldn't help but think of the people we had lost to the war. Auntie Shakeh was in Père-Lachaise. And what of our neighbors the Lipskis, and Denise and Henri Rozenbaum? Who knew where they were? Zaven and Barkev were still in a German camp somewhere, and no one had heard a word from them. Sometimes missing Zavig would hit me like an illness for which there was no medicine.

After the meal, as I carried the dinner plates into the kitchen, my mother said, "You're thinking about Zaven, aren't you?"

I asked, "How can you tell?"

"You get this pitiful look on your face."

"I've seen that same expression on yours."

"So many lost, so many not yet returned. When he comes back, my girl, he may be changed. What you see in a war marks you forever."

I said, "Sometimes I worry that he's not coming back. I doubt they feed them much and I'm sure the work is hard.

He was so thin the last time I saw him. And now with all the fighting and the bombing over Germany . . ."

"We'll go to church next week and light a candle for Auntie Shakeh, God rest her soul, and we'll light two more for Zaven's and Barkev's safe return."

The next Sunday when my mother and I arrived at the church, the *badarak* had already started. At the back of the sanctuary we lit three candles and then crossed ourselves and slid into an empty pew. The priest and deacon led a procession around the altar and down into the nave. Smoky incense clouded the air as the gold thurible was swung from side to side. The deacons chanted the divine liturgy.

As the service continued, I glanced around the nave at the other churchgoers, most of them old widows with black lace covering their heads, and some families with school-age children. In the opposite row, there was a young man who looked familiar, but I couldn't remember where I had seen him before. He must have felt my gaze because he turned and stared straight at me, his eyes sharp with recognition. When he smiled and nodded, I remembered a German uniform. What was his name? Andon. Andon Shirvanian. Jacqueline and I had met him the night of the folkloric dance concert.

At the end of the service he approached us.

"Oryort Pegorian?" he asked. "Pardon my boldness. Do you remember me?"

"Of course," I answered. "Mairig, this is Andon Shirvanian."

"I am happy to make your acquaintance, Digin Pegorian." He bowed his head. "I had the pleasure of meeting your daughter at a cultural evening about a year ago. I am surprised that she remembered my name."

"You are from the Soviet Armenia?" my mother asked.

He replied, "Born in Leninakan. But my family is originally from Moush."

"My husband's family is from there," my mother said as we made our way to the exit.

Out in the churchyard, people she hadn't seen since Auntie Shakeh's funeral quickly surrounded my mother. I stood nearby with Andon. Snowflakes were slowly filtering down.

"You cut your hair," he said. "It is very becoming."

"Thank you."

"I am flattered that you remembered my name," he said.

"You remembered my name as well."

"But that is different. I was a stranger, wearing a German uniform, and you were kind."

"I wasn't that friendly," I said, remembering how I had deflected his offer to meet again. "What are you doing here?"

"I came to light a candle for my mother," he said.

"Is she ill?"

"She died some months after I left for the war. This is the third anniversary."

"I'm sorry for your loss."

"In a time of war, no one is without losses. But you and I managed to survive this one, did we not?"

"It seems that way," I answered. "But I really meant what are you doing here in Paris?"

"That is too long a story to tell while standing in this cold churchyard. Will you be friendlier to me now than you were before? Will you agree to see me another time?"

"It seems possible now that you aren't dressed in a German uniform."

"Will you invite me to pay a call at your home?" he asked with a wry smile. "Or perhaps we could meet for a coffee? It is less formal."

When he smiled at me like that, I felt a feather of excitement brush behind my ribs. Then I was immediately ashamed. I stared sternly down at my hands. I had just lit a candle for Zaven's safe return, and here I was entertaining an invitation from another man. I looked up at Andon's face; now it was sincere and a little wistful, as though he could sense how close I was to saying no.

We made a plan to meet later in the week at a café not far from the Sorbonne, after I finished my afternoon shift at the library.

On the way home on the Métro, my mother observed, "That Andon's a nice-looking boy. His Armenian is beautiful, and he has good manners."

"And clean fingernails, if you had a chance to inspect them," I said. "But he's not Zaven."

My mother grew serious. "No, he's not."

I approached the café near the Panthéon and saw Andon seated at a table by the window. When he spied me he broke into a full smile and waved. He rose as I came over and pulled out the chair for me.

"I'm so glad to see you, Oryort Pegorian," he said. "I wasn't sure that you would come."

"You don't know me well," I answered.

"This is true. We do not know each other well. But I would like to know you better."

His smile made me feel as though my foot had slipped on

a tread in the stairwell. I had to catch the handrail to keep myself from falling.

I blurted out, "Listen, Andon, you should know that my boyfriend was deported. And when he comes back, we'll be getting married."

"Are you engaged?" he asked.

"Nothing formal, but a promise," I said.

"He was deported for what reason?" he asked.

"He was caught distributing Resistance tracts."

"Have you heard from him?"

I shook my head. "No one has."

"And how long has he been gone?"

"Since May." I didn't mention that it had been a full year since I had last seen Zaven.

He nodded slowly. "I see."

"You and I can be friends," I said.

"I would very much like to be your friend, Oryort Pegorian."

"Please call me Maral."

"Maral."

"You promised to tell me what you are doing now," I said, anxious to change the subject.

"I am working for my father's cousin. He has a rug shop not far from here. The carpet trade is one my family knows, among others. I learned as a boy how to repair them and now I am learning to appraise them as well."

"How long have you been in Paris?"

"Since late September."

"And what were you doing before that?"

"It is a rather long story . . ."

I glanced at the clock over the bar. "I have at least an hour."

"That's more than enough time to recount the tale. Soon after I met you, they sent us to the Atlantic coast to work on the construction of the barriers. But, of course, the Allies invaded in a different location, and the walls we made served no purpose. Then they ordered us onto trains heading to Germany. We were told we would be working in an armaments factory. That job would have made us a prime target for Allied bombers. But we never got there.

"As our train crossed the Belgian border, the Americans dropped a bomb that hit the front of the train and tore up the tracks. My friends and I jumped out of the back of the train and took to the woods. We wandered around for some days until we found a Resistance unit and asked if we could join them. They put us under arrest while they contacted their leaders for instructions. Word came back that the Allies had made a deal with Stalin. So they were sorry, but we couldn't join the Resistance. All Soviet prisoners of war were to be held for eventual repatriation to the Soviet Union."

"Then what happened?" I asked.

"It was a choice of waiting as a prisoner of war knowing that I would eventually be sent back to the Soviet Union or escaping and finding a way to stay in France. My presence here tells you what I decided. I left on my own. I imagine that my friends will be on trains heading east as soon as the war is over."

"You didn't want to go home? What about your family?"

"I am disappointed that I may not see my family for a long

time, but let me put it this way: We soldiers were expected to
die on the battlefield defending the motherland, and doing
anything less than that, such as being taken prisoner, will not
be looked on with much lenience. Then there is the issue of
the German uniform."

"Why did you join the German army?"

"General Dro came to the POW camp . . . Do you know
who he is?"

I shook my head.

"He was a hero of the Russian Caucasus Army during the
First World War, and he saved many Armenian lives during the Deportations. He was the first defense minister of
the Armenian Republic, and a leader in the Dashnak Party.
When he came to the POW camp, he said, 'Men, we do not
know how this war will end, but when it does, Hayastan will
need you, so put on this German uniform.' The Germans
had promised an independent Armenia if the Soviets were
defeated. A few of the Dashnak leaders, including General
Dro, thought this was their best hope. It is now evident that
they wagered wrongly.

"In that camp, they had us on a diet that didn't kill you
right away. I calculated a man could last perhaps two years
on the rations they provided, if he found a way to avoid hard
labor and managed to steer clear of the illnesses that felled
the weaker ones in droves. I had already been in the camp
for sixteen months, so I put on the German uniform. But
this is a kind of reasoning for which I assume Stalin has no
patience."

"My father says that Stalin is an assassin."

"Yes, well, I don't want to speak more about Stalin, but I

should like to meet your father sometime. What is his profession?"

"He was trained as a shoemaker in the orphanage workshops in Lebanon, and now he has his own cobbling shop."

"Do you have any brothers or sisters?"

"One older brother. Missak. He works for a printer. He forged documents for the Resistance."

"I should also like to meet this brother," Andon said. "Your mother is an admirable woman. And you . . ." He stopped.

"Yes."

"I'm not sure whether it is the proper way to address a friend," he said.

I knew I shouldn't, but I wanted him to say it. "I'll be the judge of that."

"Nothing original. It is an old Armenian expression. Perhaps you have heard it before: You are so beautiful that you shed light on dark walls."

"No, I don't believe that's proper to tell a friend, even though it might be the most poetic thing anyone has ever said to me."

"Will you forgive me?" he asked with a smile.

23

I CONVINCED MYSELF THAT as long as I didn't plan to meet Andon, there could be nothing wrong with our chance encounters. My decision to go to the cathedral each Sunday, I reasoned, had nothing to do with him. Nor did the time I spent in front of the mirror on Sunday morning arranging my hair six different ways before finding the one that suited.

My father asked, "How did an atheist like me end up with a child who goes to church every week? Is she turning into a religious fanatic?"

"Don't call yourself an atheist," my mother admonished.

"What do you think I am?" my father asked.

"I don't know what you are, but don't call yourself that. It can't bring anything good," my mother replied. "And she's not a religious fanatic. She used to go to church with Shakeh all the time when she was a little girl, and Shakeh wasn't a fanatic."

Missak asked, "Did you fix your hair like that to impress the priest?"

I said, "I'm leaving now. Feel free to continue this discussion without me."

"Will you be back for lunch?" my mother asked. "The Kacherians are coming, and Auntie Shushan is bringing *kadayif.*"

I entered the cathedral and anxiously scanned the parishioners. I saw the back of Andon's head halfway down the nave, recognizing him by his black Sunday suit, his crisp white collar, and the straight hair that dipped a bit at the center of his neck. I reached the pew directly across from him and settled into the aisle seat. He turned to smile at me and then turned back, and for the rest of the service we both faced forward, though each of us occasionally stole a glance at the other.

Afterward, we stood talking in the wintry churchyard until I started to shiver.

"You are cold. We should go," Andon said.

I nodded reluctantly.

"May I accompany you home?" he asked.

"Oh, I'm sorry. My parents are having guests today."

"I hope you did not assume that I was inviting myself to your home. I meant only to take you to your door."

"There's no reason for you to go that far out of your way," I said, worrying that the Kacherians or some curious neighbors might see us.

"Except that it would give me pleasure," he answered. "May I at least walk you to the Métro?"

Despite the cold, we walked to the nearest station slowly.

"How were your classes this week?" he asked.

"Fine. The English-novel seminar is my favorite, but the books are so long and we have to read one a week. I am up late most nights reading. How is your work?"

"My cousin is a good man, and I enjoy showing the carpets to customers, but I must admit that the days are long. When I am alone in the shop and the repairs are finished, I study French grammar. I have written some sentences and I was hoping to trouble you to correct them for me. If it is too much bother and you don't have the time, I understand."

"It's no bother at all," I said.

He pulled a folded sheet of paper from his coat pocket and handed it to me. As I started to open it, he objected. "Oh, not now. Later. When you are at a table with a pen in your hand. I am serious. I want you to correct my mistakes so that I may learn."

The train came, and as the Métro rattled from one station to the next, I read his paragraph. *My name is André Shirvanian*, he wrote in French. He had already given himself a French name. *I was born in Leninakan, Armenia. I have one sister and one brother. I have brown eyes and black hair. I live in Ivry with my cousin. The weather today is cloudy.* They were all short, declarative sentences. His handwriting was meticulous, as though he had copied the printed letters exactly. There were only a few small mistakes with the articles, accents, and pronouns, which I would correct, as he'd suggested, with a pen in my hand.

When I reached our apartment, everyone, including the Kacherians, Missak, and Jacqueline, was already seated at the table in the front room.

"Where have you been?" my mother asked as she paused in the hall holding a steaming pot of rice pilaf with a dish-towel. "We've been waiting for you."

"Sorry I'm late," I answered.

I followed her to the table, and when I looked at the Kacherians, I saw Zaven's dark eyes in his father's face, and I felt a spasm of remorse. Quickly I assured myself that there was no reason to feel guilty. Andon Shirvanian was simply my friend.

Winter gave way to early spring, and the Sunday ritual re-mained the same, except that instead of walking to the clos-est Métro station, we strolled to the one on the place de la Concorde. Each week Andon would give me another paragraph to correct, and in that way I learned more about him: he had no favorite color; his sister's name was Anna; his brother's name was Samvel; and his beard grew so quickly that he often shaved twice a day. As his French improved, he began to practice using tenses other than the present, and he wrote small stories about his childhood that were amus-ing and sometimes touching. He asked me to tell him an anecdote about myself in exchange for each one he wrote. As the plane trees and the chestnuts came into leaf, I looked forward all week to our Sunday promenade on the Champs Élysées.

Then one Sunday, he wasn't in the cathedral when I arrived. I sat in the pew glancing over my shoulder as the latecomers straggled in. When he hadn't appeared twenty minutes into the service, my mood darkened, and the dron-ing liturgy was so tedious I wanted to weep. What if something had happened to him? Perhaps there had been an accident. Or maybe he had decided he was tired of wasting his Sundays on me.

I realized then how much I had come to depend on him. I liked the way he listened with his full attention, as though each word that came out of my mouth were a revelation. I enjoyed the way that he talked—the formal diction and the precision of his descriptions—and what he had to say about people, ideas, and books; it turned out that he liked to read. As his French improved, he had started to make his way through the fables of La Fontaine and other simple classics.

At the sound of footsteps in the aisle, I turned and saw Andon slip into the pew across from me. He offered an apologetic smile.

After nodding my head in acknowledgment, I stared straight ahead, my face stern with annoyance. But with whom was I annoyed? Was I angry with him for being late? No, I was angry with myself. I couldn't pretend anymore that we were merely friends. What I felt toward him was more than friendly and I knew my feelings were reciprocated. I would have to stop going to church on Sunday and pretending that I was interested in something in that cathedral other than Andon Shirvanian.

After the service, I agreed to walk with him, but only to the closest Métro stop.

He said, "I am so sorry that I was late. I overslept because I was reading until the early hours, and then there was a problem with the train. I apologize if I disappointed you."

"It's nothing that you've done. It's me."

"And what could you have possibly done?" he asked.

"I'm going to be honest with you: I've made a mistake. I thought we could be friends, but I realized just now that it wasn't possible."

"Why can we not be friends?"

"Don't make me say it. The war will be over any day now. I'll be expecting Zaven back. And it's not right that I should let myself have these feelings about you. It's not fair to Zaven, or to you."

"But what if he does not return, Maral? What then?"

"I can't think like that."

We had reached the Métro entrance.

"I have to go," I said.

"And you will not be at the cathedral next Sunday?" he asked.

"I won't," I told him.

"If I had been on time today, perhaps this would not be happening?"

"Maybe not today, but one Sunday soon."

He frowned. "You know, it is possible to have these complicated feelings, Maral, and also be a friend. I will always be your friend, and should you ever need anything, you can find me at my cousin's shop. May I still give you the story I wrote?" He held out a folded sheet of paper.

Sitting on the bench on the Métro platform, I read his last story.

When I arrived in Paris dressed in a hated uniform, I met a pretty girl who was kind to me. The entire time that I was near the sea, I thought about that girl. Perhaps she was only someone I had imagined to make myself feel less alone. But when my war was over, I hoped to meet her again. I did find her in the cathedral and she was just as beautiful as I remembered. As time went by, she was no longer simply a pretty girl, but my friend. In a strange country and in a new language, she was my companion.

I sat on the bench for a long time, letting one train after the next pass through the station before I finally boarded one to go home.

The following Sunday, when I was still in my nightgown and robe after breakfast, my father asked, "What? Have you lost your religion? You aren't going to the church to commune with your God and His hooded henchmen?"

My mother said, "Can you please keep your blasphemy to yourself?"

"I have too much studying to do," I answered. And once again I turned to my books.

24

A S   I   W A S   W A L K I N G   H O M E along the rue de Belleville, I saw a crowd gathered around the corner newsstand. I crossed the street and threaded my way to the counter, where I caught sight of the paper that had drawn people's interest. On the front page there were pictures of skeletal men in striped uniforms standing behind barbed wire, emaciated men lying on wooden shelves stacked from floor to ceiling, half-naked bodies piled like cordwood, and charred bones in what were called human ovens. My mind flinched away from the images—they were too horrific to be real. With trembling hands I put down a coin, folded the paper, and tucked it into my satchel.

When I entered the apartment, my mother took one look at my face and said, "*Yavrum,* what is it? What's the matter?"

I held up the paper. "Buchenwald."

My mother glanced at the photos, put her hand to her cheek, and whispered, "*Aman.*"

Sitting at the table in the front room with the paper, I studied the black-and-white faces of the gaunt, haggard survivors, not sure that Zaven and Barkev would even be recognizable.

My mother sat nearby, shaking her head and moaning. "*Ahkh, ahkh, ahkh. Vhy, vhy, vhy.* Stop looking at those pictures, Maral. You will make yourself sick."

I threw the newspaper to the floor. "You're right. It's sickening."

My mother said, "God should rain down fire and destroy us all."

When my father and Missak arrived from work that evening, both of them were grim-faced. My father glanced from my mother's drawn countenance to my red-rimmed eyes. He sighed heavily, but said nothing.

At the end of dinner, my father said, "I'm going to the Kacherians'."

Missak said, "I'll go with you."

"Should I?" I asked. In fact, I couldn't imagine anything I wanted to do less than visit Zaven's mother on the day she had seen those pictures.

My father shook his head. "You stay with your mother."

I went to bed early and lay staring at the children in Missak's sketch, which was still tacked to the wall. When I closed my eyes, the photographs from the paper were etched inside my eyelids.

I fell asleep and dreamed that Zaven was lying in the mud on a torn blanket next to a barbed-wire fence. He was staring at me with enormous, pensive eyes. He was so thin that I could see the pulse beat in his temple, so thin that his upper arm was smaller than my wrist. I gently picked him up as though he were an injured child. "You're too late," he whispered. I started up the steep hill with Zaven in my arms, and as I walked he grew smaller. Finally he was no bigger than a doll made from a castoff sock.

The next evening, my mother and I paid a call on the Kacherians. When we entered the apartment, we saw that the work of grieving had begun in earnest. In the parlor, Auntie Shushan moaned on the divan; my mother joined her, while I sat in a chair next to pale and solemn Virginie. The hard rations of the war had kept her from growing tall—she was diminutive and thin—but at almost fifteen, she was no longer a little girl.

Virginie said, "They're coming back, Maral. I know they are."

A few weeks later, we heard that the first deportees had started returning from the camps. Missak found out that the Red Cross had set up a service for returnees at the Hôtel Lutetia, so Auntie Shushan went there every few days to look for her sons. Our two families agreed it was unwise for her to make the trek alone, so my mother, Virginie, and I took turns accompanying her. The routine was the same. We combed the lists for Zaven's and Barkev's names, and then scoured the halls for their faces. We didn't find them the first week, or the second, or the third. By the fourth week, I began to give up hope of ever seeing Zaven among the frail and worn survivors in the hotel's corridors.

One evening toward the end of May, Missak strode into the front room, where my mother and I were setting the dinner table, and announced, "Barkev arrived this afternoon."

"Thank God," my mother said.

"Did you see him?" I asked.

"Yes," he said. "I saw him."

"And Zaven?"

He shook his head. And then Missak sank into a chair, dropping his face into his hands.

My mother started with the litany: "*Ahkh, ahkh, vhy, vhy, vhy.*" And I stood behind my brother with one hand on his heaving shoulder. I didn't know what to feel or think. I observed the three of us from above, small people in a small apartment, bent with grief. This scene was playing itself out in apartments and houses all across the city, all across the continent, and all around the world. The war was a great factory of suffering, all of it fashioned by human hands.

I said suddenly, "I have to see him."

Minutes later, Virginie opened the door of their apartment. "Come in. He's in the parlor." She spoke in the hushed tones customarily used when there was an illness in the family.

As I entered the room, Barkev looked up from where he was seated, his face all angles and planes, his jaw muscles visible beneath taut flesh, and a shadow of a beard across his cheeks. There were charcoal-colored rings under his eyes. He said nothing, but he pushed on the arms of the chair and slowly stood up.

His mother and father, whom I had barely noticed were there, slipped out of the room.

"Oh, please sit down," I said. Even though I had seen the photos and all the returnees at the Lutetia, still I was unprepared.

He looked like a sick old man, and he was barely twenty-three years old.

"I'm so sorry, Maral," he said. "Don't cry."

I saw the distress in his face, so I pulled my own countenance into what I hoped was a neutral mask.

"You cut your hair," he said, carefully settling back into his chair.

"I did," I replied, taking a seat on the end of the sofa near him.

"It looks nice."

This conversation about my hair was banal and absurd, but I didn't know what else to say. We said nothing for a while, the air heavy with unspoken questions. It didn't seem right to ask about Zaven yet, but Zaven was all I could think about at that moment.

"Maral, I'm sorry that Zaven didn't come back," he said, as though reading my mind.

"I'm sorry, Barkev. I'm so sorry for both of us."

When I put my hand on his skinny forearm, he dropped his head, and something wet fell onto the back of my hand.

Just then his parents and sister came into the room, and I saw a wave of exhaustion pass over Barkev's face.

"I should go," I said.

"Please come back tomorrow," Barkev said. "We can talk more, and maybe take a walk."

A few minutes later, I sat on the bench in the courtyard of my building under the round moon's harsh light. Long shadows moved over the ground and walls of the courtyard. Only the chirping of a few crickets in the bushes and the sound of an occasional passing car interrupted the stillness. Finally I trudged up the stairs to our apartment, thinking my family would all be asleep, but my mother was sitting in the front room in her robe with her long hair down.

"You shouldn't have waited up for me."

She sighed. "I couldn't sleep."

"I don't really want to talk."

"That's okay. It's past time for bed," she answered wearily.

I went to my bedroom and lay on the bed fully clothed, silently repeating to myself, *Zaven is dead. Zaven won't be coming back. Zaven is gone for good,* but the words were meaningless. My body felt hollow, as though it had been gutted of blood, muscle, bone, and all sensation.

No one woke me up the next morning so I missed my classes and didn't get up until midday. The food my mother offered me at lunchtime appeared inedible.

In the afternoon, I went to see Barkev. His mother ushered me into the parlor, where he was sitting in the same armchair he had been in the day before, but he was wearing a clean shirt and he had shaved.

"It's a beautiful day," I said. "Should we go to the Buttes Chaumont?"

His mother objected. "You can't walk all that way, Barkev."

"Maybe not," he said, looking apologetically at me. "Maybe the park around the corner would be better."

We made our way slowly down the stairs, Barkev holding the railing and taking each step carefully as though he were unsure of his footing.

When we reached the bustling rue de Belleville, we paused, and Barkev said, "Everything here seems the same. Except for me."

"You'll soon be back to your same old self," I said.

He glanced at me doubtfully. "Maybe."

Seeing how tired even this short walk had made him, I said, "I'm thirsty. Why don't we go to the café on the corner."

So we settled at a table on the sidewalk after giving our order to the barman.

"Barkev," I said, "is it okay for you to talk about what happened?"

"What do you want to know?" His voice was small and tight, as though he were bracing himself for a blow. The barman brought our coffee.

I wanted to know what had happened to Zaven—how and when he had died. I wanted to know what the camp had been like for the two of them, and how Barkev had managed to survive when his brother had not. But he wasn't ready for all these questions, so I decided to start from the beginning with one simple query.

"So after you left Fresnes, you went to Buchenwald?" I asked.

"From Fresnes we went to Compiègne, and from there they put us onto a train to Buchenwald. Do you know what the word *buchenwald* means in German?" he asked. "'Beech forest.' You might want to take a holiday in a place with a name like that."

I watched as he picked up his coffee cup, his hand unsteady, and brought it to his lips. He lifted his eyes to mine.

All the unspeakable images from the newspapers flashed through my mind. "What happened to Zaven?"

"There's a short answer and a long one. He died of typhus in March." He put down his cup.

"And the long answer?"

He said, "I'm not ready for the long answer. Maybe tomorrow."

He picked up his cup again, but his hand was shaking so hard that he gave up and returned it to the saucer. "It's strange about my hands," he said, staring at them as though they belonged to someone else. "Often they are fine. And then, like just now, I have no control over them."

I said, "You've got to have patience. It will take some time."

"And if it doesn't get better, what work will I be able to do?"

"I promise you, it will get better."

He said, "Now you're a fortuneteller."

"No," I told him. "But you've been making shoes since you were eight. You'll be able to do that again."

I accompanied him to the entrance of his building, but he didn't want me to walk up the stairs with him. I think he didn't want me to witness how difficult it was for him to mount the steps.

As I turned to go, he said, "You'll come tomorrow?"

"I'll stop by when I'm finished with classes."

The next afternoon we made it to the Parc de Belleville and sat on a bench in the shade.

It was a brilliant spring afternoon. There were several small children playing in the sandbox with shovels and a pail, their mothers chatting nearby. An old woman sat on another bench with a grizzled mongrel in her lap.

Barkev said, "I'm still not ready to tell the long story. But I can give you the middle-size version."

I nodded.

He started. "When we arrived at the camp, they asked what work we did. I said shoemaker. Zaven said small-appliance repair. It was bad luck they didn't need another person to do what he did. I worked in the shoe-repair shop in the officers' school. They put Zaven on the work crew moving stones, shoveling dirt, and grading roads. We had already been hungry for months, so after a few weeks of that work and the slop they gave us to eat, he was as thin as a stick. I had it easy with an inside job. The outside details were brutal. After three months, I was able to fix it so he was transferred to shoe repair. But he was already weak.

"When the weather turned, everyone started getting sick. We thought the war would be over by Christmas, but it wasn't. The week after Christmas, dozens of guys died because they had given up hope. Later, Zaven came down with typhus. His temperature was so high he couldn't sit up at the workbench. They sent him to what they called the infirmary. That was another German joke. It was a barracks where they put the sick on wooden boards to get well or die.

"I visited him in the evening. He wouldn't eat. He might take a little water. Half the time when he talked he made no sense. The last night he was suddenly calm, and when he looked at me I could see the old Zaven in his eyes. He made me promise I'd go home for my mother and you."

Barkev bowed his head. I noticed that his hands were clenched into tight fists on his lap.

He said, "A month later they liberated the camp."

We walked slowly home and as we were parting, he asked, "Will you come again tomorrow?"

"Not tomorrow," I said. "I have classes and then work at the library."

"The next day?" he asked.

"Not until the weekend," I said.

On Sunday afternoon, I noticed that Barkev was already looking less gaunt. His mother, my mother, and a few other Armenian women in the neighborhood were putting their concerted efforts into fattening him, believing that good food could cure any ailment.

He suggested that we go to the Buttes Chaumont.

"Are you sure that's not too far?" I asked.

"I went there myself yesterday and the day before," he assured me.

So we strolled slowly to the park and chose a bench under a broad chestnut tree near the entrance.

Barkev said, "When I told you what happened to Zaven, I left parts of the story out." He pulled a grubby bit of dark yarn from his breast pocket and held it out to me with a slight tremble in his hand. "He made me promise to give you this."

I took the yarn. It was no longer possible to tell what color it had been, and its strands were frayed.

"I knew it was important. It wasn't easy holding on to anything in the camp, not even something so worthless that no one would want to steal it. How could I let him down and not bring this to you? Guys were dying all over the place up to the last hours before they liberated the camp, and even after."

He stared down as he continued talking. "After Zaven died, I had this dream about you a lot of nights. You were standing in the cathedral lighting candles. Always you lit two candles—one for Zaven and one for me."

He stopped here, an unasked question suspended in the air between us.

Then Barkev said, "Surviving was almost all luck. But even with luck, you needed something to keep yourself from giving up. Maybe it was a wife or a mother. Maybe not wanting to let the Germans win. For me it was this."

He reached into his shirt pocket and held out with a steady hand a tiny pencil stub. The lead and eraser were long gone; the yellow wood was chipped and dented. It was the one he had used to trace my feet on cardboard that long-ago Sunday afternoon.

He lifted his eyes to me then, and they were dark and fierce in his narrow face. It was impossible for me to imagine saying no.

25

ONE FRIDAY IN JUNE, not long after my nineteenth birthday, my father dropped an envelope beside my plate at the dinner table. "A young man came to the shop today. He brought a pair of shoes for repair and left this for you."

I instantly recognized the handwriting.

"Aren't you going to open it?" my mother asked.

"Not now," I said.

"He was polite," my father said. "His heels were worn down, but they were good shoes."

"If it was that Andon I met at church, he seemed like a nice boy," my mother added.

Missak asked, "You met him?"

"Of course I did," my mother said. "His family is from Moush."

"When did you tell him the shoes would be ready?" I asked.

"Monday afternoon," my father answered.

"Can you have them done tomorrow?"

My father shrugged. "If you want. He isn't some kind of a suitor, is he?"

"Of course he's not a suitor," the mother said. "Maral's engaged."

"He's a friend," I said. "I gave him French lessons."

"The same kind of French lessons you gave that American soldier?" Missak asked.

I elbowed him. "He was Armenian."

"What American soldier?" my mother asked.

Neither of us replied.

Later, when I was alone in my room, I carefully unsealed the envelope and unfolded the sheet of writing paper.

Dear Maral,

If you should need to get in touch with me for any reason, you may reach me at my cousin's shop. I can be found there during business hours each day except for Sunday. For the next three Sundays I will be at the service at the cathedral.

Your friend,

Andon

The address and phone number of the store, Tapis Shirvan, were printed at the bottom of the note.

That Sunday I entered the church carrying a brown-paper parcel. When I sighted Andon seated halfway up the nave on the left side, I became flustered and paused, trying to decide where to go. I walked slowly forward and slid into a pew on the right side a few rows behind him. When the congregation stood as the clergy's procession made its way up the aisle, I watched him as he turned to scan the nave. His eyes passed over the crowd and he smiled when he recognized me. I had hoped I would feel nothing, but my heart beat suddenly faster. The chanting of the liturgy continued, with the congregants rising and sitting, and the incense burning, and it went on for what seemed like hours.

Finally the service was over, and I allowed myself to be pulled along by the crowd as it spilled out of the cathedral. I waited in the courtyard, anxiously smoothing my hair and straightening my skirt. Then, among the stream of gray parishioners, his handsome face appeared.

"Compliments of my father," I said, holding out the parcel.

Andon took the package and untied the string. He lifted one of the shoes to examine the new heel. "But I must pay him."

"My father won't accept your money."

"But I insist," he said.

"No, my father insists."

Andon bowed his head slightly. "Tell your father thank you for his kindness and that I appreciate his fine work. Would you care to go for a stroll? It's a beautiful day."

We walked along the Champs Élysées under clear blue skies and a dazzling sun. I almost wished it were raining. If rain were pelting down, Andon would have held up a large black umbrella. He would have taken my hand to help me across the flooded gutters.

"Well, my friend, it has been a long time," he said.

"Very long," I said.

"Your man did not return, but his brother did," he said.

"How did you know?"

"News has no borders."

"Did you also hear that I'm engaged?"

"In fact, I had heard this. But I thought perhaps you would come to tell me yourself, one friend to another. I wrote you the note hoping to give you such an opportunity."

"My brother and my best friend, Jacqueline, announced they were engaged. The next day Barkev asked me to marry him."

"And you said yes."

"Evidently."

"Evidently," he repeated.

"My brother put his foot down—he didn't want a church wedding. Jacqueline couldn't convince him. Barkev didn't care, and so the four of us will be married at the *mairie* on the same day."

"When will that be?"

I hesitated. "In two weeks."

"So soon?"

"Yes."

"And you are sure this is what you want?" There was a tight smile on his face.

"Yes," I said.

"Well, if you were not, I would offer you an alternative." The smile was gone.

I said nothing and stared down at our shoes moving over the pavement.

"I must tell you, I was disappointed to learn you had substituted the brother without giving me at least an opportunity," Andon said.

We continued walking in silence.

When we reached the Métro entrance, he shook my hand and looked gravely into my eyes. "I wish you the greatest happiness. Should you ever have need, you know how to reach me. Goodbye, my friend."

"Goodbye," I said.

After running headlong down the Métro stairs, I sat on the bench once again, letting several trains pass before I boarded a car to go home. I stared out the window into the hurtling darkness, seeing Andon's face and then Barkev's, and then Zaven's. They flew by faster and faster, until the three faces blended into one. When I was a schoolgirl, I had believed that happiness was a question of finding one's true love, the way it happened in so many of the novels I read. But as the train sped through the tunnel, I realized you could love more than one person at the same time, and that marriage was not just about love. It was also about duty.

When I went to visit with Barkev and his family later that afternoon, I was unable to keep up the cheerful banter I thought of as a remedy for him. I wasn't in the mood to tell an amusing story about a street musician with a four-stringed guitar and a small white dog dancing on its hind legs.

"Are you all right?" Barkev asked.

"Just a little tired. I was up late studying. You look tired too."

"I don't sleep so well."

I felt a rush of sympathy, and I put my hand on his arm. "Maybe we'll both sleep better with company."

I threw myself into preparations for the wedding. My mother and I worked to turn my bedroom into a home for

Missak and Jacqueline. We pushed the two narrow beds together, cleared the bureau, and put down new shelf paper in the drawers. As I swept and mopped the floor, washed the window, and laundered the curtains, I assumed that at the Kacherians' apartment, Auntie Shushan and Virginie were doing much the same in the room Barkev and I would share. I couldn't quite imagine what my new life would be like.

For the wedding dresses, my mother chose white chiffon fabrics—Jacqueline's had purple flowers, and mine had pink ones. Jacqueline and I pored over a fashion magazine looking for a style that she could copy. The sewing machine whirred in the evenings as my mother pieced together first one dress and then the other. Finally Jacqueline and I stood on chairs in the front room while our respective mothers pinned up our hems.

"*Peh!* They both look very beautiful," said Sophie Sahadian, leaning back on her heels to gaze up at us. "What a good job you did, Azniv. The dresses fit perfectly."

"We have to hem them tonight. Can you believe it's only two more days until our girls will be married?" my mother said.

"I can't get used to the idea that my baby is going to be moving out."

"Your baby? Don't worry, you have plenty more babies to keep you company, and I'm not going far! Just across the street," Jacqueline said. "And believe me, I'm looking forward to sharing a bed with just one person. We've been three sisters to a bed for too long. It was okay when we were little, but now I have bruises from all those knees and elbows."

"Enough talking. Go take those off. We have to hem them." My mother shooed us out of the room.

In the bedroom, as we shimmied out of the dresses, Jacqueline said, "Are you ready for your wedding night?"

I glanced at her. "Are you?"

Jacqueline laughed and bounced onto the bed in her white lace-trimmed slip. "We've been practicing."

I pulled a robe over my own white slip. "I don't want to hear about it."

Jacqueline asked, "Haven't you and Barkev—"

"That's none of your business," I interrupted.

"Oh, don't be such a prude," Jacqueline said. "You're almost a married woman."

"No, we haven't, as a matter of fact."

"Well, if you want any advice, let me know."

I swept up the two dresses from the bed. "I'm a nice Armenian girl and I have nothing more to say to you on the topic."

The next day, the women from the three wedding families gathered in the Kacherians' kitchen and started cooking. Food was still rationed, but Donabedian the Magnificent had produced a lamb shank, as well as dates, apricots, and almonds for the wedding pilaf. The Alfortville cousins had offered up several chickens, a dozen eggs, and a pound of butter. My mother rolled out phyllo dough for the pastries. Sophie Sahadian dusted a tray of crescent-shaped butter cookies with powdered sugar.

Jacqueline asked, "Can I have one?"

"Of course not," her mother said. "If you have one, your sisters will want them too. Then we might not have enough for the guests."

"Just one?" Jacqueline reached toward the tray on the

table. "The girls don't need them. I'm the bride and I'm hungry."

Her mother swatted her hand away. "Go find a bread stick."

On a sunny, hot July day, Missak and Jacqueline, and Barkev and I, were married at the *mairie* of the Twentieth Arrondissement with our families in attendance. Afterward, we spread out a feast on blankets near the lake in the Buttes Chaumont. All the Sahadians, Kacherians, Nazarians, and Meguerditchians were there. So were Jacqueline's lawyer boss and his wife, Missak's boss and his wife, and several neighbors. Hagop brought along his oud and two musician friends, so after the meal there was dancing.

"Do you want to dance?" I asked Barkev when the playing started. We were sitting together on a blanket on the grass. He had taken off his suit jacket and loosened his tie.

He shook his head. "You go ahead."

"Are you sure?"

"You go with them." As he gestured toward the forming lines of dancers with Missak at the head of one and Jacqueline at the head of the other, the gold wedding band on his finger glinted in the sun.

I thought briefly of joining the dancers, but when I glanced back at Barkev, I saw a shadow pass over his face.

"I want to sit with you," I said.

"It's miserable that he's not here, but then if he were . . ." His sentence trailed off.

"Don't," I told him. "This is our day."

"He told me about the red yarn." He looked down and plucked a blade of grass.

"Oh," I said. "So you know."

Just then Jacqueline passed by at the head of the line of dancers. She waved at me with her free hand.

"Come on, Maral!" she called.

"I'm watching you!" I called back.

Barkev leaned toward me, pushing a strand of hair out of my eyes. "Sorry to be such an old man."

"But you are my old man now, aren't you?"

That night, when we closed the door on our new, shared bedroom, I carefully arranged the set of gilt-edged combs and brushes my parents had given me as a wedding gift on the top of the dresser. With my back turned to Barkev, I slipped on the lace-trimmed summer nightgown my mother had made, and in the dresser mirror I saw Barkev, with his back turned to me, change into a pair of striped pajamas. We had so little privacy, with his parents and sister in the same apartment and with the whole neighborhood's windows flung open because of the summer heat. But now there was a gold ring on my left hand, and a gold ring on his, and no one could disapprove.

I folded back the sheet and lay down on the bed. He stretched out beside me, running his fingers down the side of my face. It was like a chord strummed on an oud's strings, full of longing. When we kissed, I felt a hot tear slide from his face onto mine.

26

SOME MORNINGS AS I was just waking up, in the anteroom between dreams and day, I thought I was still in my family's apartment in the bedroom I had shared with my aunt. Then I would open my eyes: the dark-haired man whose head was on the pillow beside me was my husband. Once, for a second, when Barkev's back was to me, I mistook him for his brother, but then I remembered. I glanced around the room, from the water stain on the ceiling over the bed to the walnut dresser with a mirror above it to the wooden chair next to the dresser, on the seat of which a pair of work pants were neatly folded. The closet door was ajar, and inside it my dresses hung next to Barkev's Sunday shirts and his wedding suit. I reminded myself: *My name is Maral Kacherian. I am married and I live with my husband's family.*

I had imagined that becoming a wife would overnight turn me into a more serious and substantial person. But no such transformation had occurred. I didn't feel like a grown woman—it was as though I had moved from being a daughter in my own family to being a daughter in his. His mother ruled in the kitchen, and his father presided at the dinner table.

Even though Barkev and I had known each other for as long as I could remember, I was still discovering my husband. I had always thought that Zaven, the younger and shorter brother, was the handsomer of the two, even though their features were similar. I realized on closer study that the main difference between them was that Barkev's face was asymmetrical, making his smile crooked and one nostril flare a little more than the other. His eyes were a lighter shade of brown, and he was quieter and more thoughtful than Zaven. If we went for a walk, he noticed before I did that I was hungry and offered me roasted chickpeas from a paper bag he carried in his pocket. He liked playing backgammon with his father in the evenings after dinner. He was a restless sleeper and had frequent nightmares that woke us both.

One morning about six weeks after we married, I opened my eyes and what I wanted more than anything was to stay in bed all day. And it wasn't just Barkev's turning, muttering, and grinding his teeth at night that left me tired. My blood was sluggish in my veins, my head hazy, and my stomach queasy.

I was soon to start my second year at the university, but it didn't make sense to continue if there was a baby coming in the spring. Deep down, I wasn't even sure what I was doing at the university; I just craved the books and the praise that came with being a student. I felt I should ferret out the knitting needles and apply to Auntie's boss for work again.

I sighed.

"What's the matter?" Barkev asked.

"Sorry," I said, turning to him. "Did I wake you?"

"No. It's time to get up. What do you see in that spot on the ceiling? You spend a lot of time staring at it."

"That's how I think."

"What were you thinking?"

"That I'm going to have a baby," I answered.

"Are you sure?"

"Let's not say anything until I see the doctor." I studied the dark circles under his eyes. "Are you pleased?"

"I'm happy about the baby. The world the baby comes into is another thing."

Barkev didn't talk about it, but I could sense when he was remembering the camp. I couldn't even think of the place's name without the newspaper images floating up like bloated corpses in a river. He must have felt alone here among people who had very little idea of what he had lived through.

Now Barkev's eyes were fastened on me, but he wasn't seeing me.

"What are you thinking?" I asked.

His eyes slowly focused. "If it's a boy, we could name him Zaven."

I recoiled inside. It was too heavy a burden to put on an infant—that he must be both himself and a loved one lost to war. There were children in our community named for fathers, mothers, or siblings killed during the Deportations, but it was not a tradition I had wanted to continue.

"You don't like the idea?" he asked.

"Not much," I admitted.

He seemed almost relieved.

My stomach suddenly lurched and I jumped from the bed, grabbing my robe as I made for the toilet on the hall landing.

"Are you all right?" Barkev called after me.

I raced past the startled faces of my mother-in-law and Virginie.

Crouching before the porcelain toilet bowl, I heaved up mostly bile. I stood and pulled the toilet handle, feeling lightheaded as the water noisily churned through the pipes. I had never fainted, but I imagined this was what it must feel like just before you did. I leaned heavily on the wall behind me taking slow deep breaths until the dizziness passed.

When I returned to the kitchen, they were all at the table having breakfast, and my mother-in-law raised one eyebrow.

Virginie asked, "Are you okay?"

My father-in-law asked, "Are you coming down with something?"

I shook my head. "It's nothing. I'm fine now."

"Sit down, honey," Shushan said with a knowing smile. She pulled out a chair at the table. "Let me make you some toast and tea."

After Virginie left for the lycée and my husband and father-in-law headed off to work, my mother-in-law asked, "Should you and I go see the doctor this week?"

"I thought I could keep it secret for a little while."

"A secret? In an apartment this size?"

After Dr. Odabashian had confirmed our suspicions, I confided in my mother and Jacqueline. My mother was initially elated and then doubt flickered across her face.

"What about the university?"

"I'm done with that," I said.

"You are sure?" my mother asked.

"Yes. I'm sure."

As the weeks went by, the nausea subsided and I began to have dreams that the baby had been born—a tiny baby, sometimes so small it would have fit into the palm of my hand. Nightly the baby suffered one calamity after the next. In one dream it was born with no arms and legs, and I planted it like a bulb in the dirt of a flowerpot; I accidentally knocked the flowerpot off the window ledge and it smashed in the courtyard below. I didn't tell my mother-in-law about the dreams because she was superstitious.

Shushan Kacherian was known for her skill in reading the future in coffee grounds at the bottom of a cup. My mother frowned on this practice because Father Avedis disapproved, but other women in the community sought Digin Shushan's readings. My mother-in-law was also a great believer in dreams as bearers of signs and portents. She consulted a small worn book with lists of objects and happenings and what they signified. If you dreamed that a person recovered from illness, this surely meant the person would die. If you wore a ring in a dream, that was bad luck, unless the ring was silver, and then it was good. I didn't want my mother-in-law to suspect what an absent-minded, neglectful mother I was in my dreams, because this could only be a bad omen.

I started knitting again—most of it piecework for Auntie's old boss that I did while sitting in the front room with my mother during the afternoons. It was like old times—I knit and my mother ran up vests on the machine. Sometimes we talked, but for long stretches we worked in companionable silence. I had plenty to occupy my thoughts—a new husband, a baby on the way, and fragmented memories from childhood and my school years that flickered across my mind's eye. Occasionally I thought of Andon. Was he sitting in the back of his cousin's shop repairing a rug? Then I would imagine Barkev at his bench, his head bent over an elegant woman's shoe with a fine hammer as he tapped tiny nails to hold the sole in place. He had told me that sometimes still his hands trembled so badly that he couldn't do his work, but it seemed this happened with less frequency.

In the late afternoons, I returned to help my mother-in-law prepare dinner. After the meal I sat with Barkev and my in-laws in the living room listening to the radio. Using slim needles, I worked baby sweaters and booties out of balls of whisper-thin white wool. I held a bootie in my palm, trying to imagine the tiny foot that would fill it.

My mother-in-law said, "Because you had such bad morning sickness, I'm sure it's a boy. If it was a girl, you would hardly have been sick at all."

My father-in-law said, "Enough of these Old Country superstitions. The baby will be what it is, and none of your predictions will have any influence."

Shushan replied, "Really, the best way to tell is how she carries the baby. Wait until her belly gets a little bigger. If it's sticking way out, that will prove it's a boy."

"And if it isn't sticking way out?" I asked.

"Well, if you're carrying lower down and broader, that means it's a girl," my mother-in-law said.

Vahan shook his head. "The only thing that will prove anything is taking a good look at the baby when it's born."

27

ONE AFTERNOON WHEN I was working at my mother's, the doorbell shrilled unexpectedly. Through the peephole, I saw on the landing a dark-haired woman with fair skin holding the hand of a light-haired child, a girl of about eight years old dressed in a blue coat.

I opened the door. "Claire!"

The girl smiled shyly, holding up a frayed rag doll with yellow yarn for hair.

"And Charlotte! You've come back. And this must be your aunt Myriam."

The woman held out her hand. "Myriam Galinski. I am so glad to meet you. Claire has told me so much about you and your family."

My mother was behind me. "Girl, what are you doing keeping these people shivering in the cold," she said in Armenian. In French she added, "Please come in."

"Madame Galinski—" I started to say.

"Please, call me Myriam."

"Myriam, this is my mother, Azniv Pegorian."

"Let me make you some tea," my mother said. "Maral, hang up their coats, give them slippers, and take them to the front room."

"I see you are expecting," Myriam said. "When is the baby due?"

I answered, "In the middle of April."

"So nice to have a new baby in the spring. You have the whole summer to be outdoors. My twins were born in May."

"How old are they?" I asked as I led them into the apartment.

"Seven. A boy and a girl," Myriam said. "I left them in Nice with my husband. You miss them, don't you, Claire?"

Claire nodded, holding her doll, face out, against her heart.

I asked, "But Claire, what happened to Charlotte's eyes? Now she has one black one and one gray. Should we try to find another gray one?"

Claire nodded.

"Or maybe you can pick two buttons of any color you want," I said. I went to my mother's sewing corner and found the tin of buttons. "Do you remember when we used to spill these on the bed and sort them?"

I remembered the overcast summer morning when Claire and I stayed in the bedroom pretending to play with the buttons while her parents were taken out of the building. I wondered how much Claire remembered from that day and the days that followed.

I plucked a gray button from the tin. "Look, it's the same

as the ones we used the first time. Should we sew this on?"

"Charlotte would like that," she said.

My mother came into the room with a tray of tea, a pitcher of milk, a platter of homemade cookies, and four plates.

"Little one," my mother said, "when you were with us before, we had nothing to offer you but toast. Do you remember? No milk, no nothing. We still have rationing, but it's possible to find the things you need now." She set the tray on the table and continued, "Look what I have for you, sweetie." She held the platter out to the child and said, "Take as many as you like."

Claire glanced at her aunt, who nodded her assent.

Claire placed two cookies on her plate. "Thank you very much, madame."

"What beautiful manners you have, Claire," my mother commented as she slipped three more cookies onto the child's plate. "And look how long your curls are now. It must be a job for your aunt to brush them out in the evening. When Maral was your age, her hair was down to her waist, and at night I brushed and brushed until her hair was shiny."

After my mother poured out the tea, an uncomfortable silence settled on the room. Should we talk about what happened to Claire's parents in front of her, or should we not? I snipped the thread holding the black button onto the face of the doll. I began to sew the gray button in its place.

Finally, my mother said, "We always wondered about what happened to Claire after they invaded the Free Zone."

"It wasn't too bad until the Italians left. After that, we thought it best to move from the city. Claire, my husband, the twins, and I went to a small village in the mountains

north of Nice. It was a difficult time," she said. "I came here
to thank you for keeping Claire and for sending her to us. I
know that wasn't easy. We are also here to see what we can
learn about my sister and her husband. We found out the
number of the convoy they were on and the camp they were
sent to, but as yet nothing more."

I turned to the child and handed her the doll. "There.
Two gray eyes, just like yours. But Charlotte's hair is a bit of
a mess, don't you think?"

Claire straightened the ragged yellow yarn.

"Want to look in the yarn bag? You could pick a new color,
but I think I might still have that yellow if you like."

Claire and I pulled out a selection of small yarn balls in
an array of colors, lining them up on the table: the bright
yellow, black, an improbable purple, and several shades of
brown.

Her aunt said, "It will take time, I suppose. But we've
made the inquiries."

"I like this one," Claire said, selecting a light tan. "My hair
is almost this color now."

With a few deft clips of the scissors, I made Charlotte bald
and then quickly sewed on a new mop of hair.

My mother said, "It shocked us, it shocked us all that they
would take Sara in her condition. And they were rounding
up the little children as well. It was disgraceful. We told Sara
and Joseph to leave Claire with us."

Myriam said, "We will always be grateful for what you
did."

I said, "Charlotte is still wearing the dress my mother
made her for your train trip."

"Charlotte and I had matching dresses," Claire said. "But mine doesn't fit anymore."

"How long will you stay in Paris?" my mother asked.

"Just a few days. Claire can't miss too much school, and my twins are waiting," Myriam said.

"I want to make you and Charlotte matching sweaters. Let me measure your shoulders and your sleeves. I will mail them to you," I said.

Claire bit her lip and looked at me intently. I sensed what she was thinking.

"Auntie Shakeh got sick and went to heaven," I said.

Claire nodded. "Yes. Probably my parents and the baby went there too."

After the door closed behind Myriam and Claire, my mother whispered in Armenian, "*Vahkh, vahkh.* The shame is on all of us. Think if we hadn't saved that child how stained our souls would be."

We were clearing the dishes from the front room when Jacqueline dashed into the apartment, breathless from running up the stairs. Her cheeks were flushed with cold and her eyes were flashing.

"It just started snowing. And guess what?" Jacqueline said as she tossed off her shoes and slid her feet into leather slippers.

"What?" I asked.

"I'm pregnant!"

"*Meghah!*" my mother said. "You too? We're going to have a houseful of babies."

"How far along are you?" I asked.

"A little more than two months. The doctor says the baby will come at the end of August."

"Does Missak know?"

"I called him from the doctor's office. Oh, Maral, won't it be so much fun? The cousins will be only four months apart."

That evening as I walked home along the icy sidewalks, snowflakes shimmered under the streetlights. It was only a few steps from my old home to the new, but I was anxious that I might slip, tumble forward onto my belly, and crush the baby. I imagined that after the baby was born, there would be many more dangers to guard against, everything from rusty nails to kidnappers. I sighed with relief as I turned into the building.

That night after Barkev and I went to bed, I told him about Claire and her aunt's visit. It was cold in the room, so we had the blankets up to our chins, and the words made little clouds in the air.

"Do you think they'll find out what happened to the parents?" I asked.

"The Germans kept good records of everything, including when people died."

"Sometimes I wonder about Denise Rozenbaum and her parents. And Henri."

"Henri came to the camp about a month after we arrived," Barkev said.

"You never told me that."

"You never asked me."

"And Denise?"

He shrugged. "From Drancy, they went to Auschwitz, and that's all Henri knew."

Lying on my side with my face inches from his, the soft light from the lamp on the nightstand coming from behind him, I stared at my husband. I wanted to ask what had happened to Henri, but I knew from Barkev's expression that Henri had died. Did it really matter how? That's why I hadn't asked Myriam what camp the Lipskis had been sent to. What good would it do Myriam or Claire to learn on what day and by which method the child's parents had been killed?

The baby turned inside me. Then there was a little jump and then another one. Pause, jump, pause, jump, pause, and jump again.

"Feel this." I took Barkev's hand and placed it on my belly.

"What is it?"

"The doctor told me that happens when the baby has hiccups."

"Does it bother you?"

"If it goes on too long. Most of the time when I sit still, the baby gets restless and starts moving around, but when I go for a walk, the baby sleeps. We're together all the time, and yet I don't know what the baby looks like, or even if it's a boy or a girl. Sometimes I worry that I won't love the baby. It seems that I will, because mothers are supposed to, but what if it doesn't happen? Wouldn't that be awful? I would have to pretend to love it, because otherwise I would be a monster. Can you imagine what your mother would think?"

Barkev raised his eyebrows. "You will be a good mother, and you will love your baby. Don't worry about my mother."

Of course he wouldn't understand. And Jacqueline wouldn't either. I didn't know why my mind was always going down such back alleys, or why my dreams were so vivid and disturbing. Barkev claimed that he didn't remember his—even when he woke up shouting, he didn't know what he had been dreaming about.

"Sometimes when I'm tired, I worry too much and talk too much. Good night, Barkev."

I rolled over onto my other side, slid my hand under the pillow, and closed my eyes, waiting for the baby's hiccupping to abate. I didn't want the dream about Claire's parents, Henri, Zaven, and the camp where starving men in tattered clothes held out empty tin cups, into each of which I dropped a shirt button. I wanted a dream about going to the park with Claire and the baby on a summer afternoon. Claire would sit on a brightly painted horse waving to the baby and me as we watched the carousel spin.

28

My father asked, "Don't you want an Armenian name?"

"I like Pierre," I said. I was the one who had carried the baby for nine months. I was the one who had been in the grip of rolling pain as the baby shouldered his way into the world. Why shouldn't I choose his name? And why shouldn't the name be French? Barkev hadn't objected.

My mother suggested, "We thought maybe you would want to name him Zaven."

I turned away from her and stared down at the small infant who was sleeping in my arms. "That name is too big for this small baby."

My father-in-law looked at Barkev. "What do you think, son?"

Barkev answered, "Pierre is okay with me. But an Armenian name would be okay too."

My mother-in-law said, "There are so many nice Armenian names to choose from. What do you think of Nazar? Isn't that nice? Or maybe Dikran?" She opened her purse, pulled out a piece of paper, and waved it like a flag. "Virginie and I made a little list."

Virginie laughed nervously. "It's your list, not mine."

The baby's face suddenly scrunched up, his small red mouth opening in an angry wail.

"Can we talk about this later? He's hungry," I said.

In the end, we took the baby home from the hospital with no name at all. We all called him Bzdigeh, or Little One. After a few tense days, I agreed to the name Bedros Pierre Kacherian. I thought, *Let them call him Bedros; to me he will be Pierre.*

Both our families gathered in the Kacherians' living room on Sunday afternoon when the baby was not quite a week old. Little Pierre was dressed from head to toe in hand-knit whites: a fine white gown that was knotted at the bottom, a white cap, and a white sweater, and he was swaddled in a white blanket.

I watched as Pierre, with a rosy face, a full head of black hair, and shining blue-black eyes, was passed from hand to hand. Even Barkev's face broke into a smile when the baby curled tiny pink fingers around his thumb.

"He's strong," Barkev said.

Jacqueline, her belly bulging under her dress, sighed. "I can't wait until our baby is born. When are you having him christened?"

Missak said, turning to Barkev, "Christened? You're not doing that, are you?"

Barkev said, "I don't care one way or the other."

"What do you mean, you don't care?" I asked. "Of course he's going to be baptized and christened at the cathedral."

"What a waste of time and money," Missak said.

My mother objected. "Both of my children were baptized in the Armenian Church, and both of my grandchildren will be as well."

Barkev's mother asked, "Have you decided on godparents?"

"We assumed they would be Missak and Jacqueline," I answered, "but if my brother doesn't want to go to the cathedral . . ."

"I didn't say I wouldn't go. I just said it would be a waste, but if that's what you want, who am I to object? I'll be happy to be the godfather."

Jacqueline said, "I hope you know that I'm planning to baptize our baby when the time comes."

"Do you all hear the way my wife is talking to me?" Missak asked.

My father shook his head. "What can we do? It's too hard to fight, boys. Just give in now."

The night was a long, bumpy road as I was knocked in and out of sleep by the sharp cries of the baby, who slept in a basket on a chair next to my side of the bed. When he started to cry, I groggily pulled him from the basket and into the bed to nurse. I didn't know how he did it, but Barkev managed to sleep through the cries, the feeding, and the change of diapers. I finally settled the baby into the basket and was about to drowse when Barkev started grinding his teeth and muttering in his sleep. I put the pillow over my head and squeezed my eyes shut, but the moaning grew louder until Barkev started out of his nightmare, jumping up in bed. I sat up, and with a handkerchief that I kept on the nightstand, I wiped the sweat from his forehead. "Go back to sleep," I murmured.

Not fully awake, Barkev stared at me with wild eyes before flopping down on the bed, gone back to whatever monsters awaited him. I dropped to sleep like a stone falling to the bottom of a pond. But my time there was all too brief. Soon the baby's cries pulled me to the surface again.

In the morning, I was jittery with exhaustion. We all had breakfast together before my father-in-law and husband headed off to their atelier. When Virginie left carrying her satchel of books and notebooks, I watched her with envy. I felt as though my brain had shriveled to the size of a walnut. Or, worse, I felt like a cow, wrapped in a hazy, wordless existence of milk and interrupted sleep that bound me to the tiny, helpless animal I now held in my arms.

My mother-in-law said, "After you feed Bedros, give him to me. You need to lie down. Don't worry about washing the diapers. I'll do that. And in the afternoon, when he sleeps, you should sleep as well. This won't last, you know. In a few weeks or maybe a month, he'll settle at night. Then it will be okay until the teeth start coming."

I stumbled back to the bedroom and paused to look at the pale face in the mirror over the chest of drawers. "You are the mother now," I told myself sternly. "You are the mother."

• • •

The next Sunday we all went to the cathedral, where naked Bedros Pierre was laid on a white christening blanket. Father Avedis lifted the baby by his back and feet and dipped him into the baptismal font. The baby squalled loudly and flailed his limbs, but when the holy father anointed his small nose and lips with the muron, invoking the blessings of God on his five senses, the baby stopped yelling and stared up soberly at the faces of the priest and the rest of us gathered around him. Father Avedis touched the oil to the baby's forehead, hands, and feet.

As we were on the way home by Métro, I said to my brother, "I hope you were listening to Father Avedis's instructions as to your responsibilities as the godfather."

Missak snorted. "You mean the part about making sure that he goes to church?"

"No. The part about your having to give him a bath three days from now and then take the water and pour it under a tree."

"Are you serious?" he asked.

My mother, who was holding the baby, said, "Of course she's serious. You can't let the holy muron go down the drain. You take the basin down to the courtyard. There's a small bush there that will be good enough. No one's asking you to go all the way to the park."

Virginie said, "You can make it a birdbath with a cup of water."

Jacqueline added, "Or a sponge bath, and then you can bury the holy sponge under the bush."

My mother-in-law admonished, "Don't joke, girls. Show some respect."

I glanced at Barkev, who seemed not to have heard a word. He was staring out the window at the passing walls of the dark tunnel.

Within a few weeks, Pierre did begin sleeping better, as my mother-in-law had predicted. Daily life began to seem more manageable. Barkev was still having bad dreams at night and was distant and distracted during the day, but the baby was starting to be entertaining. His skin was soft as an apricot's and he stared soulfully up at my face.

I smiled down at him. "That's right, Pierre, I'm your mother."

Then one day—as I was holding him in my lap, speaking nonsense in a high-pitched voice that would have seemed ridiculous to me only a few months before—Pierre smiled. It was a funny, pink-gummed smile, but it was thrilling nonetheless and made up for sleepless nights and chapped hands.

Later that afternoon Jacqueline stopped by the apartment and said, "I have a surprise for you downstairs."

"Why did you leave it down there?" I asked.

"It was too big for me to carry up."

"What is it? A washing machine? How did you know?"

Jacqueline said, "Come with me. And bring the baby."

"The baby?"

"You heard me. It's a beautiful day and the two of you need some fresh air. You've been spending too much time cooped up in this apartment."

We reached the ground floor, and there was a tall black-and-chrome perambulator sitting next to the mailboxes.

"Oh!" I gasped. "It's beautiful. Where did you get the money for something like that?"

Jacqueline took the baby from me and placed him in the

carriage. "I found this at the flea market. Your mother reupholstered the inside and sewed some new sheets. Look at this sweet quilt she made. Missak painted the outside and polished the chrome. Your father put on new springs and wheels. And here it is. Ready for the prince pasha."

I pushed the pram out to the sidewalk. "Buttes Chaumont?"

Jacqueline said, "Let's go."

As we strolled toward the park, I noted the approving faces that peered into the carriage to admire my baby. Pierre, who was staring up at the tree branches under which we passed, cooed and gurgled and mewed and bleated.

Jacqueline said, "Listen to him!"

"Sometimes he sounds like a whole barnyard."

We reached the park, and we sat on a sunny bench near the lake. I turned the stroller so the sleeping baby was in the shade.

"It's perfect," I said, gesturing toward the perambulator. "When your baby comes we can take turns using it."

Jacqueline took a deep breath. "Probably not."

"Why not?"

"We're moving to Alfortville next month," she answered.

"What? Why?"

"Missak found a job with a printer out there. He's an old guy who wants to work only a few more years, and he doesn't have anyone to leave his business to. Missak hopes to buy him out when he retires."

"Where will you live?"

"The chicken king is going to rent us one of his houses. It's only a few blocks from the printer. It's a ten-minute walk to the church. We'll do the christening there instead of at the cathedral."

"Do my parents know?" I asked.

"We're going to tell them tonight. They will be upset at first, especially your mother. But Maral, it's tough living all piled on top of one another the way we are. Your mother has her own way of keeping house and she wants everything done just so. The glasses must be washed before the plates, the laundry must be folded so the shirt fronts have no creases, and there's even a special method for sweeping. She's always looking over my shoulder. Can you imagine what that will be like after the baby is born?"

"What do you think it's like with my mother-in-law?"

"But you are used to it. Your mother and your mother-in-law are alike. In our apartment, we had so many kids underfoot, my mother didn't care if every pin was in its place or not. I love your mother, but she's driving me crazy."

That night while the baby was sleeping and the two of us were lying side by side in the bed with the lights out, I reported the news to Barkev.

He said, "Your brother told me."

"What do you think?"

"It's a good plan for them."

"What about for us?"

"Not now," Barkev answered.

"But maybe later?"

"Maybe. I don't know."

"Because of money? Cousin Karnig would give us a deal."

"Of course it's money. But not just that."

"What else?"

"Other things."

"Well, talk to me. I'm your wife."

He said sharply, "I'm having trouble at work."

"What kind of trouble?"

"It's not just my hands now. Sometimes I lay the leather out in front of me and can't remember how to assemble the parts."

"What do you do then?" I asked.

"I have to leave and walk around for twenty minutes until it stops. When I come back, my hands are steady and I can piece the shoe together with my eyes closed. But I can't tell when it's going to happen."

"Does your boss know?"

"Yes," he said. "He's been okay. But it can't go on like this. On a bad day, I do half the work I should."

I didn't know what to say. It occurred to me that the baby and I were a burden to him. "I wish there were something I could do for you."

"There's nothing you can do."

"Do you dream about the camp?" I asked.

"I told you I don't remember my dreams," he said.

"Do you ever see any of the others who came back?"

"No."

He said this one word in such a way that no others were possible.

In the silence that followed, I heard the baby sigh in his sleep. The clock on the nightstand ticked. The darkness in the room expanded until it stretched as wide as the sky. There were no stars and there was no moon, no point of light anywhere at all.

29

THE SUNDAY AFTER MISSAK and Jacqueline's baby was born, my father borrowed a car so we could drive to Alfort-ville. My parents sat in the front seat; Barkev and I were in the back, with Pierre sitting on my lap. It was a hot August day and I smoothed back the baby's damp hair. Once the car passed the city limits and picked up speed, the rush of air coming in the windows brought relief from the stifling heat.

We pulled into the driveway of the gray stucco house with gold shutters on a tree-lined street, and Jacqueline's mother waved to us from the front door.

"Welcome, welcome," Sophie Sahadian said, gesturing us in. "Missak went to the bakery for bread, but he'll be back any minute now."

Jacqueline, who was dressed in a housecoat and slippers, sat on the couch holding the new baby. "Look at this little monster. He eats all the time, and he's killing me." She thrust the baby at her mother. "Burp him, will you? I want to show Maral the house."

I handed Pierre, who seemed big and noisy in comparison to the newborn, to my mother.

Jacqueline led the way up the stairs to the second floor. "Did it hurt when you started nursing? It feels like that baby has teeth. It makes me want to cry."

"I was a little sore in the beginning. He's still so tiny!"

"Are you kidding? He's giant. That was some delivery."

"Alexandre is a nice name. You can call him Alex for short. Does he have a baptism name?"

"To please your parents and the priest, we picked Avedis. The baby's bedroom is here," Jacqueline said as we reached the second-floor landing; she pointed into a sunny nursery, where there was an oak crib with frolicking lambs carved into the footboard.

"What a beautiful crib!"

"Cousin Karnig made it," Jacqueline said, closing the nursery door. "The bathroom is here in the middle. Look at that big bathtub! No more zinc basin."

"Do you just sit in there and soak?"

Jacqueline shut the bathroom door. "Who has time? And our room is on this side. Come take a look while I get dressed."

"It's so bright and green," I said, gazing out the bedroom window at the backyard as Jacqueline changed into a skirt and blouse.

"Come see the rest," Jacqueline said.

I followed her down the stairs to the kitchen, which held a small table with four stools and had a long white counter along one wall. The stovetop had four burners, and the oven was big enough for two trays of bread sticks to bake at once. Jacqueline flipped a light switch on the wall and opened a door to another flight of stairs that led down to the basement. In the low-ceilinged cellar, damp diapers were pinned to a rope line strung between two pipes. In one corner there was a new washing machine with an agitator and a wringer. No more washboards for Jacqueline. I looked down at my chapped, roughened hands.

"Girls," Sophie Sahadian called from the top of the stairs, "it's time for lunch."

Lunch was spread on a picnic table in the backyard. I laid Pierre on a blanket in the grass while Alexandre slept in a perambulator nearby.

My father clapped Missak on the back. "A boy to carry on the family name."

Missak said, "He was the biggest baby in the hospital."

Jacqueline said, "You sound so proud, like you had something to do with it."

"Oh, no," Missak answered, "I know it was all you, *anoushig*."

"Since when do you talk like that? What have you done to him, Jacqueline?" I asked.

"He's gone soft in the head since the baby was born," Jacqueline said.

When we arrived home that night, the apartment felt more cramped than usual. So did our bedroom; the baby had graduated from the basket to a crib, and it blocked access to one side of the bed. After I was in my nightgown, I put the baby on the top of the bureau to change his diaper. Barkev sat on the bed as he took off his shoes.

He asked, "Are you sorry you married me?"

"Why would you say that?"

"When you see Jacqueline's house, don't you wish you married someone else?"

"No, I don't."

"Sometimes I wonder if you married me out of pity."

"Barkev, that's not right."

"Well, why did you?"

"Because you asked me, and because I cared for you."

"Or because you loved my brother but I was the one who came back?"

By this time, Pierre was in his pajamas. I took him to the small armchair in the corner to feed him.

"You are in a wretched mood," I said. "And I don't like the way you are talking to me."

The only sounds in the room were the noise of the baby snuffling as he nursed and the clock ticking. A few minutes later, I put Pierre in the crib. I changed into my nightdress and climbed past Barkev's legs to my side of the bed.

Barkev switched off the nightstand lamp.

"You tell me you want me to talk, and when I do, you say you don't like the way I'm talking," he said into the dark.

"You are so miserable lately. Is it something I'm doing?"

"It's not you."

"What is it?"

"Now that my son can carry on the family name, my duty's done."

"Barkev, what would I do without you? And what about your son?"

"You should be able to find someone else to make you happy."

"Your suffering has made you unkind."

"I'm sorry." He reached out for me across the dark.

A few weeks later, my mother-in-law and I were at the kitchen table rolling out dough for *cheoregs* when Paul Sahadian knocked at the front door.

"What is it?" I wiped my buttery palms on my apron. "What happened? My father?"

"They called your father's shop. There's been an accident."

I felt sick, my heart swooping down inside my body as though it had been dropped at the end of a long rope.

"What happened?" asked my mother-in-law, who came up behind me in the hall.

Paul said, "It's Barkev. There's been an accident."

Shushan Kacherian pressed her hands to her heart. "God help us."

"What happened?" I asked again.

Paul finally answered, "He was hit by a truck."

"But he'll be okay?" I asked.

Paul's face was grim. "By the time the ambulance got there . . . I'm sorry."

My mother-in-law groaned and her eyes rolled back in her head. Paul and I caught her before she hit the floor and carried her to the sofa in the living room. Just then the baby woke from his nap and cried from the crib in the other room.

"Paul, I don't think I can take care of both of them. Will you please get my mother?" I asked.

"Your father went first to tell her—she should be here any minute now—and then he went to meet Mr. Kacherian at the hospital. I'll sit with her until they arrive."

I went to the bedroom and reached for Pierre. I laid him on the bed to change him. He stared up at me, kicking his legs and waving his arms as I pinned on the new diaper. Somewhere in a corner of my mind, I understood that Barkev was gone, irrevocably gone, but it didn't seem real. Here was the bed that we shared, and there was the pillow on which his head had rested that morning. Here was our child, a little boy whose bright, dark eyes were much like his father's.

The poor thing, I thought as I lifted Pierre from the bed, *he's not even five months old and already fatherless. He won't remember Barkev. He won't know anything about him except what's in the stories we tell.*

By the time my father and father-in-law arrived, I was in the front room with Paul, my mother, my mother-in-law, and the baby. Shushan Kacherian's eyes were rimmed with red and she held a sodden handkerchief to her cheek. My father gave the orders, telling us who would go where and do what. My assignment was to take care of the baby. Paul was dispatched to find Virginie at the lycée. My father-in-law went in search of the undertaker, and my father went back to his shop, where he could make the necessary call to the priest from the recently installed telephone. Once the men had left, my mother and mother-in-law wept in each other's arms, and their sobs were soon joined by those of Virginie, Sophie, and Alice Sahadian.

By evening, the front room was jammed with family and friends. Vahan Kacherian recounted the story of what had happened to Barkev several times for the benefit of newcomers. The story went like this: Barkev was having one of his bad days, and as he was unable to assemble the uppers of the shoes, the boss decided to send him on errands, including buying some skins from a leather merchant in the neighborhood. Barkev left the atelier, and according to people who were walking by, a few blocks away from the shop he stepped into the street to cross as a delivery truck came barreling down the hill.

"Oh, my sons, my sons," my mother-in-law wept. "How is it possible that God took both of them? Why? Why? Why?"

There was a fresh round of weeping each time the story was told, but I was dry-eyed. I sat in the corner holding the baby, having instinctively pulled some kind of hard, protective shell over myself for the sake of Pierre. He was tense and fretful, so I bounced him up and down. As the evening gave way to night, I carried the baby into the bedroom, away from all the commotion, changed and fed him, and then laid him in the crib. I leaned over the rail and rubbed circles on his back until he fell asleep.

Finally Missak and Jacqueline arrived. They had borrowed the Nazarians' car and driven from Alfortville with little Alex. When Jacqueline handed the baby to my brother and put her arms around me, I leaned into her.

"Oh God, sweetie," Jacqueline said into my ear. "I'm so sorry."

"I think my heart is breaking, but I'm not sure because I can't feel a thing." Only then did I start crying.

When people finally cleared out of the apartment, I was wooden with exhaustion. In the bedroom, I pulled on my nightgown and climbed into the bed with sheets that smelled of Barkev. I turned onto my side, and when I slid my hand under the pillow, I felt it—the pencil stub. It had been to Buchenwald and back and was always in his pocket, but he must have put it under the pillow before he'd left for work that morning. Since the night of the party in Alfortville, he hadn't mentioned any problems, and I had hoped his situation was improving. He had carried his burden alone to the end. His farewell message was wordless and it was for me alone, a last secret between us.

The next day Father Avedis came to the apartment to preside over the home service. Barkev's mother had insisted on all three offices: the home, the church, and the cemetery services, and not only for Barkev but also for Zaven, who according to her had never been properly laid to rest. I didn't think Barkev would have wanted all this, but he would have shrugged and gone along for his mother's sake. And, as my father pointed out, funerals were for the living and not the dead. The open casket was in the front room. All the injuries, I had been told, were on his torso, where they didn't show, except for a small bruise on his right cheek. His face was smooth and he looked younger than he had in a long time. All the worry was gone, and all the memories erased. No more nightmares. No more trembling hands. His war was over.

After the liturgy at the cathedral, we made the trek to Père-Lachaise. The sun was pitiless, and the climb up the hills of the cemetery left me panting and sticky with sweat. Barkev was to be buried not far from Auntie Shakeh. On the simple gravestone, the names and dates were carved:

Barkev Kacherian, b. 1922–d. 1946
Zaven Kacherian, b. 1924–d. 1945

After the forty or so black-clad mourners reached the gravesite, Father Avedis intoned the ritual hymn.

Let Your loving compassion flow over me. Wash my sins from Your spring of life. O wise Physician and Architect; our Hope and Savior, heal the sickness of my soul.

I was transported back to the cold, snowy day of Auntie Shakeh's funeral and remembered how, when I had slipped on the steps, Zaven had caught me by the elbow. A wave of sorrow swept over me like nausea and I closed my eyes.

The period of ritual mourning at the Kacherian apartment was like being locked in a dark, airless closet. In the morning I put on a black dress and black stockings before going out to the kitchen, where my mother-in-law had already started the day's weeping. Virginie poured tea for her mother and handed her a plate of toast, which her mother wouldn't touch. Shushan Kacherian's despair was a flood that drowned everything in its path, so I tried to spend as much of the day as possible in the bedroom. From there I heard the voices of the visitors and the muffled sounds of crying. Feet shuffled in and out of the apartment as neighbors brought casseroles, stews, and other dishes. I played with the baby, who was miraculously sunny, and when he slept, I tried, with little success, to read one of a stack of books Paul Sahadian had borrowed for me from the municipal library.

I came out of the room at mealtimes and put some of the tasteless foods into my mouth because it was important to keep my strength up for Pierre. *Poor baby*, I thought. *Trapped here in this apartment with all these weeping women.* It was late September—the beginning of autumn—and it would have been pleasant, although inappropriate during the period of mourning, to take him for a stroll to the park.

One afternoon I dared to push the perambulator around the corner to visit my mother.

"Oh, honey," my mother said, "you don't look good."

"I'll be okay."

"I don't know," my mother said doubtfully. "You need to eat. You need some sun. I don't like this custom for a young girl like you, or for the baby."

"It's day thirty-five. Only five more days."

The next afternoon I took the stroller out again, stopping by my father's shop, where I was lucky to find him alone—no customers, and Paul was off on an errand.

He asked, "How is Shushan today?"

"She is an endless fountain of tears. Grieving has become a full-time job." I was surprised at the hard edge in my voice.

My father eyed me. "Are you all right, my girl?"

"It's like I've been buried alive. And there is no room for my feelings because hers take up all the space. She doesn't need me for anything—she has Virginie, thank God. Now that Barkev is gone, I'm just a burden to them. And I'm worried about the baby. Every time my mother-in-law looks at him, she starts crying. I think she hates me."

"Why should she hate you?"

"It's my fault her sons are dead. Maybe loving me is a curse. Or maybe she resents that I'm still aboveground when they are not."

"I will talk with them. You should come home."

"Do you think they'll let me? What will people say? She doesn't want me to go to the park for fear of what people will say. It is like I'm behind a black curtain, and I can't feel anything at all."

"I have lived behind such a curtain myself. It was a time I don't talk about, but maybe it will help you to know. During the Massacres, the Turks burned Moush to the ground, killing everyone they could with torture, with swords, with fire. And the ones that survived, they drove out. My father was killed, my grandparents, and my uncle's whole family, so my mother took us, me and my brother, Missak, and two small sisters—they must have been about two and four years old—and we went with the other deportees from our town. I can't tell you, I won't tell you what I saw—I don't want my words to live in your head the way these images are burned into mine. We walked, we walked, and we had next to nothing to eat. After two weeks, we were near the river and I saw a village in the distance. I told my mother that Missak and I would go try to find some food. Beg, steal, whatever. So I left her sitting on a rock near the river with those two little girls on her lap. One was called Arpi and the other was Nazani. We were gone maybe an hour and a half, two hours. When we came back with the bread—it was a miracle, we had managed to convince the village baker to give us half a loaf—the rock was empty. I asked people where my mother and the girls had gone, and no one seemed to know. Had Kurds kidnapped them? Had they been killed? Had my mother thrown herself and the babies into the river? We looked for them for days. Each place we stopped, I looked and asked for them. But we never found them."

"Oh, Baba," I said.

"Don't cry, my girl. Rivers of tears could not bring them back. I stopped believing in God after what I witnessed. And just now, again, there was this war that made so much suffering. When I saw those pictures in the paper, I thought, *If those boys come back, those memories come with them.* Both heaven and hell are here in this world.

"Right now, you are lost, but you have a beautiful child. You will think about poor Barkev, who came back broken. You will remember also Zaven, how he once was so strong and full of life. And then you will go on. Because of Bedros, and because you are twenty years old with a life ahead of you. Because also you are my daughter, and if we are anything, my girl, we are tough and we are *jarbig.*"

"Clever or not, Babig," I said, "I want to come home."

30

FOR CHRISTMAS, JACQUELINE GAVE me a ginger kitten, a fuzzy thing with a pink nose and hazel eyes. By February, when Jacqueline and Alex came for a Sunday visit, the kitten had more than doubled in size, and her fur was sleek and shiny. I tossed the kitten a ball of green yarn that she batted around on the carpet while Pierre watched excitedly from my lap.

"What did you decide to call her?" Jacqueline asked, holding Alex, who was wearing a bib to catch his bounteous drool.

"We've been calling her Saffron."

"That's sweet. Why don't you let the baby down on the floor to play with her?"

"He tries to grab her tail. Have you seen how fast he crawls? He moves like a beetle."

"The cat can take care of herself," Jacqueline said. "You watch."

I put Pierre on the floor, and he made a beeline for the kitten, which quickly scampered under my father's armchair. Pierre lay on his belly, grasping for the kitten that was just out of reach.

Pierre screeched in disappointment. I offered him a set of metal measuring spoons and a wooden rattle. He grabbed them both, one with each hand.

"I can't wait for this one to crawl." Jacqueline bounced Alex up and down on her knee. "He's just started sitting up, but he falls over and hits his head on the floor. I put pillows around him, but he always seems to fall where the pillows aren't."

"By springtime, he'll probably be crawling, and you'll be complaining because he'll be getting into mischief. I expect Pierre will be walking by then, with me chasing along behind. Look at him now."

Pierre had dropped the toys and pulled himself to standing in front of the armchair. He turned to see if I was watching, and he grinned and showed his new teeth.

Jacqueline said, "Speaking of spring, how long are you going to wear black? You look like one of the old widows at the church. You could at least put on a little lipstick."

"Glamour is not for a widow," I said.

"Says who? Your mother-in-law? According to her, you should wear black for the rest of your life. It's been almost six months. Isn't that enough?"

"If I didn't see Pierre grow, I would have no way of keeping track of time. The weeks are all the same—knitting, taking the sweaters to the workshop, and picking up more yarn.

Helping my mother clean and cook. Scrubbing Pierre's diapers."

"You can't stay cooped in this apartment waiting for white hairs. How about a community dance? Or, I don't know, at least go to the cinema with a friend."

"I don't have anyone to go with. I've lost touch with all my old schoolmates."

"What about Virginie?"

"When she's not at school or studying, she's waiting on her mother. I think my mother-in-law is going to insist that girl wear black at her own wedding, if she even lets her marry. I wish you didn't live so far away."

"I know. I was lucky to catch a ride in today with Cousin Karnig. Your brother's so lazy on Sunday, all he wants to do is putter around the house. There's always something broken he needs to fix. Sometimes I leave the baby with him and go to church just to keep up with the gossip. You're welcome to visit. But maybe you should leave the baby with your mother and go to the cathedral. How could your mother-in-law criticize you for going to church?"

"She finally stopped complaining about the fact that we moved out. But now she's sure that someone is going to put the evil eye on Pierre. She sewed a blue bead onto his hat and wants me to make him wear it. He pulls it off the minute I put it on. So then she chases behind him with garlic and a blue ribbon."

Pierre, who had been sitting on the floor sucking on the spoons, suddenly lost interest in them, threw them, and chanted lustily, "Ba, ba, ba, ba."

I said, "Yes, we're talking about you. And it's time for lunch."

That night I lay in my bed thinking about what Jacqueline had said. My mother-in-law's philosophy had cast a pall over me. To be happy, to laugh, to show an interest in anything outside the daily chores was to betray the memory of Barkev. But it wasn't right. Barkev would not have wanted a life of sequestered mourning for me or for Pierre.

I hadn't been to the cathedral since the fortieth-day requiem service for Barkev. I could put on my best black dress and go there on a Sunday for a change of scenery. The only cost would be the Métro fare and the coins for the offering plate.

A few mornings later, Pierre, whose nose had been runny the day before, woke up with red cheeks and a slight fever. He had been up several times in the night, whimpering to be held. The third time, I had just taken him into the bed, thinking this would be more restful for both of us, but instead he had moaned, turned, and kicked, repeatedly interrupting my sleep. In the morning as Pierre nursed, he sniffed and grunted, not seeming really hungry. I carried him to the front room, where my mother was setting breakfast on the table.

My mother touched his forehead. "He's warm."

"He has a cold." I put him in the high chair and tried to feed him some cereal, but he turned his head, pushing the spoon away. He then started to wail.

As my father entered the room, he accidentally stepped on the kitten's tail. The kitten yowled, the baby continued howling, and my father shouted, "What is this bedlam? Why is that cat always underfoot? Why is that baby screaming? Can't a man have any peace?"

My father's shouting only made Pierre cry harder. Now he pulled on both ears while snot streamed from his nose. I plucked him out of the high chair, wiping his face with a damp washcloth.

My mother said loudly over his wails, "I think he has an ear infection. Maybe a double ear infection. I'm going to warm some oil."

"Damn it, woman, why are you shouting?" my father barked.

"If he has an ear infection, don't you think we should take him to the doctor?" I asked as his crying reached a crescendo.

With a dismissive hand, my mother swatted away the idea. "Warm olive oil and a cotton ball in each ear is the best medicine."

"I'm going to the shop," my father announced. And with that he marched off without his breakfast.

After my mother poured the drops of oil and stuffed the cotton into Pierre's ears, I took him to the bedroom. We sat in the wooden rocking chair my parents had given me for Christmas. As the chair's runners creaked across the floorboards, and the baby relaxed in my arms, I sang a lullaby until he dozed.

I continued rocking and humming. My house of memory had many rooms, and there was one dedicated to Barkev, one for Zaven, and one for Auntie Shakeh. I imagined each room in detail—the chairs, the table, the carpet, and the pictures on the walls showing scenes from the person's life. I

put a vase of flowers on the table in each room: red tulips for
Auntie Shakeh, lilacs for Zaven, and my poor Barkev had
Lenten roses. After a while, I felt my eyes grow heavy, pulling me toward dreams. *Let them be good ones*, I thought, *or let
me not remember them.*

The next afternoon when I stopped by my father's shop,
Paul was alone. He dropped the hammer and shoe onto the
bench and rushed forward to greet me.

"Your father should be back in about fifteen minutes. Do
you want to wait?"

"That's all right. Tell him I'll see him when he comes
home."

"Before you go, Maral, I wanted to ask you . . ."

He stopped midsentence, and I noticed that his ears,
which still stood away from his head like two handles, had
turned crimson.

"Yes?" I asked.

"Well, there is a dance on Saturday."

"Thank you, Paul. That's sweet. Your sister has been saying I should get out among people more, but I'm just not
ready."

As I walked out of the shop, it occurred to me that, like a
rudderless ship, I could end up drifting into the wrong harbor.

I entered the cathedral a few minutes after the liturgy had
begun and paused to drop coins into the box and to light
three candles. I walked down the aisle, facing forward, the
velvet dots of my black veil floating in front of me as I looked
out of the corners of my eyes at the people in the pews I

passed. I stood when I was supposed to stand and sat when the congregation sat, but I was distracted.

When it was time, I recited the creed in unison with the congregation. I loved these words: *God of God, light of light, very God of very God, begotten and not made; Himself of the nature of the Father, by Whom all things came into being in heaven and on earth, visible and invisible* . . .

When I had come to the church with Auntie Shakeh as a small child, I had thrilled at the repetition of these words. What did it mean to be begotten and not made? When I asked Auntie Shakeh, she told me it was a mystery, saying it in such a way that I knew I should not have asked. So much in the church was mysterious—what the priests did behind the curtain in the middle of the service, what they wore under their long robes, and how the communion host was transformed so it wasn't just a wafer but actually Jesus's body. I had wished I could touch the invisible things that God had made. I would glance at the seemingly empty air inside the vaulted church and imagine the angels. If the priest swung the censer near them, would it be possible to see their outlines in the smoke? Might I hear the rustle of their wings? Did angels smell like heaven?

These were the kinds of questions that made me feel both special and lonely when I was a child. *Now*, I thought, *I'm no longer special; I'm just lonely.*

After the service ended, I talked with a few familiar faces in the vestibule. Some of the older women asked after my mother. I promised to convey their greetings. Jacqueline was right. It did me good to be out in the world, talking with people, even if it was mostly idle chatter.

When I stopped to say hello to Father Avedis, I screwed up the courage to ask him about Andon.

He said, "Shirvanian? I believe he was here a month or so ago to light a candle for his mother."

I asked, "No funerals? No weddings? No baptisms?"

Father Avedis eyed me. "No weddings that I've heard about, young lady."

At home I searched through my letters and found the note he had given me with the address for Tapis Shirvan. I put the address in my coat pocket, where it burned like a hot coal.

I made the weekly trip to my boss's atelier one beautiful, sunny afternoon in late March. The early perennials popping up in planters and garden beds heralded spring's arrival. I undid the buttons of my black winter coat. Coming back, not wanting to rush home, I meandered to the English library at the Sorbonne.

The librarian said, "Maral! It's so good to see you. What brings you here?"

"I had business in the neighborhood and thought I'd stop to say hello. I know I'm not enrolled, but I was wondering if I might borrow a book."

"For you we can make an exception. Go find what you want."

A half an hour later, as I stood on the street corner outside the library with a bag of wool slung over one shoulder and Charlotte Brontë's *Villette* tucked under the other arm, I reached into my pocket for the slip of paper. I already knew the address by heart, but I stared at Andon's perfect handwriting. It was a fifteen-minute walk away. I looked at my watch. My mother probably wouldn't notice an extra half an hour, and the baby was likely still having his afternoon nap.

I stood nervously in front of the plate-glass window that said in gold letters TAPIS SHIRVAN. Inside, deeply colored rugs hung on the walls and there were stacks of carpets on the floor. A balding, middle-aged man sat at a desk in the center of the showroom—it had to be Andon's cousin—but no one else was in the shop. Of course, there would be a back room where the rugs were repaired, and if he was in the shop, Andon would be found there.

The bell above the door jangled as I crossed the threshold. The man at the desk glanced up.

"May I help you?" he asked in heavily accented French.

I replied in French, "Oh, yes, thank you. I'm looking for Andon Shirvanian."

"He stepped out for a bit. He went for lunch and then to the post office. Would you like to leave him a message?"

"Thank you, I would. Do you have a piece of paper that I might use?"

He slid a pad of paper and a pen across the desk to me.

I paused for a second, the pen poised over the page. Then I wrote in Armenian, *I was passing through the neighborhood. Sorry to have missed you. Will be at church on Sunday. Maral.*

I pushed the pad back to him.

He glanced at what I had written and smiled broadly. Then he reached out to shake my hand and said in Armenian, "Maral! I'm Andon's cousin Hrair Shirvanian. Andon has spoken so much about you. I am so happy to meet you. You are the one who helped him with his French. It's beautiful now. He writes all my letters. He's taking English classes at night. Do you want to wait for him? Sit down and I'll make us some tea."

"Oh, no, thank you. I'm afraid I can't stay. I'm expected at home."

I hurried to the avenue and the nearest Métro station, my cheeks burning with embarrassment. My mother-in-law would be scandalized. I paused to catch my breath and briefly surveyed my image in a shop window. I tucked my hair behind my ears and straightened the collar of my coat. There was nothing to do now except wait for Sunday.

31

"She's going to church again this week. Next thing you know she's going to take up with the Protestants and then we'll know she's a fanatic," my father said.

My mother said, "Maral, please tell Father Avedis I say hello."

Pierre, who had already finished breakfast and was standing holding on to the sofa, said, "Mama."

"Look at him," my mother said.

Pierre let go of the couch and took a step. He stood unsupported for a few seconds with a look of utter surprise on his face.

I laughed. "Good for you, Pierre!"

"Aman!" My mother clapped her hands. "He's walking."

"Of course he's walking. What do you think? Babies eventually walk and talk and use the toilet and do what humans do," said my father.

"Okay, you cranky old man. My grandson just took his

first step and to me that's amazing," my mother answered.

The baby lost his balance and sat heavily on his bottom. He turned, crawled back to the couch, and pulled himself up again. He grinned at his audience and took another step.

I arrived at the cathedral early and sat in the pew twisting a white lace-trimmed hankie. When I looked down and saw that the fabric was thoroughly wrinkled, I smoothed it on my lap, neatly folded it, and put it in my purse. I mustered the self-restraint to keep from craning my neck around as I heard the footsteps of churchgoers making their way down the nave. But finally, I was compelled to look over my shoulder and there he was. He was wearing his black suit with the starched white shirt and a red tie. He smiled and dipped his head in greeting, sliding into the pew on the other side of the aisle. I returned his smile, feeling myself flush. I faced forward, still smiling.

When the service finally came to a close, the exiting crowd pulled us toward the vestibule.

Andon said, "The café on Marbeuf?"

I nodded. He had chosen a place nearby but far enough away that we were unlikely to be spotted. We instinctively wanted to avoid anything that might set the church ladies gossiping.

The parishioners spilled out into the sunny courtyard, where they gathered in eddies and pools. After Andon and I briefly exchanged glances, he headed to the street while I paused to talk with one of my mother's friends. I calculated that five minutes should be sufficient and so engaged in a painful conversation about the exact number of teeth Bedros now had, and how Jacqueline and Missak were doing in Alfortville. Just as I extricated myself, Father Avedis approached.

"So, I saw that Shirvanian was here today," he said.

"Yes. I saw him too." I blushed. So he had noticed, which meant others likely had as well. In this village, our lives were like laundry flapping on an outdoor line.

Father Avedis smiled. "It's a pretty afternoon. Have a good day, my child."

"Thank you, Der Hayr." I bobbed my head.

When Father Avedis turned to a family standing on the other side, I walked out of the courtyard, headed up the block, and then broke into a trot. I was out of breath when I reached the café where Andon waited.

As I approached the table, he stood and reached to shake my hand.

"Oh, Andon, please don't be so formal." I quickly leaned to offer one cheek and then the other.

"I presumed to order you tea with lemon. I hope that is what you wanted."

"It's nice you remembered."

"Two years is not so long that I should forget."

"Has it already been two years?"

"Not quite two years. Not until June."

"What have you been doing all this time?" I asked.

"There is not so very much to report. I live in the same place. I do the same work. I have learned English."

"Your cousin told me. That's wonderful."

"And you?"

"Well, you knew that I got married. Then I quit the university. I had a baby. After Barkev died, I moved back with my parents and took up my old work."

"Please accept my condolences. To have survived the war only to die in an accident that way is a tragedy . . ."

"So you heard."

"Yes," he said. "And how is the baby?"

"He's well—happy, healthy, and about to have his first birthday."

"Bedros Pierre is a fine name," he said.

"Did Father Avedis tell you?"

"The church bulletin mentioned the baptism."

"I wonder if they might put 'Maral Pegorian Kacherian has a run in her stocking' in the church bulletin."

"You seem different," he said.

"In a good way or a bad?"

"I'm not sure. I think I am a little afraid of you."

I laughed. "That's good."

"You were so cautious before," he said. "Now I will get to know you better."

When it was time for me to go, we walked toward the Métro together. I slipped my arm through his almost casually. We kept our eyes straight ahead, but I felt the blood churning inside me.

"When can we meet again?" he asked.

"Next Sunday," I answered.

"At the cathedral?"

I said, "The weather is getting so nice, it seems a waste to spend the whole morning inside. How about we meet at the café?"

• • •

After dinner that evening, my mother and I discussed arrangements for Pierre's birthday party, which was to be held at Missak and Jacqueline's in two weeks. The Kacherians and the Sahadians would be there. My mother was making a new outfit for the baby—a white jacket with white shorts, which seemed impractical, but she insisted. Jacqueline had offered to bake the cake. Vahan Kacherian had taken the measure of Pierre's feet for the baby's first pair of shoes.

While we talked, Pierre, who was fresh from his bath and dressed in pajamas, tried to go from taking one step to taking two. He worked on this project assiduously, crawling back to the couch after each time he landed heavily on his seat. The cat, from a safe perch on the back of the couch, at first followed the baby's movements and then dozed. Finally, after a series of attempts, Pierre gave up and sat, rubbing his eyes with small fists.

Pierre was quickly asleep in his crib. I put on my nightgown and got into bed with the Brontë novel. That night, however, instead of reading, I clasped the book to my chest and stared up at the ceiling. Monday, Tuesday, Wednesday, Thursday . . . It was a long time until I would see Andon again.

The following Sunday, the weather was warm and sunny. I couldn't bring myself to wear full mourning on such a day. I dutifully stepped into a black cotton skirt, then put on a white blouse and finished with an emerald-green scarf.

My father eyed me over his newspaper. He grunted. "About time you stopped with all that black."

My mother nodded. "You look nice."

"Please don't tell my mother-in-law," I told them.

"What should she have to say about it?" my father asked.

My mother, who was holding Pierre in her lap, replied, "The poor thing still can't bear anyone else's happiness."

"I might be a little late today," I said. "If you don't mind, I thought I'd go for a walk."

"That's fine," my mother said. "I'm taking Pierre over to see Shushan and Virginie this morning. Don't worry—I won't mention a thing. After lunch the little one will take a nap."

I paused on the landing to pull out a compact mirror and apply some lipstick. Then I ran down the stairs, through the courtyard, and onto the bright street. I enjoyed the swish of my full skirt and the sound of my heels clicking on the pavement.

As I approached the café, I saw Andon sitting at the same table as the week before, anxiously scanning the street. He hadn't seen me yet. When his eye caught mine, he waved and smiled.

"Am I late?" I glanced up at the clock on the wall as I slid into my chair. "Only three minutes. That's not late, is it?"

He shook his head. "I'll order. Tea for you?"

I nodded and he gestured to the waiter.

"How was your week?" I asked.

"Long. And how was yours?"

"Very long," I answered. "You seem irritated."

"Not irritated. I arrived too early and then I sat here worrying that you might not come."

"Why would you think that?"

"Because I wanted to see you so very much."

"I've been looking forward to this all week."

"Maral, I want you to know that my intentions are honorable," said Andon.

"I never thought they were dishonorable."

"I'm quite serious. I should like to speak to your father," he answered.

"Oh, Andon, I'm quite serious myself, but not enough time has passed."

"When I heard about your husband, I waited for you to contact me. If you think of how long we have known each other, I have been waiting a very long time."

"It's too soon."

"Are you sure it is a question of timing? Perhaps it is something else."

"Such as?"

"The circumstances of my departure from Poland, and the uniform I was wearing when we met. I am not ashamed but neither am I proud of what I did. It is perhaps best a story left untold for many years. General Dro was lately expelled from his party. The men I was with did not go back to Yerevan; they went straight to camps in Siberia."

"Oh, Andon, I'm so sorry to hear about your friends. But that's not it. I just need a little more time."

"As you may have surmised by now, I am a patient man."

Under clear blue skies, we went for a walk along the river, strolling across one bridge to the Left Bank and then crossing at the Île Saint-Louis and going back to the Right. We ended up at the place des Vosges, just a few blocks from my old lycée. Too soon it was midafternoon and time for me to head back to Belleville. As we started toward the Métro station, I wanted more than anything for Andon to kiss me, but I knew he was too polite to do such a thing.

"There's something I want to show you before we say goodbye," I said.

"What is that?" he asked.

"Follow me." I led him to a small passageway—a little alley where some of the older Victor Hugo girls had gone with their boyfriends.

"This is it?" he asked, looking around.

"Not quite all of it," I said.

When I kissed him it was like a glass of raki that filled me up and set the world on fire.

When I put my cheek against his, he whispered, "You light up dark walls."

We walked hand in hand to the Métro entrance, where he asked, "Next Sunday?"

I groaned. "Next Sunday we're going to Alfortville for Pierre's birthday."

"Two weeks?"

"Such a long time. Let's meet at the Buttes Chaumont. Maybe I'll bring Pierre."

When I arrived home, Missak, Jacqueline, and Alex were at our apartment. I had missed Sunday dinner, but my mother had covered a plate for me and left it on the counter. My father and brother played backgammon in the front room, and my mother put the babies down for a nap in the bedroom. I stood in the kitchen with my food as Jacqueline washed the dishes.

"You look happy," she said. "Was there good gossip after the service?"

"I'm the news. Don't say anything. I went for a walk with Andon."

"Shouldn't he be in Leninakan?"

"He didn't go back. He's working at a rug shop on the Left Bank."

"Paul will be disappointed. But he never had much of a chance."

"He should try to pry Virginie loose from my mother-in-law. She's more his age."

That night Zaven appeared in my dreams. We were in our building's stairwell. It was a cold, dark night, and I heard the drone of planes in the distance. Zaven put his arm around me, and I rested my head on his shoulder.

He whispered, "I should never have left you."

Then he was suddenly gone, and I was alone in the court-yard.

I heard footsteps approaching, and out of the shadows came Henri and Denise, and the Lipskis, and behind them Auntie Shakeh, wearing a black dress that hung on her skinny frame like a sack. A throng of people moved forward to join them, and I recognized, among the many faces, the Latin and Greek teacher Mademoiselle Lévy, two Jewish girls from my class at the lycée, and Missak Manouchian. All of them stood silently in the courtyard with somber faces. Finally Barkev emerged, walking with a limp and weaving through the crowd toward me. I put my hand to a dark bruise on his cheek. He said, "It's lonely without you, Maro Jan."

32

My mother waved to me from the shade, where she was sitting in a row of lawn chairs with my mother-in-law and Jacqueline's mother. "Maral, that baby is going to ruin his suit. Look—he already has grass stains on his shorts."

"So, I'll use bleach," I answered, watching as Pierre tottered across the lawn toward my father-in-law, who was waiting open-armed near the men gathered around the grill. "It's his birthday."

Jacqueline walked past with a steaming casserole. "The shish is off the fire, so come to the table before the pilaf gets cold."

When the meal was over Hagop Meguerditchian played his oud, while his wife, Alice, sang along. Missak circled the table pouring raki into the men's glasses.

My father-in-law raised his glass. "Here's to the health of my grandson Bedros."

"*Genatz!*" my father added.

"To my godson, Bedros Pierre!" said Missak, and then he downed the raki.

I picked Pierre up and kissed him on the neck. "The birthday boy!"

My mother-in-law gave a strangled moan. Shushan Kacherian's lips were trembling, and tears started rolling down her face.

My mother took her hand and said, "Don't cry, honey. He's watching from heaven."

Shushan groaned through her tears. "That baby will never know his father."

Virginie flew to her mother's side. "It's okay. Let's go in."

Shushan sobbed as Virginie led her away. "Why, O Lord? What did I do to deserve this kind of suffering?"

As the back door closed behind them, Jacqueline murmured into my ear, "She knows how to ruin a party."

I answered, "Maybe it's better than if no one had said anything."

"She's not the only one who lost them. She never thinks of you, and Missak isn't over it . . ."

"I wonder if it's something you get over, or if you just wear it like a scar."

She said, "Don't talk like that. You'll be happy again. I know you will."

"Let's go for a walk," I said. "I want to tell you something without the whole world hearing."

We put Pierre and Alex into the perambulator, and before we had rounded the first corner, both of them were asleep. Before we rounded the second corner, I told Jacqueline that Andon had asked me to marry him.

"But how can you marry him after what he did?" she asked.

"What do you mean?"

"You know very well what I mean. You saw the uniform he was wearing."

"But Jacqueline, at the time you didn't mind the uniform. In fact, you defended him. Remember?"

"It's different now. The war is over. And I'm married to Missak."

"What does he have to say about it?"

"When I told him about you and Andon, he didn't like the idea at all. Missak risked his life in the Resistance. And after what happened to Zaven and Barkev, it just doesn't seem right."

"Missak has never met Andon, and Andon wasn't a Nazi. He was an Armenian prisoner of war who had a choice between dying and putting on a German uniform. He built a useless wall along the coast."

She shrugged. "Don't argue with me. He's your brother. You talk to him."

But I didn't want to talk to him. I could imagine the way the conversation would go, my arguments only pushing him to cling more tightly to his mule-headed judgments.

Back in our Belleville apartment that night, I lay in my narrow bed thinking about Andon and my brother. If I married Andon over my brother's objections, would the family be riven for years? I wasn't concerned about my mother, but I would have to talk to my father before Missak did.

Here I was, having lost two husbands, making plans for taking a third. Was it my fault that I had lost them? If I had thrown my arms around Zaven's neck and insisted that he shouldn't leave, would he have stayed? If I had loved the first one less and the second one more, would it have made a difference? Was there something I could have said that last morning that would have lessened Barkev's suffering?

My sense of obligation suddenly felt like an intolerable burden. For a moment I imagined myself packing a suitcase and running away with Andon, maybe as far away as America. But I knew it was impossible. The one duty I could never shirk was my responsibility to my son, and it was that small life that tethered me in a thousand ways.

Finally I fell asleep, but I woke and twisted in my sheets, repeatedly switching on the light to check the slow-moving hands of the clock.

I dreamed I was walking down a dark street. Moonlight cast long shadows across the cobblestones. I saw Zaven standing in the doorway of a building ahead. As I walked toward him, he ducked inside. "Zaven, wait!" I said, quickening my pace to follow. But when I reached the entrance hall, it was pitch-dark. Someone struck a match. The flame cast a circle of light on his face, and I saw it was Harry from the Bronx. He lit the cigarette that dangled from his mouth. "This damn war's still not over," he said. Behind me came the sound of boots hammering on the cobblestones. I woke up with my heart pounding.

That week the baby was fretful because his first molars were coming in. My mother rubbed his gums with peppermint oil, but soon after he was drooling and whining again. Everything felt intolerable. At meals, I couldn't believe how loud my father's chewing sounded, and I was equally appalled by the way my mother gulped down food without chewing it at all. When I wasn't knitting or doing dishes or taking care of the baby, I tried to read, but I found myself going over the same paragraph several times without registering what it said. One afternoon in the middle of the week I went out in the neighborhood, but it was like looking in a funhouse mirror where faces were distorted with pettiness and self-regard. The next day, people I passed on the street seemed to be on the verge of tears.

Later in the week I went by my father's shop at the end of the day as he and Paul were closing down the machines and sweeping up. After we said goodbye to Paul, I told my father all about Andon: the prisoner-of-war camp, General Dro, the German uniform, the folkloric party, the Atlantic wall, the end of the war, his wanting to marry me, and my brother's objections.

My father said, "When you've seen what I have, where a decision to go one way or another turned out to be a matter of life or death, you give people more room to do what is human. Don't misunderstand. Cruelty is one thing. The Nazi puppet earned his firing squad, and Delattre got better than he deserved. I understand your brother's feelings, but I also understand your young man."

"What should I do, Babig?"

"Strange as it sounds, I can't tell you. I don't know if your brother will come around. You have to decide for yourself what kind of husband and father you think Andon will be."

The responsibility was then mine alone. Missak would be angry, and even if they never found out about the German uniform, the Kacherians, particularly my mother-in-law, would be displeased. I envied Andon that his family was half a world away.

When Sunday morning finally arrived, I decided I wouldn't take Pierre to the park. Given the misanthropic mood I had been in all week, I was apprehensive about meeting Andon and didn't want the added distraction of a possibly fractious baby. It had been two long weeks since our last meeting, and I had no idea what I would feel when I saw him.

At breakfast, my mother said, "That dress looks nice. Are you going to church?"

I answered, "I'm going to the park. Would you watch the baby?"

"I'm glad you're not taking him. It looks like rain."

I said, "I hope not."

"Well, if it does rain, you should bring that boy home for lunch."

"What boy?"

"After all this time, do you think I'm really so stupid?"

When I reached the park, Andon was standing by the entrance in his Sunday suit. He smiled and waved at me with a tall black umbrella as I approached. Under his other arm he was holding a large, odd-shaped package wrapped in brown paper.

He kissed me on both cheeks. "I feared you might not come because of the weather."

"I didn't bring the baby."

"Not with the rain about to come down. I brought something for his birthday." He handed me the parcel. "Please open it."

I tore off the paper, and inside was a black wooden horse set on four red wheels.

"It's beautiful. Did you make it?" I turned the toy in my hands. The details were exquisite, from the trimmed woolen mane to the colorful saddle.

Andon nodded. "The saddle is a piece of an old rug."

"It's wonderful. Pierre will adore it."

"I think we have a little time before the rain. Let's go for a walk. This is my first visit here, and you must know it very well."

"I've been coming here since I was a little girl." *In fact,* I thought, *my initials are carved with Zaven's in the trunk of that tree over there, and Barkev and I celebrated our wedding party on the lawn by the lake.* "This time of year, there are new flowers blooming each day."

"We should come every Sunday. You know, during the week, when I read something, I imagine what you might say about it," Andon said, and here he pulled out a small notebook. "I even have a place where I write questions I want to ask you."

There were many men in the world, and there was likely another man that I could have met and married if I had turned away from Andon that morning. But I didn't, and I never regretted it a day in my life.

"Why are you crying?" he asked.

I shook my head and shrugged.

He offered me his handkerchief.

A large drop of rain landed on my arm. I glanced up at the sky, which had grown darker and more ominous as storm clouds rolled in. The leaves on the trees stirred against one another. A few more droplets of rain fell, spattering at our feet. As drops pelted down faster, Andon opened his big umbrella and held it over us.

"What do you suggest we do now?" he asked.

"I thought you might want to speak to my father."

And then the rain suddenly began to pour down in sheets; a bolt of lightning flickered jaggedly in the sky. Steering the umbrella against the wind, we ran for home.

About the Author

© James Schamus

NANCY KRICORIAN IS THE author of the novels *Zabelle* and *Dreams of Bread and Fire*. Her essays and poems have been published in numerous literary journals and magazines. Kricorian grew up in the Armenian community of Watertown, Massachusetts, and she earned her undergraduate degree in Comparative Literature at Dartmouth College; she spent the following year studying semiotics at the University of Paris. After completing a Master of Fine Arts in Poetry at Columbia University, Kricorian taught at Barnard, Rutgers, Queens and Yale. She subsequently worked for ten years as a literary scout for foreign publishers, and since 2003 has been on the staff of CODEPINK Women for Peace. She lives in New York City.

Selected Titles From She Writes Press

She Writes Press is an independent publishing company founded to serve women writers everywhere. Visit us at www.shewritespress.com.

THE BELIEF IN ANGELS by J. Dylan Yates. $16.95, 978-1-938314-64-3. From the Majdonek death camp to a volatile hippie household on the East Coast, this narrative of tragedy, survival, and hope spans more than fifty years, from the 1920s to the 1970s.

THE SWEETNESS by Sande Boritz Berger. $16.95, 978-1-63152-907-8. A compelling and powerful story of two girls—cousins living on separate continents—whose strikingly different lives are forever changed when the Nazis invade Vilna, Lithuania.

PORTRAIT OF A WOMAN IN WHITE by Susan Winkler. $16.95, 978-1-938314-83-4. When the Nazis steal a Matisse portrait from the eccentric, art-loving Rosenswigs, the Parisian family is thrust into the tumult of war and separation, their fates intertwined with that of their beloved portrait.

FAINT PROMISE OF RAIN by Anjali Mitter Duva. $16.95, 978-1-938314-97-1. Adhira, a young girl born to a family of Hindu temple dancers, is raised to be dutiful—but ultimately, as the world around her changes, it is her own bold choice that will determine the fate of her family and of their tradition.

SHANGHAI LOVE by Layne Wong. $16.95, 978-1-938314-18-6. The enthralling story of an unlikely romance between a Chinese herbalist and a Jewish refugee in Shanghai during World War II.

BEAUTIFUL GARBAGE by Jill DiDonato. $16.95, 978-1-938314-01-8. Talented but troubled young artist Jodi Plum leaves suburbia for the excitement of the city—and is soon swept up in the sexual politics and downtown art scene of 1980s New York.